Manhattan is my Beat

'Highly original and very entertaining;
Alfred Hitchcock magazine

'Deaver writes with clarity, compassion, and
intelligence, and with a decidedly human and
contemporary slant'
Publishers Weekly

'Deaver is a master of ticking-bomb suspense'
People Magazine

Jeffery Deaver

'Deaver is a terrific storyteller, and he takes the
reader on a rollercoaster of suspense, violence and
mystery . . . Good entertainment'
Susanna Yager, *Daily Telegraph*
on *The Devil's Teardrop*

'The best psychological thriller writer around'
The Times

Also by Jeffery Deaver

The Lesson of Her Death
Praying for Sleep
A Maiden's Grave
The Bone Collector
The Coffin Dancer
Speaking in Tongues
The Devil's Teardrop
The Empty Chair

Manhattan is my Beat

Jeffery Deaver

CORONET BOOKS

Hodder & Stoughton

Originally published in the United States in 1988 by Bantam.

First published in Great Britain in 2000
by Hodder and Stoughton
First published in paperback in 2000
by Hodder and Stoughton
A division of Hodder Headline

A Coronet Paperback

22

ISBN 978-0-340-79311-4

Printed and bound in Great Britain by Clays Ltd, St Ives plc

Hodder and Stoughton
A division of Hodder Headline
338 Euston Road
London NW1 3BH

The land of faery:
where nobody gets old and godly and grave,
where nobody gets old and crafty and wise,
where nobody gets old and bitter of tongue.

—*William Butler Yeats*

CHAPTER ONE

He believed he was safe.

For the first time in six months.

Two identities and three residences behind him, he finally believed he was safe.

An odd feeling came over him—comfort, he finally decided. Yeah, that was it. A feeling he hadn't experienced for a long time, and he sat on the bed in this fair-to-middling hotel, overlooking that weird silver arch that crowned the riverfront in St. Louis. Smelling the midwestern spring air.

An old movie was on television. He loved old movies. This was *Touch of Evil*. Orson Welles directing. Charlton Heston playing a Mexican. The actor didn't look like a Mexican. But then, he probably didn't look like Moses either.

Arnold Gittleman laughed to himself at his little joke and told it to a sullen man sitting nearby, reading a *Guns & Ammo* magazine. The man glanced at the screen.

"Mexican?" he asked. Stared at the screen for a minute. "Oh." He went back to his magazine.

Gittleman lay back in the bed, thinking that it was damn well about time he had some funny thoughts like the one about Heston. Frivolous thoughts. Amount-to-nothing thoughts. He wanted to think about gardening or painting lawn furniture or taking his grandson to a ball game. About taking his daughter and her husband to his wife's grave—a place he'd been too afraid to visit for over six months.

"So," the sullen man said, looking up from the magazine, "what's it gonna be? We gonna do deli tonight?"

Gittleman, who'd lost 30 pounds since Christmas—he was down to 204—said, "Sure. Sounds good. Deli."

And he realized it *did* sound good. He hadn't looked forward to food for a long time. A nice fat deli sandwich. Pastrami. His mouth started to water. Mustard. Rye bread. A pickle.

"Naw," said a third man, stepping out of the bathroom. "Pizza. Let's get pizza."

The sullen man who read about guns all the time and the pizza man were U.S. marshals. Both were young and stony-faced and gruff and wore cheap suits that fit very badly. But Gittleman knew that these were exactly the kind of men you wanted to be watching over you. Besides, Gittleman had led a pretty tough life himself, and he realized that when you looked past their facade these two were pretty decent and smart guys—street-smart, at least. Which was all that really counted in life.

Gittleman had taken a liking to them over the past five months. And since he couldn't have his family around him he'd informally adopted them. He called them Son One and Son Two. He told them that. They weren't sure what to make of it but he sensed they got a kick out of him saying the words. For one thing, they said, most of the people they protected were complete shits and Gittleman knew that, whatever else, he wasn't that.

Son One was the man reading the guns magazine, the man who'd suggested deli. He was the fatter of them. Son Two grumbled again that he wanted pizza.

"Forgetaboutit. We did pizza yesterday."

An irrefutable argument. So it was pastrami and cole slaw.

Good.

"On rye," Gittleman said. "And a pickle. Don't forget the pickle."

"They come with pickles."

"Then *extra* pickles."

"Hey, go for it, Arnie," Son One said.

Son Two spoke into the microphone pinned to his chest. A wire ran to a black Motorola Handi-Talkie, clipped onto his belt, right next to a big gun that might very well have been reviewed in the magazine his partner was reading. He spoke to the third marshal on the team, sitting by the elevator up the hall. "It's Sal. I'm coming out."

"Okay," the staticky voice responded. "Elevator's on its way."

"You wanta beer, Arnie?"

"No," Gittleman said firmly.

Son Two looked at him curiously.

"I want *two* goddamn beers."

The marshal cracked a faint smile. The most response to humor Gittleman had ever seen in his tough face.

"Good for you," Son One said. The marshals had been after him to lighten up, enjoy life more. Relax.

"You don't like dark beer, right?" asked his partner.

"Not so much," Gittleman responded.

"How do they make dark beer anyway?" Son One asked, studying something in the well-thumbed magazine. Gittleman looked. It was a pistol, dark as dark beer, and it looked a lot nastier than the guns his surrogate sons wore.

"Make it?" Gittleman asked absently. He didn't know. He knew money and how and where to hide it. He knew movies and horse racing and grandchildren. He *drank* beer but he didn't know anything about making it. Maybe he'd take that up as a hobby too—in addition to gardening. Home brewing. He was fifty-six. Too young for retirement from the financial services and accounting profession—but, after the RICO trial, he was definitely going to be retired from now on.

"Clear," came the radio voice from the hallway.

Son Two disappeared out the door.

Gittleman lay back and watched the movie. Janet Leigh was on screen now. He'd always had a crush on her. Was still pissed at Hitchcock for killing her in the shower. Gittleman liked women with short hair.

Smelling the spring air.

Thinking about a sandwich.

Pastrami on rye.

And a pickle.

Feeling safe.

Thinking: the Marshals Service was doing a good job at making sure he stayed that way. The rooms on either side of this one had adjoining doors but they'd been bolted shut and the rooms were unoccupied; the U.S. government actually paid for all three rooms. The hallway was covered by the marshal near the elevator. The nearest shooting position a sniper could find was two miles away, across the Mississippi River, and Son One—the *Guns & Ammo* subscriber—had told him there was nobody in the universe who could make a shot like that.

Feeling comfortable.

Thinking that tomorrow he'd be on his way to California, with a new identity. There'd be some plastic surgery. He'd be safe. The people who wanted to kill him would eventually forget about him.

Relaxing.

Letting himself get lost in the movie with Moses and Janet Leigh.

It was really a great film. The very opening scene was somebody setting the hands of the timer on a bomb to three minutes and twenty seconds. Then planting it. Welles had made one continuous shot for that exact amount of time, until the bomb went off, setting the story in motion.

Talk about building the suspense.

Talk about—

Wait. . . .

What was that?

Gittleman glanced out the window. He sat up slightly.

Outside the window was . . . What *was* that?

It seemed like a small box of some sort. Sitting on the window ledge. Connected to it was a thin wire, which ran upward and disappeared out of view. As if somebody'd lowered the little box from the room above.

Because of the movie—the opening scene—his first thought was that the box was a bomb. But now, as he lunged forward, he saw that, no, it looked like a camera, a small video camera.

He rolled off the bed, walked to the window. Looked at the box closely.

Yep. That's what it was. A camera.

"Arnie, you know the drill," Son One said. Because he was heavy he sweated a lot and he sweated now. He wiped his face. "Stay away from the windows."

"But . . . what's that?" Gittleman pointed.

The marshal dropped the magazine to the floor, rose, and stepped to the window.

"A video camera?" Gittleman asked.

"Well, it looks like it. It does. Yeah."

"Is it . . . But it's not yours, is it?"

"No," the marshal muttered, frowning. "We don't have surveillance outside."

The marshal glanced at the thin cable that disappeared up, presumably to the room above them. His eyes continued upward until they came to rest on the ceiling.

"Shit!" he said, reaching for his radio.

The first cluster of bullets from the silenced machine gun tore through the plaster above them and ripped into Son One, who danced like a puppet. He dropped to the floor, bloody and torn. Shivering as he died.

"No!" Gittleman cried. "Jesus, *no!*"

He leapt toward the phone. A stream of bullets followed him; upstairs the killer would be watching on the video camera, knowing exactly where Gittleman was.

Gittleman pressed himself flat against the wall. The gunman fired another shot. A single. It was close. Then two more. Inches away. Teasing him, it seemed like. Nobody would hear. The only sound was the cracking of plaster and wood.

More shots followed him as he dodged toward the bathroom. Debris flew around him. There was a pause. He hoped the killer had given up and fled. But it turned out that he was after the phone—so Gittleman couldn't call for help. Two bullets cracked through the ceiling, hit the beige telephone unit, and shattered it into a hundred pieces.

"Help!" he cried, nauseated with fear. But, of course, the rooms on either side of this one were empty—a fact so reassuring a few moments ago, so horrifying now.

Tears of fright in his eyes . . .

He rolled into a corner, knocked a lamp over to darken the room.

More bullets crashed down. Closer, testing. Trying to find him. The gunman upstairs, watching a TV screen of his own, just like Gittleman had been watching Charlton Heston a few minutes ago.

Do something, Gittleman raged to himself. *Come on!*

He eased forward again and shoved the TV set, on a roller stand, toward the window. It slammed into the pane, cracked it, and blocked the view the video camera had of the room.

There were several more shots but the gunman was blind now.

"Please," Gittleman prayed quietly. "Please. Someone help me."

Hugging the walls, he moved to the doorway. He fumbled the chain and dead bolt, shivering in panic, certain the man was right above him, aiming down. About to pull the trigger.

But there were no more shots and he swung the door open fast and leapt into the hallway. Calling to the marshal at the elevator—not one of the Sons, an officer named Gibson. "He's shooting—there's a man upstairs with a gun! You—"

But Gittleman stopped speaking. At the end of the hallway Gibson lay facedown. Blood pooled around his head. Another puppet—this one with cut strings.

"Oh, no," he gasped. Turned around to run.

He stopped. Looking at what he now realized was the inevitable.

A handsome man, dark-complected, wearing a well-cut suit, standing in the hallway. He carried a Polaroid camera in one hand and, in the other, a black pistol mounted with a silencer.

"You're Gittleman, aren't you?" the man asked. He sounded polite, as if he were merely curious.

Gittleman couldn't respond. But the man squinted and then nodded. "Yeah, sure you are."

"But . . ." Gittleman looked back into his hotel room.

"Oh, my partner wasn't trying to hit you in there. Just to flush you. We need to get you outside and confirm the kill." The man gave a little shrug, nodding at the camera. " 'Causa what we're getting paid they want proof. You know."

And he shot Gittleman three times in the chest.

In the hotel corridor, which used to smell of Lysol and now smelled of Lysol and cordite from the gunshots, Haarte unscrewed the suppressor and dropped it and the Walther into his pocket. He glanced at the Polaroid picture of the dead man as it developed. Then put it in the same pocket as the gun.

From his belt he took his own walkie-talkie—more expensive than the Marshals' and, unlike theirs, sensibly equipped with a three-level-encryption scrambler—and spoke to Zane, his partner, upstairs, the one so proficient with automatic weapons. "He's dead. I've got the snap. Get out."

"On my way," Zane replied.

Haarte glanced at his watch. If the other marshal had gone to get food—which he probably had, since it was dinnertime—he could be back in six or seven minutes. That's how much time it took to walk to the restaurant closest to the hotel, order take-out, and return. He obviously hadn't gone to the restaurant *in* the hotel because they would just have ordered room service.

Haarte walked slowly down the four flights of stairs and outside into the warm spring evening. He checked the streets. Nearly deserted. No sirens. No flashing lights of silent roll-ups.

His earphone crackled. Haarte's partner said, "I'm in the car. Back at the Hilton in thirty."

"See you then."

Haarte got into their second rental car and drove out

of downtown to a park in University City, a pleasant suburb west of the city.

He pulled up beside a maroon Lincoln Continental.

Overhead a jet, making its approach to Lambert Field, roared past.

Haarte got out of the car and walked to the Lincoln. He got in the backseat, checking out the driver, kept his hand in his pocket around the grip of the now-unsilenced pistol. The man sitting in the rear of the car, a heavy, jowly man of about 60, gave a faint nod, his eyes aimed toward the front seat, meaning: The driver's okay; you don't have to worry.

Haarte didn't care what the man's eyes said. Haarte worried all the time. He'd worried when he'd been a cop in the toughest precinct of Newark, New Jersey. He'd worried as a soldier in the Dominican Republic. He'd worried as a mercenary in Zaire and Burma. He'd come to believe that worry was a kind of drug. One that kept you alive.

Once he finished his own appraisal of the driver he released his grip on the pistol and took his hand out of his pocket.

The man said in a flat midwestern accent, "There's nothing on the news yet."

"There will be," Haarte reassured him. He flashed the Polaroid.

The man shook his head. "All for money. Death of an innocent. And it's all for money." He sounded genuinely troubled as he said this. He looked up from the picture. Haarte had learned that Polaroids never show blood the right color; it always looks darker.

"That bother you?" the man asked Haarte. "Death of an innocent?"

Haarte said nothing. Innocence or guilt, just like fault and mercy, were concepts that had no meaning to him.

But the man didn't seem to want an answer.

"Here." The man handed him an envelope. Haarte had received a lot of envelopes like this. He always thought they felt like blocks of wood. Which in a way they were. Money was paper, paper was wood. He didn't look inside. He put the envelope in his pocket. No one had ever tried to cheat him.

"What about the other guy you wanted done?" Haarte asked.

The man shook his head. "Gone to ground. Somewhere in Manhattan. We aren't sure where yet. We should find out soon. You interested in the job?"

"New York?" Haarte considered. "It'll cost more. There's more heat, it's more complicated. We'd need backup and we probably should make it look accidental. Or at least set up a fall guy."

"Whatever," the man said lackadaisically, not much interest in the details of Haarte's craft. "What'll it cost?"

"Double." Haarte touched his breast pocket, where the money now rested.

A lifted gray eyebrow. "You pick up all expenses? The cost of backup? Equipment?"

Haarte waited a moment and said, "Add ten points for the backup?"

"I can go there," the man said.

They shook hands and Haarte returned to his own car.

He called Zane on the radio once more. "We're on again. This time in our own backyard."

CHAPTER TWO

Rune got elected to pick up the videotape and her life was never the same after that.

She argued with her boss about picking up the tape—Tony, the manager of Washington Square Video on Eighth Street in Greenwich Village, where she was a clerk. Oh, she argued with him.

Rewinding a tape, playing with the VCR, snapping the controls, she stared at the fat, bearded man. "Forget it. No way." She reminded him how he'd agreed she didn't have to do pickups or deliveries and that was the deal when he'd hired her.

"So," she said. "There."

Tony peered at her from under flecked, bushy eyebrows and, for some reason, decided to be reasonable. He explained how Frankie Greek and Eddie were busy fixing monitors or something—though she guessed they were probably just figuring out how to get comped into the Palladium for a concert that night—and so she *had* to do the pickups.

"I don't see why I *have* to at all, Tony. I mean, I just don't see where the have-to part comes in."

And right about then he changed his mind about being reasonable. "Okay, here's where it comes in, Rune. It's the part where I'm fucking *telling* you to. You know, as your boss. Anyway, whatsa big deal? There's only one pickup."

"That's like a total waste of time."

"Your life is a waste of time, Rune."

"Look," she began, not too patiently, and went on with her argument until he said, "Thin ice, honey. Get your ass outa here. Now."

She tried, "Not in the job description." Only because it wasn't in her nature to give in too quickly and then she saw him go all still and before he exploded she stood up and said, "Oh, will you just *chill,* Tony?" In that exasperated, sly way of hers that would probably get her fired someday but so far hadn't.

Then he'd looked at an invoice and said, "Christ, it's only a few blocks from here. Avenue B. Guy's name is Robert Kelly."

Oh, Rune thought, Mr. Kelly? Well, that was different.

She took the receipt, snagging the retro, fake-leopard-skin bag she'd found in a used-clothing store on Broadway. She pushed out the door, into the cool spring air, saying, "All right, all right. I'll do it." Putting just the right tone in her voice to let Tony know he owed her one for this. In her two decades on earth Rune had learned that if she wanted to live life the way she did, it was probably a good idea to collect as many obligations from people as she could.

Rune was five two, one hundred pounds. Today she wore black stretch pants, a black T-shirt under an business-man's Arrow shirt she'd cut the sleeves out of, so it looked like a white pinstripe vest. Black ankle boots. There were twenty-seven silver bracelets, all different, on her left forearm.

Her lips varied in size, compressing, expanding. A barometer of her mood. She had a round face; her nose pleased her. Her friends sometimes said she looked like certain actresses who appeared in independent films. But there were few present-day actresses she cared about or tried to look like; if you took Audrey Hepburn and put her in a Downtown, New Wave version of *Breakfast at Tiffany's*—that's who Rune wanted to resemble and in many ways she did.

She paused, looked at herself in a mirror sitting in an antiques shop window, the words WHOLESALE ONLY larger than the name of the place. Several months ago she'd gotten tired of her spiky black-purple haircut, had rinsed out the frightening colors, and had stopped trimming the do herself. The strands were longer now and the natural chestnut was emerging. Staring at the mirror, she now teased the hair out with her fingers. Then patted it back down. It wasn't long, it wasn't short. The ambivalence of it made her feel more homeless than she normally did.

She started once more on her journey to the East Village.

Rune glanced down at the receipt again.

Robert Kelly.

If Tony'd told her right away who the customer was, she wouldn't have given him so much crap.

Kelly, Robert. Member since: May 2. Deposit: Cash.

Robert Kelly.

"My boyfriend."

That's what she'd told Frankie Greek and Eddie at the store. They'd blinked, trying to figure out what *that* meant. But then she'd laughed and made it sound like a joke—before they grinned and sneered and asked what was it like to be in bed with a seventy-year-old man?

Though she'd added, "Well, we *have* been out on a date." Which left enough doubt to make it fun.

Robert Kelly *was* her friend. More of a friend than most of the men she'd met in the store. And he *was* also the only one she'd ever gone out with—in her three months' working there. Tony had a rule against going out with customers—not that any rule of Tony's would slow her up for more than a half-second. But the only men she ever seemed to meet at the store were either long domesticated or about what you'd expect from somebody who picks up clerks in a Greenwich Village video store.

Hi, I'm John, Fred, Stan, Sam, call me Sammie, I live up the street, this's an Armani, you like it, I'm a fashion photographer, I work for Morgan-Stanley, I got some blow, hey, you wanna go to my place and fuck?

Kelly, Robert, deposit: cash, wore a suit and tie every time she'd seen him. He was fifty years older than she was. And when she'd offered to do him a favor, a little thing, copy a tape for him, for free, he'd looked down, blushing, and he'd asked her out to lunch to thank her.

They'd gone to a highly turquoise 1950s revival soda shop, called the Soda Shop, on St. Marks, and, surrounded by NYU students who managed to be both morbidly serious and giddy at the same time, had eaten grilled cheese sandwiches with pickles. She'd ordered a martini. He'd laughed in surprise and said in a whisper he'd thought she was sixteen. The waitress had somehow accepted the fake ID, which showed her age to be 23. According to the authentic documentation—her Ohio driver's license—Rune was twenty.

At lunch he'd been a little awkward at first. But that didn't matter. Rune was an old hand at keeping the conversation going. Then he warmed up and they'd had a great time. Talking about New York City—he knew it real well even though he'd been born in the Midwest. How he used to go to clubs in Hell's Kitchen, west of Midtown. How he'd have picnics in Battery Park. How he used to go for hikes in Central Park with a "lady friend" of his— Rune loved that expression. When she was old she hoped she'd be somebody's lady friend. She'd—

Oh, damn . . .

Rune stopped in the middle of the sidewalk. *Goddamn.* She reached into her bag and found that she'd forgotten the tape she'd made for him. Which was too bad for Mr. Kelly because he'd be looking forward to it. But mostly it was too bad for her—because she'd left it at the store and if Tony found she'd made a bootleg of a store tape, Jesus, he'd kick her right out on her ass. No pleas for mercy accepted at Washington Square Video.

But she couldn't very well go back now and pull it out from underneath the counter where she'd hidden it. She'd bring it to Mr. Kelly in a day or two. Or slip it to him the next time he stopped in.

Would Tony find it? Would he fire her?

And if he did? *Well, them's the breaks.* Which is what she usually said, or at least *thought,* when she found herself back in line at the New York State Department of Labor, a place where she was a regular and where she'd made some of her best friends in the city.

Them's the Breaks. Her mantra of unemployment. Of fate in general too, she supposed.

Except that today, trying to be cavalier about it, she decided she didn't want to get fired. For her, this was a curious sensation—one that went beyond the usual pain-in-the-butt inconvenience of job searching that began to loom when a boss would motion her over and say, "Rune, let's you and me talk." Or "This isn't going to be easy . . ."

Though it usually was *very* easy.

Rune took the firings better than most employees. She had the routine down. So why was she worried about getting canned now?

She couldn't figure. Something in the air maybe . . . As good an explanation as any.

Rune continued east, through the area that NYU and the real estate developers were decimating for dorms and boring cinder-block apartments. A large woman thrust a petition toward her. "Save our Neighborhood" it said. Rune passed the woman by. That was one thing about New York. It always changed, like a snake shedding skins. If your favorite area vanished or turned into something you didn't like, there was always another one that'd suit you. All it took was a subway token to find it.

She glanced again at Mr. Kelly's address. 380 East Tenth. Apartment 2B.

She crossed the street and continued past Avenue A, Avenue B. Alphabet soup, alphabet city. The neighborhood growing darker, shabbier, more sullen.

Scarier.

Save our neighborhood . . .

CHAPTER THREE

███████ Haarte didn't like the East Village.

When it came to the coin-toss to see who was going to stake out the target's apartment three weeks ago, after they'd gotten back from the Gittleman hit in St. Louis, he was glad Zane'd won.

He paused on East Tenth and looked for surveillance in front of the tenement. Zane'd been there for a half hour and had said the block looked clean. They'd learned that a while ago the target had vanished from his apartment on the Upper West Side—the apartment the U.S. Marshals Service had provided for him—and he'd given the slip to his minders. But that info was old. The feds might've tracked him down again—those pricks could find anybody if they wanted to—and be checking this building out. So this morning Haarte paused, scanned the street carefully, looking for any signs of baby-sitters. He saw none.

Haarte continued along the sidewalk. The streets

were piled with garbage, moldy books and magazines, old furniture. Cars doubled-parked on the narrow streets. Several moving vans too. People in the Village always seemed to be moving out. Haarte was surprised anybody moved *in*. He'd get the fuck out of this neighborhood as fast as he could.

Today Haarte was wearing an exterminator's uniform, pale blue. He carried a plastic toolbox which contained not the tools of the bug-killers' trade but his Walther automatic on which was mounted his Lansing Arms suppressor. Also inside the box was the Polaroid camera. This uniform wouldn't work everywhere but whenever he had a job in New York—which wasn't often because he lived there—he knew the one thing that people would never be suspicious about was an exterminator.

"I'm almost there," he said into his lapel mike. The other thing about New York was that you could seem to be talking to yourself and nobody thought it was weird.

As Haarte approached the building, 380 East Tenth Street, Zane—parked a block away in a green Pontiac—said, "Street's clear. Saw a shadow in his apartment. Asshole's in there. Or somebody is."

For this hit, the way they'd worked it out, Haarte was going to be the shooter, Zane was getaway.

He said, "Three minutes till I'm inside. Drive around back. Into the alley. Anything goes wrong we split up. Meet me back at my place."

"Okay."

He walked into the foyer of the building. Stinks in here, he thought. Dog pee. Maybe human pee. He shivered slightly. Haarte made over a hundred thousand dollars a year and lived in a very nice town house several miles from here, overlooking the Hudson River and New Jersey. So nice he didn't even *need* an exterminator.

Haarte checked out the lobby and hallway carefully. The target might not be thinking about a hit and Haarte could possibly just call up on the intercom and say that he was there to spray for roaches. The target might just let him in.

But he might also come to the top of the stairway, aim into the foyer with his own piece, and start shooting.

So Haarte decided on the silent approach. He jimmied the front-door lock with a thin piece of steel. The cheap lock clicked open easily.

He stepped inside and took the pistol from his toolbox. Started down the hall to Apartment 2B.

Rune was surprised, seeing Robert Kelly's building.

Surprised the way people sometimes are when they come to visit a friend for the first time. She'd seen his modest clothes and had expected modest quarters. But she was looking at piss-poor. The brick was scaly, diseased, shedding its schoolhouse-red paint in dusty flakes. The wooden window frames were rotting. Rust water had trickled down from the roof and left huge streaks on the front step and sidewalk. Some tenants had patched broken panes with cardboard and cloth and yellowing newspaper.

Of course she'd known that the East Village wasn't the greatest neighborhood—she came to clubs here a lot and hung out with friends in Tompkins Square Park on Avenue A, dodging the druggies and the wanna-be gangsters. But, picturing the gentlemanly Mr. Kelly, the image that had come to mind of his home was a proper English town house with frilly plaster moldings and flowered wallpaper. Outside would be a black wrought-iron fence and a neat garden.

Like the set in a movie she'd seen as a little girl, sitting next to her father—*My Fair Lady*. Kelly would sit in the parlor like Rex Harrison, in front of the fire, and drink tea. He would take small sips (a cup of tea lasted forever in English movies) and read a newspaper that didn't have any comics.

She felt uncomfortable, embarrassed for him. Almost wished that she hadn't come.

Rune walked closer to the building. A three-legged chair lay on its side in the bare-dirt garden outside the front stairs. A bicycle frame was fastened with a Kryptonite lock to a no-parking sign. The wheels, chain, and handlebars had been stolen.

Who else lived in the building? she wondered. Elderly people, she supposed. There were a lot of retirees around there. She herself would rather spend her final years there than in Tampa or San Diego.

But how had they happened to end up there? she wondered.

There'd be a million answers.

Them's the breaks. . . .

The building just across the alley from Mr. Kelly's was much nicer, painted, clean, a fancy security gate on the front door. A blond woman in an expensive pink jogger's outfit and fancy running shoes pushed out the doorway and stepped into the alley. She started her stretching exercises. She was pretty and looked disgustingly pert and professional.

Save our neighborhood . . .

Rune continued to the front stairs of Mr. Kelly's building. An idea occurred to her. She'd pick up the tape but instead of going back to the store she'd take a few hours off. She and Mr. Kelly could go have an adventure.

She'd take him for a long walk beside the Hudson.

"Let's look for sea monsters!" she'd suggest.

And she had this weird idea that he'd play along. There was something about him that made her think they were similar. He was . . . well, mysterious. There was nothing literal about him—being *un*literal was Rune's highest compliment.

She walked into the entryway of his building. Beneath the filth and cobwebs she noticed elaborate mosaic tiles, brass fixtures, carved mahogany trim. If it were scrubbed up and painted, she thought, this'd be a totally excellent place. . . .

She pushed the buzzer to 2B.

That'd be a fun job, she thought. Finding junky old buildings and fixing them up. But people did that for a living, of course. Rich people. Even places like this could cost hundreds of thousands. Anyway, she'd want to paint murals of fairy tales on the walls and decorate the place with stuffed animals and put magical gardens in all the apartments. She supposed there wasn't much of a market for that kind of look.

The intercom crackled. There was a pause. Then a voice said, "Yes?"

"Mr. Kelly?"

"Who is it?" the staticky voice asked.

"Here's Johnnyyyyyyy," she said, trying to impersonate Jack Nicholson in *The Shining*. She and Mr. Kelly had talked about horror films. He seemed to know a lot about movies and they'd joked about how scary the Kubrick film was even though it was so brightly lit.

But apparently he didn't remember. "Who?"

She was disappointed that he didn't get it.

"It's Rune. You know—from Washington Square Video. I'm here to pick up the tape."

Silence.

"Hello?" she called.

Static again. "I'll be there in a minute."

"Is this Mr. Kelly?" The voice didn't sound quite right. Maybe it wasn't him. Maybe he had a visitor.

"A minute."

"I can come up."

A pause. "Wait there," the voice commanded.

This was weird. He'd always seemed so polite. He didn't sound that way now. Must be the intercom.

Several minutes passed. She paced around the entryway.

She was looking outside when, finally, she heard footsteps from inside, coming down the stairs.

Rune walked to the inner door, peered through the greasy glass. She couldn't see through it. A figure walked forward slowly. Was it Mr. Kelly? She couldn't tell.

The door opened.

"Oh," she said in surprise, looking up.

The woman in her fifties, with olive-tinted skin, stepped out, glanced at her. She made sure the door closed before she left the entryway so Rune couldn't get inside—standard New York City security procedures when unknown visitors were in the lobby. The woman carried a bag of empty soda and beer cans. She took them out to the curb and dropped them in a recycling bin.

"Mr. Kelly?" Rune called again into the intercom. "You all right?"

There was no answer.

The woman returned and looked over Rune carefully. "Help you?" She had a thick Caribbean accent.

"I'm a friend of Mr. Kelly's."

"Oh." Her face relaxed.

"I just called him. He was going to come down."

"He's on the second floor."

"I know. I'm supposed to pick up a videotape. I called five minutes ago and he said he'd be right out."

"I just walked past his door an' it was open," she said. "I live up the hall."

Rune pushed the buzzer and said, "Mr. Kelly? Hello? Hello?"

There was no answer.

"I'ma go see," the woman said. "You wait here."

She disappeared inside. After a moment Rune grew impatient and buzzed again. No answer. She tried the door. Then she wondered if there was another door— maybe in the side or in the back of the building.

She stepped outside. Walked to the sidewalk and then continued on to the alley. The pert yuppie woman was still there, stretching. The only exercise Rune got was dancing at her favorite clubs: World or Area or Limelight (dancing was aerobic and she also built upper-body strength by pushing away drunk lawyers and account execs in the clubs' co-ed rest rooms).

No, there was nobody else. Maybe she—

Then she heard the scream.

She turned fast and looked at Mr. Kelly's building. Heard a woman's voice, in panic, calling for help. Rune believed the voice had an accent—maybe the woman she'd just met, the woman who knew Mr. Kelly. "Somebody," the voice cried, "call the police. Oh, please, help!"

Rune glanced at the woman jogger, who stared at Rune with an equally shocked expression on her face.

Then a huge squeal of tires from behind them.

At the end of the alley a green car skidded around the corner and made straight for Rune and the jogger. They both froze in panic as the car bore down on them.

What's he doing, what's he doing, what's he doing? Rune thought madly.

No, no, no . . .

When the car was only feet away she flung herself backward out of the alley. The jogger leapt the opposite way. But the woman in pink hadn't moved as fast as Rune and she was struck by the side-view mirror of the car. She was thrown into the brick wall of her building. She hit the wall and tumbled to the ground.

The car skidded onto Tenth Street and vanished.

Rune ran to the woman, who was alive but unconscious, blood pouring from a gash on her forehead. Rune
sprinted up the street to find a pay phone. It took her
four phones, and three blocks, before she found one that
worked.

CHAPTER FOUR

Mr. Kelly's door was open.

Rune stopped in the doorway, stared in shock at the eight people who stood in the room. No one seemed to be moving. They stood or crouched, singly or in groups, like the mannequins she'd seen in the import store on University Place.

Gasping, she rested against the doorjamb. She'd raced back from the pay phone and charged up the stairs. No trouble getting in this time; the cops or the Emergency Medical Service medics had wedged the building door open.

She watched them: six men and two women, some in police uniforms, some in suits.

Her eyes fell on the ninth person in the room and her hands began to tremble.

Oh, no . . . oh, no . . .

The ninth person—the man whose apartment it was. Robert Kelly. He sat in an old armchair, arms out-

stretched, limp, palms up, eyes open and staring sky-
ward, like Jesus or some saint in those weird religious
paintings at the Met. His flesh was very pale—everywhere except his chest. Which was brown-red from all
the blood. There was a lot of it.

Oh, no . . .

Her breath shrank to nothing, short gasps, she was
dizzy. Oh, goddamn him! Tony! For making her pick up
the tape and see this. God*damn* Frankie Greek, god*damn*
Eddie for pretending to fix the fucking monitors when all
they were really doing was figuring out how to get into a
concert for free . . .

Her eyes pricked with tears. *Goddamn.*

But then Rune had a curious thought. That, no, no, if
this *had* to happen, it was better that *she* was there, rather
than them. At least she was Mr. Kelly's friend. Eddie or
Frankie would've walked in and said, "Wow, cool, a
shooting," and it was better for her to be the one to see
this, out of respect for him.

No one noticed her. Two men in business suits gave
instructions to a third, who nodded. The uniformed cops
were crouched down, writing notes, some were putting a
white powder on dark things, a black powder on light.

Rune studied the faces of the cops. She couldn't look
away. There was something odd about them and she
couldn't figure it out at first. They just seemed like everybody else—amused or bored or curious about something. Then she realized: *that's* what was odd. That there
was nothing out of the ordinary about them. They all had
a workaday glaze in their eyes. They weren't horrified or
sickened by what they were looking at.

God, they seemed just like the clerks in Washington
Square Video.

They looked just like me, doing what I do, renting
movies eight hours a day, four days a week: just doing
the job. The Big Boring J.

They didn't even seem to notice, or to care, that somebody had just been killed.

Her eyes moved around the apartment slowly. Mr. Kelly lived *here*? Grease-spotted wallpaper sagged. The carpet was orange and made out of thick, stubby strands. The whole place smelled like sour meat. There was no art on the walls: some old-time movie posters in frames leaned against a shabby couch. A dozen boxes were scattered on the floor. It seemed he'd been living out of them. Even his clothes and dishes were stacked in cartons. He must have moved in recently, maybe around the time he'd joined the video club, a month before.

She remembered the first time he'd come into Washington Square Video.

"Can you spell your name?" Rune'd asked, filling out his application.

"Yes, I can," he'd answered, offhand. "I'm of above-average intelligence. Now, do you *want* me to?"

She'd loved that and they'd laughed. Then she'd taken down the rest of the facts about Kelly, Robert, deposit: cash. Address: 380 East Tenth Street, Apt. 2B. He'd wanted a detective film, and, thinking about the old *Dragnet* series, she'd said, "All we want is the facts, sir, just the facts."

He'd laughed again.

No credit cards. She remembered thinking that was definitely one thing they had in common.

What were the words? You knew them real well at one time. How did they go?

Rune's eyes were on *him* now. A dead man who was a little heavy, tall, dignified, seventh-decade balding.

All that the father giveth me, he that raised up Jesus from the dead will also quicken up our mortal bodies . . .

What bothered her most, she decided, was the completely still way Mr. Kelly lay. A human being not moving at all. She shuddered. That stillness made the mystery of life all the more astonishing and precious.

I heard a voice from Heaven saying ashes to ashes, dust to dust, sure and certain I hope for Resurrection, and the sea shall give up . . .

The words coming fast now. She pictured her father, laid out by the talented siblings of Charles & Sons in Shaker Heights. Five years before. Rune had a vivid recollection of the man, lying in the satiny upholstery. But that day her father had been a stranger—a caricature of the human being he'd been when alive. With the makeup, the new suit, the smoothed hair, there was something slick and phony about him. He didn't even seem dead: he just seemed odd.

There was something far more real about Mr. Kelly. He wasn't a sculpture; he wasn't unreal at all. And death was staring right back at her. She felt the room tilting and had to concentrate on breathing. The tears tickled her cheeks with a painful irritation.

The Lord be with you and with thy spirit blessed be the name of the Lord. . . .

One of the men near the body noticed her. A short man in a suit, mustachioed. Trimmed black hair flowing away from his center part, held close to his head with spray. His eyes were close together and that made Rune think he was stupid.

"You're one of the witnesses? You're the one called nine one one?"

She nodded.

The man noticed where her eyes were aimed. He stepped between her and Mr. Kelly's body.

"I'm Detective Manelli. You know the deceased?"

"What happened?" Her mouth was dry and the words vanished in her throat. She repeated the question.

The detective, watching her face, probably trying to figure out where she fit on the spectrum of relationships, said, "That's what we're trying to find out. Did you know him?"

She nodded. She couldn't see the body; her eyes fell to a small metal suitcase stenciled with the words CRIME SCENE UNIT. They fixed on the case, wouldn't let go.

"The tape. I was supposed to pick up the tape. For my job."

"Tape? What tape?"

She pointed to a plastic bag with blue letters, WSV, printed on it. "That's my store. He rented a movie yesterday. I was supposed to pick it up."

"You have some ID?"

She handed Manelli her real driver's license and her employee discount card. He jotted down some information. "You have a New York address?"

She gave it to him. This he wrote down too. Handed back the cards. He didn't seem to think she was involved. Maybe in his line of work you got a feel for who was a real killer.

In a soft voice Rune said, "I was the one who rented the tape to him. It was me. Yesterday." She whispered manically, "I just saw him yesterday. I . . . He was fine then. I talked to him just a few minutes ago."

"You talked to him?"

"I just called on the intercom."

"You're sure it was him?" the detective asked.

She felt a thud in her chest. Recalling that the voice sounded different. Maybe it was the killer she'd talked to. Her legs went weak. "No, I'm not."

"Did you recognize the voice?"

"No. But . . . it didn't sound like Mr. Kelly. I didn't think anything about it. I don't know—I thought maybe I woke him up or something."

"The voice? Young, old, black, Hispanic?"

She shook her head. "I don't know. I couldn't tell."

"You were outside? Did you see anything?"

"I was in the alley. This green car tried to run us down."

"Us?" Manelli repeated. "You and the woman from next door?"

"Right."

"What kind of car was it?"

"I don't know."

"Dark green or light?"

"Dark."

"Tags?"

"What?" Rune asked.

"The license plate number. You notice it?"

"He was trying to run me down, the driver."

"You didn't see the number, you mean?"

"That's what I mean. I didn't see it."

"How 'bout the state?" the detective asked.

"No."

He sighed. "You see the driver?"

"No. There was too much glare."

Another man in a suit came up to them. He smelled of bitter cigarettes. "Whatta we got?"

Manelli said to him, "Here's what it looks like, Captain. This lady comes to pick up a videotape. She calls on the intercom and we think the perp answers. Probably after he does the vic."

Does the vic. Rune stared at the detective, furious at the callousness.

"Pops him three in the chest. No defensive wounds, so it happened fast. He never even tried to dodge. And one in the TV."

"The TV?"

Rune followed their eyes. The killer had shot out the TV set. A spidery fracture surrounded a small black hole in the upper right. It was, she noticed, a very old, cheap set.

Manelli continued. "Then this neighbor up the

hall—" He looked at his notebook. "Amanda LeClerc. She comes upstairs and finds him dead."

"Nobody hears anything?" the captain asked.

"No. Not even the shots . . . Okay, then the killer or his backup's in a car in the alley. He bolts and takes out one witness."

And nearly me too, Rune thought. As if they care.

Manelli consulted his notebook again. "Name's Susan Edelman. Lives next door." He nodded toward the building where Rune had seen the jogger stretching.

"Ice her?" the captain asked.

Ice . . . do . . . These people had no respect for human beings.

"No," Manelli said. "But Edelman's in no shape to say anything. Not for a while."

Rune remembered the woman lying on the greasy cobblestones of the alley. Blood on her pink jogging suit. Remembered feeling guilty that she'd put down the poor woman for being a yuppie, for being pert.

"This young lady"—Nodding at Rune—"saw the car too. Says she didn't see much."

"Yeah?" the captain asked. "You get a look at the perp?"

"The what?"

"Perp."

Rune shook her head. "I speak English. It's my native language."

"The driver."

"No."

"How many people were in the car?" the captain continued.

"I don't know. There was glare. I told *him* that."

"Yeah," the captain said doubtfully. "Some people think there's glare when they just don't *want* to see anything. But you don't hafta worry. We take care of witnesses. You'll be safe."

"I wasn't a witness. I didn't see anything. I was getting out of the way of a car that was trying to run me over. It's a little distracting. . . ."

Her eyes strayed again to the corpse; she found she'd eased to the side of the slow detective. Finally she forced herself to look away. She glanced up at Manelli.

"The tape," she said.

"What?"

"Can I get the tape? I'm supposed to take it back to where I work."

She saw the cover for the cassette. *Manhattan Is My Beat.*

Manelli walked over to the VCR and pushed eject. A clatter of the mechanism. The tape eased out. Manelli motioned to a crime-scene cop, who walked over. The detective asked, "Whatta you think? Can she have it?"

"One of my biggest fears." The crime-scene officer's latex-gloved hand lifted the cassette out of the VCR; he looked it over.

"What's that?" Manelli asked the officer.

"I rent *Debbie Does Dallas* and get hit by a bus before I can return it. My widow gets a bill for two thousand bucks for some sleazy porn and—"

Rune said angrily, "That's *not* what he rented and I don't think you should joke."

The technician cleared his throat, kept an awkward grin on his face. He didn't apologize. He said, "Thing is, look at the TV. You know, him shooting it out? Maybe it's a coincidence but I'd say we better dust this tape pretty careful. Maybe the perp looked at it. And we do that, well, I'll tell you I wouldn't run it through *my* VCR with powder on it. This shit'll gum up anything."

Rune said, "You can't just take our tape."

She didn't care about Washington Square Video's inventory. No, what bothered her was that the cops were keeping the one thing that connected her to Robert Kelly. Stupid, she thought. But she wanted that tape.

"We can actually. Yeah."

"No, you can't. It's ours. And I want it."

The captain was irritated with her but Manelli, even if he too was pissed off, was trying to remain civil-servant polite. He said, "Why don't we go downstairs? You're not supposed to be here anyway."

Rune glanced one last time at Robert Kelly, then followed the detective into the hall, which was hot and filled with the smells of dust and mold and cooking food. They walked down the stairs.

Outside, leaning on an unmarked police car, Manelli said to her, "About the tape—we've gotta keep it. Sorry. Your boss wants to complain, have him or his lawyer call the corporation counsel. But we gotta. Might be evidence."

"Why? You think the killer watched the movie?" she asked.

The detective said, "He may have picked it up to see if it was worth taking."

"And then shot the TV because it wasn't?"

The detective said, "Maybe."

"That's crazy," Rune said.

"Murder's crazy."

She was remembering the pattern the blood made on Mr. Kelly's chest.

He asked, "Tell me true. How well did you know him?"

Rune didn't answer for a moment. She wiped her eyes and nose with the tail of her shirt-vest. "Not well. He was a customer is all."

"You couldn't tell us anything about him?"

Rune started to say, sure, but then realized that, no, she couldn't. Everything she thought she knew, which was a lot, she'd just made up: the wife who was dead of cancer, the children who'd moved away, a distinguished military career in the Pacific, a job in the garment district, a totally cool retirement party he still talked about ten years later. In the past few years he'd met a group of retirees in the East Village, getting to know them over the months at the A&P or Social Security or one of the shabby drugstores or coffee shops on Avenues A or B. Gradually—he'd have been shy about it—he would've suggested getting together for a game of bridge or a trip to Atlantic City to play the slots or saved their money to hear a rehearsal at the Met.

These were scenes she could picture perfectly. Scenes from movies she'd seen a dozen times.

Only none of it was true.

All she could tell this cop was that Kelly, Robert, deposit: cash, wore suits and ties even in retirement. He liked to laugh. He was polite. He had the courage to eat in restaurants by himself on holidays.

And he was a lot like her.

Rune said to the cop, "Nothing. I don't really know a thing."

The detective handed her one of his cards. "And you really didn't see anything?"

"No."

He accepted this. "All right. You think of something, call me. Sometimes that happens. A day or two goes by and people remember things."

When he'd turned away and started up the stairs she said, "Hey."

He paused, looked back.

"You get the asshole that did this, that would be a real good thing, you know?"

"That's why I do what I do." He continued up the stairs.

The Crime Scene cop passed him and walked outside, carrying his metal suitcase. Rune glanced at him, started to walk away, then turned back. He looked at her, then away as he continued to his station wagon.

She called to him, "Oh, one thing. For your information, Mr. Kelly didn't rent dirty movies. For some reason—don't ask me why—he liked movies about cops."

⎯⎯⎯

How big a problem was it?

Haarte considered this, walking quickly toward the subway.

The day was plenty cool—nothing like a muggy spring day around the Mississippi River when they'd gotten Gittleman—but he was sweating like crazy. He'd ditched the exterminator coveralls—they were tossaways, standard procedure after a job—but he was still hot.

He reflected on what'd happened. Part of it was bad luck but he was also at fault. For one thing, he'd decided against hiring local backup because the vic wasn't being minded by the marshals or anybody else. So there was just Zane and him for both surveillance and shooting. Which had worked fine for the St. Louis hit. But here he should've known that some innocents might show up. New York was a big fucking city. More people, more bystanders.

Then, he decided, he'd sent Zane down the alley too early. He just wasn't thinking. So they hadn't had any warning about whoever that girl was who showed up and rang the buzzer, which happened just as Haarte was about to shoot. The vic had risen from his chair and seen Haarte. Haarte had shot him. The old guy had fallen on the remote control and the sound on the TV had gone way up. So Haarte had shot the TV set out too. Which made another loud noise and filled the apartment with a gassy, smoky smell.

Then the girl called on the intercom again. She

sounded concerned. And a moment later there was a call from *another* woman.

Grand Central Station, Jesus . . .

He knew they were suspicious and that they'd be coming upstairs to check on the vic at any minute.

So Haarte decided to split up. He'd told Zane to get back to Haarte's apartment. He'd go by surface transportation. It wasn't a moment too soon. As he climbed out the fire escape window on the east side of the building he'd heard the scream. Then Zane took off and Haarte jumped into the alley and disappeared.

When they'd talked ten minutes later Zane, to his dismay, told him there were witnesses. Two women. One of them had been hit by the Pontiac but the other jumped out of the way in time.

"ID you?" Haarte asked.

"Couldn't tell. I already changed the tags but I think we oughta get the fuck out of town for a while."

Haarte considered this. The broker in St. Louis wouldn't pay without some confirmation of the vic's death. And Haarte hadn't had time to take a Polaroid. He also didn't want to leave the witnesses alive.

"No," he'd told Zane. "We stay. Listen, we need that backup now. Find out who's in town."

"What kind of backup?" Zane asked.

"Somebody who can shoot."

――――――

"Hi, there."

Rune, leaning on the fence in front of Robert Kelly's building, turned. The woman she'd met in the entryway, the woman with the bag of cans, was standing unsteadily on the stoop, arms crossed, tears running down her face.

They'd just brought the old man's body out. Rune had started to leave, after Manelli returned to the apartment, but then she'd decided to stay. She wasn't sure why.

"Your name's Amanda?"

The woman wiped her face with a paper towel and nodded. "That's right. How you know?"

"The cops mentioned it. I'm Rune."

"Rune . . ." She spoke absently.

Other tenants had come downstairs, gossiped about the shooting, then returned to their rooms or headed up the street.

The two detectives left. Manelli said, "Good-bye." The captain hadn't even glanced at her.

Amanda cried some more.

Unable to stop herself, Rune cried too. Wiped her face with the tail of the shirt again.

"How you know him?" Amanda had an accent, Rune decided, that sounded like a female Bob Marley's. Low and sexy.

"From the video store. Washington Square Video. Where he rented movies."

Amanda looked at her like a VCR and renting movies were a luxury she couldn't even imagine.

Rune asked, "How'd *you* know him?"

"Neighbors. Met him when he move in, a month ago. But we got close real fast. What it was, about Robert, he *talk* to you. Nobody else here talk to you. He always ask about my kids, ask where I came from. You know . . . So hard to find somebody who just likes to listen."

Amen, Rune thought.

"He asked me a lot about me too. But he no say much about himself."

"Yeah, that's true. He never seemed to like to talk about the past."

"I no believe this happen. What do you think it was? Why somebody do this?"

Rune shrugged. "Drugs, I'll bet. Around here . . . What else?"

"I no understand why they kill him. He wasn't no threat. If they want to rob him they could take it and just let him be. Why kill?"

Murder's crazy . . .

"He so nice," Amanda continued, speaking softly. "So nice. When I have problems with the landlord, problems with INS, Mr. Kelly help me out. I only know him one month but he write letters for me. He real smart." More tears. "What'm I gonna do?"

Rune put her arm around the woman.

"He help me with my rent. The INS, they took my check. My paycheck. I working but they took my check. I applied for the card, you know. I was trying to do it right, I no cheat nobody or anything. But they wouldn't let me have any money. . . . But Mr. Kelly, he lend me money for the rent. What'm I gonna do now?"

"They going to send you back home?"

She shrugged.

"Where's that?" Rune asked. "Home?"

"I *come* from the Dominican Republic," Amanda said, then added defiantly, "but *this* is my home now. New York City is my home. . . ." She looked back at the building. "Why they kill somebody like him? There're so many bad people out there, so many people with bad hearts. Why they kill somebody like Robert?"

There was no answer for that, of course.

"I have to go," Rune said.

Amanda nodded, wiped her eyes with the shredding paper towel. "Thank you."

Rune asked, "For what?"

"Waiting till they take him away. To say good-bye. That was good of you. That was very good."

CHAPTER FIVE

Near quitting time, Tony came back to the store.

"So where the hell were you this afternoon?"

"I needed to clear my head," Rune told him.

Tony snickered. "That'd take more than one afternoon."

"Tony, no crap. *Por favor.*"

He dropped his backpack in front of the counter and dodged around a cardboard cutout of Sylvester Stallone, who brandished a large cardboard gun. He checked the receipts. "You should've argued with the cop. Christ, that tape . . . it's over a hundred bucks wholesale."

"I gave you the name of the cop to talk to, you want," she shot back. "It's not *my* job. You're the manager."

"Yeah, well, at least you should've come back after. Frankie Greek was here by himself. He gets overloaded when he's got to work by himself."

She said in a low voice, "He gets overloaded when he has to tie his shoes by himself."

Frankie, a scrawny aspiring rock star and high school dropout, had long, curly hair and reminded Rune of the poodle on the pink skirt she'd bought last week at Second-Hand Rose, a vintage clothing store on Broadway. He was in the back room at the moment.

"Well, where *were* you?" Tony persisted.

"Walking around," Rune said. "I didn't feel like coming back. I mean, he was dead. I saw him. Right in front of me."

"Whoa. You see the bullet holes and everything?"

"Oh, Jesus Christ. Hang it up, okay?"

"Are they like in the movies?"

She turned away, kept wiping the counter with Windex. Tony and Frankie both smoked. It made the glass filthy.

"Well, you shoulda called. I was worried."

"Worried? Like, I'm *sure*," she said.

"Just call next time."

Rune had a feel for it now. He was backing down. No trips to unemployment this week. *Them's the breaks* . . . She felt like pushing so she pushed. "There won't *be* a next time. I don't do any more pickups, okay? That's a rule."

"Hey, we're all simpatico here, no? The Washington Square Video family." Tony glanced at Frankie as the skinny young man came out of the back room.

"Think I can fix that monitor," Frankie said.

"Yeah, well, that's not your priority. Locking up's your priority."

The large man slung his dirty red nylon backpack over his shoulder again and disappeared out the front door.

Frankie said, "Like, I heard you talking to Tony."

"And?"

"How come you didn't make up something? About

coming in late today? Like say your mother got sick or something?"

Rune said, "Why would I lie to *Tony*? You only lie to people who have power over you. . . . So what happened with the Palladium?"

Frankie was crestfallen. "We only got one pass and Eddie, like, won the toss. Man. It was Blondie too."

He glanced at a stack of porn tapes that had been returned and needed to be reshelved. One title seemed to interest him. He put it aside. He said, "That guy who was killed. He was that old guy you liked, right?"

"Yeah."

"I don't remember him too good. Was he cool?"

She leaned on the counter, playing with her bracelets. She looked outside. The city had these weird orange streetlamps. It was close to eleven P.M. but the light made the city look like afternoon during a partial eclipse. "Yeah, he was cool." She dug under the counter and found the bootleg tape she'd made for Kelly. Turned it over in her hands. "Also, he was kind of different."

"Like, what? Weird?"

"Not weird the way *you* mean."

"What, uhm, way do I mean?"

She didn't answer. A thought was in her mind. "But there was one thing weird about him. Not him personally. He was the nicest old guy you'd ever want to meet. Polite."

"So what was weird about him?"

"Well, he'd only been a member for a month."

"And?"

"He rented the same movie a lot."

"A lot?"

Rune typed on the keyboard of the little Kaypro portable computer on the counter. Then she read from the screen. "Eighteen times."

"Wow," Frankie said, "that's weird."

"*Manhattan Is My Beat,*" Rune said.

"Never heard of it. About a, like, reporter?"

"A cop. Walking a beat. One of those old-time cop movies from the forties. You know, all the men wearing those big drapey double-breasted suits and have their hair slicked back. Nobody really famous in it. Dana Mitchell, Charlotte Goodman, Ruby Dahl."

"Who're they?"

"You wouldn't know them. They're not part of the Brat Pack. Anyway, the movie just came out on tape a month ago. I'm not surprised nobody was in a hurry to release it. I watched it but it wasn't my style. I like the black and white though. I hate colorization. It's a political issue with me.

"Anyway, Mr. Kelly shows up the day after it's released. We had a poster up in the window. The distributor sent it. . . . Uh, there it is, in the back. . . ."

Frankie glanced. "Oh, yeah, I remember it."

Rune continued. "He comes in and wants to rent it. He wasn't a member so he asks about joining. Then— this *is* weirdness for you—he asks how he puts tapes in his TV. Can you believe it? He doesn't know about VCRs! So I tell him if he doesn't have a player he's got to get one and I tell him where Audio Exchange and Crazy Eddie's are. Well, he doesn't have much money, I can tell, cause he goes, 'Do you think they'll take a check? See, I just moved and it doesn't have my address on it. . . .' That kind of stuff. And I was thinking, yeah, right, the reason they won't take the check isn't the address, it's that there's no money in the account. So I tell him about this place on Canal where they have all kinds of used stuff and he can probably get a VCR for fifty bucks."

"Beta only, I'll bet." Frankie sneered.

"No, they've got VHS. And he leaves and I think

that's the last I'll see of him. But the next day he's back when the store opens and he says he found a player. And he joins and rents this movie he's so interested in. Turns out he's a real sweetheart, we bullshit some, talk movies. . . ."

"Yeah, your date," Frankie observed. "I remember him."

"And he's not flirting or anything. He's just talking. Takes the film home. Eddie picks it up the next day. Okay, couple days later, he calls a delivery in. Rents something I don't know what it is and what else? *Manhattan Is My Beat* again. This goes on for weeks."

Frankie nodded, his shaggy hair bobbing.

"Christ," Rune told him, "I feel so sorry for the guy— I picture him spending all his Social Security check on this stupid movie. I told him just to buy it. But you know Tony. How he marks up? He was charging almost two hundred. What a rip-off. So I tell Mr. Kelly I'm going to copy it for him."

"Man, Tony'd be super pissed, he finds out," Frankie said, lowering his voice as if the store were bugged.

"Yeah, whatever," Rune said. She pictured Mr. Kelly again. "You should've seen his eyes. I thought he was going to cry, he was so happy. Anyway, it was, like, noon or something and he asked if he could take me to lunch, you know, to thank me."

"So did you make the dupe for him?"

Rune's face fell. After a moment she said, "I did, yeah. But it was just a couple days ago. I never got the chance to give it to him. I wish I had. I wish he'd seen it once at least—the tape I'd made, I mean. He said he didn't have anything much to give me now but when he got rich, he'd remember me."

"Yeah, right, I've heard that before."

"I don't know. He said it in a funny way. Like, *when*

his ship came in. It was like . . . Hey, you know fairy stories?"

"Uhm . . . I don't know. You mean, like, Jack and the cornstalk?"

She rolled her eyes. "I was thinking about this one from Japan. About the fisherman Urashima."

"Like, who?" Frankie Greek's eyes were close together too. Like the detective in Mr. Kelly's apartment. Manelli.

"Urashima saved a turtle from some children who were stoning it. He helped it back to the ocean. Only it turned out to be a magic turtle and took him to the sea lord's palace under the ocean."

"How could he breathe underwater?"

"He just could."

"But—"

"Don't worry about it. He could breathe, okay? Anyway, the lord's daughter gave him money and pearls and jewels. Maybe everlasting youth too, I don't remember."

"Man, not too shabby," Frankie said. "Happily ever after."

Rune didn't say anything for a moment. "Not exactly. He blew it."

"What happened?" Frankie seemed marginally interested.

"One of the things the daughter gave him was a box he wasn't supposed to open."

"Why not?"

"Doesn't matter. But he *did* open it and, bang, got turned into an old man in about five seconds flat. See, fairy tales have rules too. You have to play by them. He didn't. You've gotta listen to magic turtles and wizards. So, that's what I was thinking of when Mr. Kelly said something about getting rich. That I did a good deed and he was going to give me a reward."

Frankie added, "Just don't open any magic boxes."

Rune looked up. "So, that's my story about Mr. Kelly. Is it totally bizarre, or what?"

"You ever ask him about it, why he rented it so often?"

"Sure. And you want to hear a sad answer? He said, 'That movie? It's the high-point of my life.' He wouldn't say anything else. I'll bet his wife and him saw it on their honeymoon. Or maybe he had a wild affair with some vampy woman the night it was released and they were in a hotel in Times Square with the premiere right outside their window."

"Like, what'd the cops say about him getting whacked? They have any idea why?"

"They don't know anything. They don't care."

Frankie flicked through the pages in a rock music magazine, undid one of his earrings, looked at it, put it into a third hole in his other ear. He said, "So, you've seen it, you think it's worth being the high-point of someone's life?"

"Depends on how low your life has been."

"Like, what's it about?" the young man asked. "This movie?"

"There's a bank robbery in the 1930s or '40s, okay? Somewhere down in Wall Street. The robbers're holed up with a hostage in the bank and this young cop—you know, in love with the girl next door's name is Mary, *that* kind of hero—goes into the bank to exchange himself for the hostage. Then he kills the robber. . . . And then what happens is the cop can't resist. See, he's in love and he wants to get married but he doesn't have enough money. So he takes the loot and sneaks it out of the bank. Then he buries it someplace. The cops find out about it and throw him off the force and arrest him and he goes to jail."

"That's all?"

"I think he gets out of jail and gets killed before he

digs up the money, only I got bored and didn't pay a lot of attention."

Frankie said, "Hey, here it is. Listen." He read from the video distributor catalogue. " '*Manhattan Is My Beat*. Nineteen forty-seven.' Oh, this is so bogus. Listen. 'A gripping drama of a young, idealistic policeman in New York City, torn between duty and greed.' "

Rune glanced at the clock. Quitting time. She locked the door. "All I know is, if I ever made a movie, I'd shoot anyone who called it a 'gripping drama.' "

Frankie said, "If I ever make a movie anybody can call it anything they want, as long as I, like, get to play on the sound track. Hey, it says here it's based on a true story. About a real bank robbery in Manhattan. Somebody got away with a million dollars. It says it was never recovered."

Really? Rune hadn't known that.

"It's late," she told Frankie. "Let's get out of here. I need to—"

A loud knock on the glass door startled them. A threesome stood outside—a man and woman, arm in arm, and another woman. In their twenties. The couple was in black. Jeans, T-shirts. She was taller than he was, with very short yellow-white hair and pale, caked makeup. Dark purple lips. The man wore high black boots. He was thin. He had a long face, handsome and angular. High cheekbones. They both had yellow Sony Walkman wires and earphones around their necks. Her cord disappeared into his pocket. The look was Downtown Chic and they displayed it like war paint.

The other woman was chubby, had spiky orange hair and she moved her head rhythmically—apparently to music that only she could hear (she *didn't* wear a Walkman headset). The cut and color of her hair reminded Rune of Woody Woodpecker's.

Another knock.

Frankie looked at the clock. "What do I say?"

"One word," Rune said. "The opposite of Open."

But then the young man in black touched the door like a curious alien and gave Rune a smile that said, *How can you do this to us?* He lifted his hands, pressed them together, praying, begging, then kissed his fingertips and looked directly into Rune's eyes.

Frankie called, "Like, we're closed."

Rune said, "Open it."

"What?"

"Open the door."

"But you said—"

"Open the door."

Frankie did.

The man outside said, "Just one tape, fair lady, just one. And then we'll depart from your life forever. . . ."

"Except to return it," Rune said.

"There's that, sure," he said. Walking into the store. "But tonight, we need some amusement. Oh, sorely."

Rune said to the blond woman, "When do you have to have him back to Bellevue?"

The woman shrugged.

The Woodpecker said nothing but walked through the racks of movies, studying them while her head rocked back and forth.

"Are you members?" Rune asked.

The blonde flashed a WSV card.

"Three minutes," Rune said. "You've got three minutes."

The man: "Such a small splinter of life, don't you think?"

"Two and three-quarters," Rune responded. "And counting."

Was this guy over the edge or not? Rune couldn't decide.

The blonde spoke. She asked Frankie, "What's good?"

"Like, I don't know, I'm new here."

"We're all new everywhere," the young man said meaningfully, looking at Rune. "All the time. Every three minutes, every two and a half minutes. David Bowie said that. You like him?"

"I *love* him," Rune said. "How'd he get two different-colored eyes?"

The man was looking at her own eyes. He didn't answer. Didn't matter; she forgot that she'd asked him a question.

Rune found her lipstick and carefully put it on. She brushed out her hair with her fingers. She decided she should be more coy. Looked at her watch. "Two minutes. Less now."

He asked her, "Want to go to a party?"

Rune looked into his eyes. Brown, swimming, paisley. She said, "Maybe. Where?"

"Your place, darling," he said.

Oh, *that* again.

But he caught the expression on her face and, suddenly sounding much more down to earth, said, "All of us, I mean. A party. Wine and Cheez-Its. Innocent. Swear."

Rune looked at Frankie. He shook his shaggy head. "My sister's gonna have her baby anytime. I gotta get home."

"Please?" Downtown Man asked.

Why not? Rune thought. Recalling that her last date had been when there was snow piled up in the gutters.

"One minute," the man said. "Our time is almost depleted." He was back in the ozone and was speaking to the blonde. She looked at the orange-haired friend and said, "We need a movie. Pick one."

"Me?" the Woodpecker asked.

"Hurry," the blonde whispered.

The man: "We have less than a minute until the floods mount, the earth will tremble. . . ."

"Do you always talk that way?" Rune asked.

He smiled.

The Woodpecker grabbed a movie from the shelf. "How about this one?"

"I can live with it," the blonde answered grudgingly.

Frankie checked them out.

The man said, "Poof. Time's up. Let's go."

CHAPTER SIX

██████████ "This is an example of Stanford White's finest work," Rune told them.

Riding up in a freight elevator. A metallic grinding sound, chains clinking. The smell was of grease and mold and wet concrete. Floors under construction, floors dark and abandoned, fell slowly past them. The sound of dripping water. It was a building in the TriBeCa neighborhood—the triangle below Canal Street—dating back to the nineteenth century.

"Stanford White?" the blonde asked.

"The architect," Rune said.

The mysterious man said, "He died for love."

He *knew* that? Rune thought. Impressed. She added, "Murdered by a jealous lover on the top floor of the original Madison Square Garden."

The blonde shrugged as if love were *never* worth dying for.

The Woodpecker said, "Is this legal, living here?"

"But what, of course, is legal?" the man mused. "I mean *whose* sets of laws apply? There are layers upon layers of laws we have to contend with. Some valid, some not."

"What *are* you talking about?" Rune asked him.

He grinned and raised his eyebrows with ambiguous significance.

His name had turned out to be Richard, which disappointed Rune. Somebody this truly renegade should have been named Jean-Paul or Vladmir.

At the top floor the car stopped and they stepped out into a small room filled with boxes stenciled with block Korean letters, suitcases, a broken TV set, an olive-drab drum of civil defense drinking water. A dozen stacks of old beauty magazines. The Woodpecker strolled over to them and studied the covers. "Historical," she said. The only door was labeled "Toilet" in blotchy black ink.

"No windows, how can you stand it?" Richard asked. But Rune didn't answer and disappeared behind a wall of cartons. She climbed an ornate metal stairway, which was in the middle of the room. From the floor above she gave a shrill whistle. "Yo, follow me. . . . Hey, you imagine the trouble I have getting groceries up here? As if I buy groceries."

The trio stopped cold when they reached the next floor. They stood in a glass turret: a huge gazebo on top of the building, its sides rising like a crown. Ten stories below, the city spread around them. The Empire State Building, distant but massive, stern like an indifferent giant out of a Maxfield Parrish illustration. Beyond it, the elegant Chrysler Building. Southward, the city swept away toward the white pillars of the Trade towers. To the east, the frilly Woolworth Building, City Hall. Farther east was a blanket of lights—Brooklyn and Queens. Opposite, the soft darkness of Jersey. Through the glass of the domed ceiling they could see low clouds, glowing pinkish from the city lights.

"She's out—my roommate," Rune explained, looking around. "She's playing Russian roulette in a singles bar. If I don't find her back by this time, eating ice cream from the carton and watching sitcoms, that means she got lucky. Well, that's how *she* describes it."

Rune pulled off her jacket; it went on a hanger, which she hooked onto the armature of a bulbless floor lamp that held an ostrich-feather boa and a fake-zebra-skin sport coat. She unlaced her boots and set them on the floor next to two battered American Touristers. She opened one, looking over shirts and underwear, which she smoothed, adjusting away creases, refolding some of the wild-colored clothes, then took off her socks and put them into the other suitcase.

To Richard she said, "Dresser and dirty clothes hamper." Nodding at the suitcases.

"You rent this?" the Woodpecker asked.

"I just live here. I don't pay any rent."

"Why not?"

"Nobody's asked me to yet."

Richard asked, "How did you get it?"

Rune shrugged. "I found it. I moved in. Nobody else was here."

He said, "It becomes you."

"Being and becoming . . . ," Rune said, recalling something she'd overheard a couple of guys talking about in the video store a week or so ago.

He lifted his eyebrows. "Hey, you know Hegel?"

"Oh, sure," Rune said. "I love movies."

The circle of the floor was divided by a cinder-block wall, which she'd painted sky blue and dabbed with white for clouds. On Rune's side of the loft were four old trunks, a TV, a VCR, three futons piled on top of one another, a dozen pillows in the corner. Two bookcases, completely filled with books, mostly old ones. A half-size refrigerator.

"Where do you cook?" asked the Woodpecker.

"What does it mean, cook?" Rune replied in a thick Hungarian accent.

Richard said, "I feel something epiphanic about this place. Very watershed, you know." He looked in the refrigerator. A bag of half-melted ice cubes, two six-packs of beer, a shriveled apple. "It's not turned on."

"It doesn't work."

"What about utilities?"

Rune pointed to an orange extension cord snaking down the stairs. "Some of the construction guys working downstairs, they let me have electricity. Isn't that nice of them?"

The Woodpecker asked, "What if the owner finds out, couldn't he kick you out?"

"I'd find someplace else."

"You're a very existential person," Richard said.

And the blonde: "I want to start our party."

Rune shut the lights out, lit a dozen candles.

She heard the rasp of another match. The flare reflected in a dozen angled windows. The ripe raw smell of hash flowed through the room. The joint was passed around. Beer too.

The blonde said to the Woodpecker, "Play the movie, the one you picked out."

Rune and Richard sat back on the pillows, watched the blonde take the cassette from the Woodpecker and open the plastic container. Rune whispered to him, "Are you two like an entity or something?" Nodding at the blonde. Then she thought about it. "Or are you *three* an entity?"

Richard's paisley eyes followed the blonde as she crouched and turned on the VCR and television. He said, "I don't know the redhead. But the other one—I met her last year at the Sorbonne, I was writing a thesis on semi-otic interpretations of textile designs."

Is this a joke?

"I was sitting outdoors on the Boulevard St. Germain, and saw her get out of a limousine. I was filled with an intense sense of pre-ordination."

"Like Calvinism," Rune said, remembering some-thing she'd heard her mother, a good Presbyterian, say once. His head turned to her. Frowning, falling out of character, suddenly analytical. He said, "Oh, predestina-tion? Well, that isn't really . . ." He nodded, as he con-sidered something. Then smiled. "Oh, you mean, sort of damned if you do, damned if you don't. . . . That's pretty good. That's perceptive."

"I get off a good one once in a while." What the hell is going on? she wondered. Didn't matter, she supposed. He *seemed* impressed. Appearances count. Though she realized she still didn't have a clue about his relationship with the sullen blonde.

Rune was about to say something cool and giddy about *Casablanca*—about Rick and Ilsa in Paris—when Richard leaned over and kissed her on the mouth.

Whoa . . .

Rune backed off, eyeing the blonde, wondering if she was going to get into a catfight here. But the woman didn't notice—or didn't care. She was stepping back, handing the joint to the Woodpecker, who was adjusting the TV.

Is this crazy? Letting three strangers into my loft.

Sure, it is.

Then, on impulse, she kissed Richard back. Didn't back away until she felt the pressure of his hand on her breast. Then she sat back. "Let's just take it a little easy, okay? I've only known you for a half hour."

"But time is relative."

She kissed his cheek, an innocent peck. Destined

never to be a tall, sultry lover, Rune had flirtatious down cold.

"I'm feeling deprived," he pouted.

She started to give him another *Oh, please* glance but he meant the joint the Woodpecker was holding. "Hey, darling, to each according to his need." The woman inhaled long and gave it to him. He took a drag then passed it to Rune.

He said, "What we'll do is assume a Tantra yoga position."

Rune said, "Tantra yoga?"

"Isn't that the sex one?" the Woodpecker asked.

Rune gave Richard an exasperated grimace.

He said, "People think sex is the thing with Tantra yoga. Wrong. It's breathing. It teaches you how to breathe the right way."

Rune said, "I *know* how to breathe. I'm good at it. I've been doing it all my life."

"Shall we assume the position?"

She was about to hit him with a pillow, when he slipped into an awkward sitting position, three feet away from her, and started to breathe deeply. "Fully clothed," he said. "I meant to add that."

Rune said, "You look like you hurt yourself in a bad fall."

The TV screen flickered, the copyright notice came on.

"Sit next to me," he said. She hesitated. Then did. Their knees touched. She felt a spark of electricity but didn't move any closer.

"What do we do now?"

"Breathe deep and watch the show."

"Yeah," Rune called to the Woodpecker, "what's the movie you picked?"

The credits for *Lesbos Lovers* came on the screen. The blonde pulled the Woodpecker groggily toward her and covered her mouth with her own. Their arms wound around each other and their fingers began undoing buttons.

Rune whispered to Richard, "Oh, you meant *that* show?"

Richard shrugged. "Either one."

In the morning, when Rune woke up, Richard was making coffee on her hot plate.

She asked, "Where're your friends?" She was looking intently for something under the cushions. She surfaced with her Colgate and toothbrush.

He looked around. "Dunno."

"You find the john?"

"Downstairs. I liked the plastic dinosaurs. You did the decorating yourself, I assume."

Rune was examining him. Now he seemed out of place, wearing the black outfit—night clothes—in the bright, open-air loft.

He said, "What's your real name? It's not really Rune, is it?"

"Everybody asks me about my name."

"What do you tell them?" he asked. "The truth?"

"But what's the truth?" Rune smiled at him ambiguously.

Richard laughed. "But the fact you've got a fake name is very interesting. Philosophically, I mean. You know what Walker Percy says about naming? He doesn't mean like first names or family names but humans giving names to things. He says that naming is different from everything else in the universe. A wholly unique act. Think about that."

She did, for a moment, then said, "A year ago, I worked in a diner over on Ninth Avenue. I was Doris then. I think I only took the job to get the name tag they gave us. It said, 'Chelsea Diner. Hi! I'm Doris.' "

He nodded uncertainly. "Doris."

She said, "So, what do you do, Richard?"

"Stuff."

"Oh. I see," she said dubiously.

"Okay. I'm working on a novel." She knew he was a writer or artist. "What's it about?"

"I don't really talk about it much. I'm at a tricky part right now."

This was even better. A mystery man writing a mysterious novel. In the throes of creative angst.

"I write," she said.

"You do?"

"A diary." Rune pulled a thick, water- and ink-stained booklet off the shelf. A picture of a knight—cut from a magazine—was pasted on the cover. "My mother's kept a diary every day of her life. I've only been doing it for a few years. But I write down everything that's major in my life." She nodded at a dozen other booklets on the shelf.

"Everything?" he asked.

"Nearly."

"You going to write anything about me?" Richard asked. He was looking at the notebooks as if he wanted a peek.

"Maybe," Rune said, combing her hair out with her fingers.

He said, "And you . . . You want to be an actress, right?"

"Guess again. You're thinking of what's-her-name: Woody Woodpecker."

"Who?"

"Your friend last night. With the orange hair. The one who ran off with your girlfriend?"

"Whoa, not my girlfriend. She's not even close to bi. I made a pass at her once—"

"You?" Rune asked sarcastically.

"I met her last week at a party. We give good image."

"You—?"

He explained. "We look good together, being chic and making entrances. That's it. Not a meaningful relationship. I don't even know her name."

"Hard to introduce her to your parents in that case."

"That's not in the offing." He carried the coffee to her, set it on the floor next to the futon.

"What about the Sorbonne?" Rune asked.

"Pas de Sorbonne."

"I thought so."

"But I've been to France."

"Jean-Pierre" would be a good name for him too. Or "François." Yeah, he definitely looked like a "François."

"Richard" had to go.

Rune glanced out the window, dug under a futon, and found some sunglasses. She put them on.

"Feeling like a celebrity?" Richard asked, nodding at the fake Ray-Bans.

Suddenly the sun came over the building to the east and the entire room filled with intense raw sunlight.

"Ouch," he said, blinded.

"I maybe'll get curtains. But I can't afford them and my roommate won't help pay."

"You're not paying rent, why have a roommate?"

"Well, she pays *me* something. Anyway, having a roommate's like trial by fire. It toughens you is what it does."

"You don't seem tough to me."

"That's part of being tough—not *looking* tough. Anyway, I'll have to be out in a few months. The owner sold the building and I'm only staying here 'cause I told the contractor that I'm the mistress of the old owner and he dumped me so they're letting me stay until they start renovating this floor. So you going to ask me out on a date?"

"A date? I haven't heard that word for a long time. It sounds, I don't know, like Swahili. I'm not used to it."

True, she supposed. Really chic people don't ask other chic people out on dates. They just *go* places together. Still, there was a certain commitment involved in the concept. So she said, "Date, date, date. There. *Now* you're used to it. So you can ask me out."

"We just spent the night together—"

"On separate futons," she pointed out.

"—and you want a date?"

"I want a date."

"How about dinner?" he asked.

"That's good."

"Okay. I asked you on a date. We'll go out. You happy?"

"It's not a date yet. You have to tell me when. And I mean exactly. Not a month, not a week."

"I'll call you."

"Oh, *that*? Are you kidding? Are men genetically programmed to say those three little words? Gimme a break."

He looked around helplessly. "I don't have my Daytimer here."

He'd *call* her and he had a Daytimer. This was scary. Richard was rapidly losing his appeal.

"Never mind," she said cheerfully.

"Okay, how about tomorrow?" he asked. "I know I'm not doing anything tomorrow."

Not too eager now—watch it. "I guess."

"Where do you want to go?" he asked.

"You can come here. I'll cook."

"I thought you didn't cook."

She said, "I don't cook *well*. But I do cook. We'll save

the Four Seasons for a special occasion." She looked at her wrist. She wore two watches. They'd both stopped working. "What time do you have?"

"Eight."

"Shit, I have to go," Rune said, slipping off her T-shirt.

She could sense Richard watching her thin body, eyes sweeping up and down. She turned to him, wearing only her Bugs Bunny panties. "So, what are you staring at?" Put her hands on her hips.

And got him to blush.

Yes! Score one for me.

"Glad you don't shop at Frederick's of Hollywood," he said.

A good recovery. This boy had potential.

As she dressed, Richard asked, "What's the hurry? I didn't think your store opened until noon."

"Oh, I'm not going to work," she said. "I'm going to the police."

CHAPTER SEVEN

"Miss Rune," Detective Manelli said, "we *are* investigating the case."

She looked at his organized desk. Here—not standing in front of a corpse—he seemed like an insurance agent. The close-together eyes weren't so noticeable; they moved quickly, surveying her, and she decided he might be smarter than she'd thought. His first name was Virgil. She looked at the nameplate twice to make sure she'd read it right.

She nodded at the file open on his desk, the one he'd been reading. "But that's not his case. Mr. Kelly's, I mean."

He took a breath, let it out. "No, it's not."

"Which one is his?" she asked stridently. "How far down is it?" She gestured at the stack of folders.

The captain—the one she'd met in Mr. Kelly's apartment—breezed in. He glanced down with a splinter of recognition but didn't say anything to her.

"They want to hear today," he told Manelli. "About the tourist killing."

"They'll hear today," Manelli said wearily.

"You got anything?"

"No."

"The mayor. You know. The *Post*. The *Daily News*."

"I know."

The captain looked at Rune once again. He left the office.

"We're doing everything according to procedures," Manelli told her.

"Who's the tourist?"

"Somebody from Iowa. Knifed in Times Square. Don't start with me on that."

She said, "Just let me get this straight: You're no closer to finding Mr. Kelly's killer than you were yesterday."

On Manelli's desk, opening up like a mutant flower, was a piece of deli tissue around a mass of corn muffin. He broke off a chunk and ate it. "How 'bout you give us a day or two to make the collar?"

"The . . . ?"

"To arrest the killer."

"I just want to know what happened."

"In New York City, we've got to deal with almost fifteen hundred homicides a year."

"How many people are working on Mr. Kelly's case?"

"Me mostly. But there're other detectives checking things out. Look, Ms. Rune . . ."

"Just Rune."

"What exactly is your interest?"

"He was a nice man."

"The decedent?"

"What a gross word that is. Mr. *Kelly* was a nice man. I liked him. He didn't deserve to get killed."

The detective reached for his coffee, drank some, put it down. "Let me tell you the way it works."

"I know how it works. I've seen enough movies."

"Then you have no idea how it works. Homicide—"

"Why do you have to use such big fancy words? Decedent, homicide. A *man* was *murdered*. Maybe if you said he was *murdered,* you'd work harder to find who did it."

"Miss, murder is only one kind of homicide. Mr. Kelly could have been a victim of manslaughter, negligent homicide, suicide. . . ."

"Suicide?" Her eyebrows lifted in disbelief. "That's a really bad joke."

Manelli snapped back, "A lot of people stage their own deaths to look like murder. Kelly could've hired somebody to do it. For the insurance."

Oh. She hadn't thought of that. Then she asked, "Did he have an insurance policy?"

Manelli hesitated. Then he said, "No."

"I see."

He continued. "Can I finish?"

Rune shrugged.

"We'll interview everybody in the building and everybody hanging around on the streets around the time of the killing. We took down every license number of every car for three blocks around the apartment and we'll interview the owners. We're going through all of the deced— through Mr. Kelly's personal effects. We'll find out if he had any relatives nearby, if any friends have suddenly left town, since most perps—"

"Wait. Perpetrators, right?"

"Yeah. Since more of 'em are friends or relatives of, or at least *know,* the vic. That's the *victim.* Maybe, we're lucky, we'll get a description of a suspect that'll go something like *male Caucasian, six feet. Male black, five eight, wearing dark hat.* Really helpful, understand?" His eyes dropped to a notepad. "Then we'll take what ballistics told us about the gun"—he hesitated—"and check that out."

She jumped on this. "So what do you know about the gun?"

He was glancing at his muffin; it wouldn't rescue him.

"You know *something*," Rune insisted. "I can see it. Something's weird, right? Come on! Tell me."

"It was a nine-millimeter, mounted with a rubber-baffled silencer. Commercial. Not home-made, like most sound suppressors are." He seemed not to want to tell her this but felt compelled to. "And the slugs . . . the bullets . . . they were Teflon coated."

"Teflon? Like with pots and pans?"

"Yeah. They go through some bulletproof vests. They're illegal."

Rune nodded. "That's weird?"

"You don't see bullets like that very often. Usually just professional killers use them. Just like only pros use commercial silencers."

"Keep going. About the investigation."

"Then sooner or later, while we're doing all that work, maybe in three or four months, we'll get a tip. Somebody got ripped off by a buddy whose cousin was at a party boasting he iced somebody in a drug robbery or something because he didn't like the way somebody looked at him. We'll bring in the suspect, we'll talk to him for hours and hours and hours and poke holes in his story until he confesses. That's the way it happens. The way it *always* happens. But you get the picture? It takes *time*. Nothing happens overnight."

"Not if you don't want it to," Rune said. And before he got mad she asked, "So you don't have *any* idea?"

Manelli sighed. "You want my gut feeling? Where he

lived, some kids from Alphabet City needed crack money and killed him for that."

"With fancy-schmancy bullets?"

"Found the gun, stole it from some OC soldier—organized crime—in Brooklyn. Happens."

Rune rolled her eyes. "And this kid who wanted money enough to kill for it shot the TV? And left the VCR? And, hey, did Mr. Kelly have any money on him?"

Manelli sighed again. Pulled a file from halfway down the stack on his desk, opened it. He read through it. "Walking-around money. Forty-two dollars. But the perp probably panicked when you showed up and ran off without taking anything."

"Was the room ransacked?"

"It didn't appear to be."

Rune said, "I want to look through it."

"The room?" The detective laughed. "No way. It's sealed. No one can go in." He studied her face. "Listen up. I've seen that look before. . . . You break in, it'll be trespassing. That's a crime. And I'd be more than happy to give your name to the prosecutor."

He broke off another piece of muffin, looked at it. Set it down on the paper. "What exactly do you want?" he asked. It wasn't a dismissal; he seemed just curious. His voice was formal and soft.

"Did you know he'd rented that movie that was in his VCR eighteen times in one month?"

"So?"

"Doesn't that seem odd?"

"I seen people jump off the Brooklyn Bridge because they think their cat's possessed by Satan. Nothing seems odd to me."

"But the movie he rented . . . get this. It was about a true crime. Some robbers stole a million dollars and the money was never found."

"When?" he asked, frowning. "I never heard about that."

"It was, like, fifty years ago."

Now Manelli got to roll his eyes.

She leaned forward, said enthusiastically, "But it's a mystery! Don't mysteries excite you?"

"No. *Solving* mysteries excites me."

"Well, this's one that oughta be solved."

"And it will be. In due time. I gotta get back to work."

"What about the other witness?" Rune asked. "Susan Edelman? The one who got hit by the car."

"She's still in the hospital."

"Has she told you anything?"

"We haven't interviewed her yet. Now, I really have to—"

Rune asked, "What'll happen with Mr. Kelly's body?"

"He doesn't seem to have any living relatives. His sister died a couple of years ago. There's a friend in the building? Amanda LeClerc? She put in a claim for permission to dispose of the body. We'll keep it in the M.E.'s office until that's approved. So. That's all I can tell you. Now, you don't mind, I have to get back to work."

Rune, feeling an odd mixture of anger and sorrow, stood and walked to the door. The detective said, "Miss?" She paused with her hand on the doorknob. "You saw what happened to Mr. Kelly. You saw what happened to Ms. Edelman. Whatever you feel, I understand. But don't try to help us out. That's a real bastard out there. This isn't the movies. People get hurt."

Rune said, "Just answer one question. Please, just one?"

Silence in the small office. From outside: the noise of computer printers, typewriters, voices from the offices around them. Rune asked, "What if Mr. Kelly was a rich banker? Would you still not give a shit?"

Manelli didn't move for a moment. Glanced at the

muffin. Didn't say anything. Rune thought: He thinks I'm a pain in the ass. He sort of likes me but I'm still a pain in the ass.

He said, "If he was from the Upper East Side? He was a partner in a big law firm? Then I wouldn't be handling the case. But if I was, the file'd still be seventh in my stack."

Rune nodded at his desk. "Take a look. It's on the top now."

CHAPTER EIGHT

She'd called Amanda LeClerc but the woman wasn't home to let her into Mr. Kelly's building.

So she had to do it the old-fashioned way. The way Detective Manelli unknowingly suggested.

Breaking and entering.

At the bodega up the street from Mr. Kelly's building she told the clerk, "Two boxes of diapers, please. Put them in two bags."

And paid twenty bucks for one pair of Playtex rubber gloves and two huge boxes of disposable diapers.

"*Muchos niños?*" the lady asked.

Rune took the bulgins bags and said, "*Sí.* The Pope, you know?"

The clerk, not much older than Rune, nodded sympathetically.

She walked out of the bodega toward Avenue B. It was already fiercely hot and a ripe, garbagey smell came from the streets. She passed an art gallery. In the window were wild canvases, violent red and black slashes of paint. She smelled steamed meat as she passed a Ukrainian restaurant. In front of a Korean deli was a sign: HOT FOOD $1.50/QTR LB.

Alphabetville . . .

At Kelly's building Rune climbed the concrete stairs to the lobby. Remembering the man's voice from the intercom. Who was it? She shivered as she stared at the webby speaker.

She tried Amanda once again but there was no answer, so she looked around. Outside there was only one person on the street, a handsome man in his thirties. A Pretty Boy, a thug, from a Martin Scorsese film. He wore a uniform of some kind—like the people who read gas and electric meters do. He sat across the street on a doorstep and read a tabloid newspaper. The headline was about the tourist who'd been knifed in Times Square. The case Detective Manelli was supposed to talk to the captain about. Rune turned back, set the bags down, opened one box of diapers, and stuffed two of the pads under her black T-shirt. She buttoned the white blouse over it. She looked about thirteen months pregnant.

Then she picked up the bags, crimped them awkwardly under her arms, and opened the huge leopardskin purse, staring into the black hole with a scowl, dipping her hand into the stew of keys, pens, makeup, candy, Kleenex, a knife, old condom boxes, scraps of paper, letters, music cassettes, a can of cheese spread. For five minutes she kept at it. Then she heard the steps, someone coming down the stairs, a young man.

Rune looked up at him. Embarrassed, letting one of the bags of diapers slide to the ground.

Just be a klutz, she told herself; Lord knows you've had plenty of practice. She picked up one of the bags and accidentally on purpose dropped her purse on the ground.

"Need a hand?" the young man asked, unlocking the outer door and pushing it open for her.

Retrieving her purse, stuffing it under her arm. "My keys are in the bottom of this mess," she said. Then, thinking she should take the initiative, she frowned and said quickly: "Wait—you new here? I don't think I've seen you before."

"Uhm. About six months." He was defensive.

She pretended to relax. She walked past him. "Sorry, but you know how it is. New York, I mean."

"Yeah, I know."

"Thanks."

"Yeah." He disappeared down the first-floor hallway.

Rune climbed to the second floor. There was a red sign on the door to Mr. Kelly's apartment. DO NOT ENTER. CRIME SCENE. NYPD. The door was locked. Rune set the diapers in the incinerator room and returned to Mr. Kelly's door. She took a hammer and a large screwdriver from her purse. Eddie, from the store, who'd made her promise to forget he'd given her a lesson in burglary, had said the only problem would be the dead bolt. And if there was a Medeco and a metal door frame she could forget it. But if it was just the door tumbler and wood and if she didn't mind a little noise . . .

Rune put on the Playtex gloves—thinking about fingerprints. They were the smallest size she could find at the bodega but were still too big and flopped around on her hands. She tapped the screwdriver into the crack between the door and the jamb just about where the bolt was. Then looked up and down the hall and took the hammer in both hands. Drew it back like a baseball bat, remembering when she used to play tomboy softball in high school. She looked around again. The corridor was empty. She swung as hard as she could at the handle of the screwdriver.

And, just like at softball, she missed completely. The

gloves slipped and with the crack of a gunshot the hammer streaked past the screwdriver and slammed through the cheap paneling of the door.

"Shit."

Trying to pull the hammer out of the thin wood, she worked a large splintery piece toward her. It cracked and fell to the floor.

She drew back again, aiming at the screwdriver, but then she noticed that the hole she'd made was large enough to get her hand through. She reached in, found the door lock and the dead bolt, and got it open. Then pushed the door wide. She stepped inside and closed the door quickly.

And she froze.

Bastards!

A tornado had hit the place. The explosive clutter of disaster. Goddamn bastards, goddamn police! Every book was on the floor, every drawer open, the couch slashed apart. The boxes dumped out, clothing scattered. One bald spot in the mess: under Kelly's floor lamp, next to the chair with its dark, horrible stain and the small bullet holes with spiny brown tufts of upholstery stuffing sprouting outward. Whoever had ransacked the room had stood there—or even sat in the terrible chair!—under the light and examined everything, then thrown it aside.

Bastards.

Her first thought had been: The police did this? And she was ready to cab it right back to the police station and give Virgil Manelli hell, the narrow-eyed son of a bitch, but she remembered the detective's neat desk, his brisk haircut and trimmed mustache. And she decided that someone else had done it. A window was open and the fire escape was right outside the sill. Anybody could've broken in. Hell, *she* had.

But it wasn't druggies either: the VCR and clock radio were still here.

Who had it been? And what were they looking for?

For an hour, Rune browsed through the mountains of Mr. Kelly's life. She looked at everything—*almost* everything. Not the clothes. Even with the gloves on, they were too spooky to touch. But the rest she studied carefully: books, letters, the start of a diary—only three entries from years ago, revealing nothing except the weather and his sister's health—boxes of food the bold roaches were already looting, bills, receipts, photos, shoeboxes.

As she sifted carefully through everything, she learned a bit about Mr. Robert Kelly.

He'd been born in 1915 in Cape Girardeau, Missouri. He'd come to New York in 1935. Then moved to California. He'd volunteered for the Army Air Corps and served with the Ninth Air Force. A sergeant, supervising ordnance. In some of his letters (he'd used the words "Dearest Sister" or "Darling Mother," which made Rune cry) he'd written about the bombs that were loaded into the A-20 airplanes on their raids against occupied France and Germany. Sometimes he'd write his name in chalk on the 500-pounders. Proud that he was helping win the war.

She found pictures of him in performances in the USO for soldiers in someplace called East Anglia. He seemed to be a sad-faced stand-up comic.

After the war there seemed to be a five-year gap in his life. There was no record of what he'd done from 1945 until 1950.

In 1952 he'd married a woman in Los Angeles and had apparently begun a series of sales jobs. Insurance for a while, then some kind of machinery that had something to do with commercial printing. His wife had died ten years ago. They'd had no children, it seemed. He was close to his sister. He took early retirement. Somehow he'd ended up back here in the New York area.

Most of what she found was simply biographical. But there were several things that troubled her.

The first was a photograph of Mr. Kelly with his sister—their names were on the back—taken five years before. (He looked exactly the same as he had last week and she decided he was the sort that aged early, like her own father, and then seemed frozen in time in their later years.) What was odd about the picture was that it had been torn into pieces. Kelly himself hadn't done it, since one square had been lying on the dried bloodstain. It had been torn by the ransackers.

The other thing that caught her attention was an old newspaper clipping. A bookmark in a battered copy of a Daphne du Maurier novel. The clipping, from the *New York Journal American,* dated 1948, read, *Movie Tells True Story of Gotham Crime.* It was underlined and asterisks were in the margin.

Fans of the hit film Manhattan Is My Beat, *now showing on Forty-second Street, may recognize on the silver screen the true story of one of New York's finest. . . .*

Footsteps sounded outside the door. Rune looked up. They passed by but she thought they'd slowed. A chill of panic touched her spine and wouldn't leave. She remembered where she was, what she was doing. Remembered that Manelli had warned her not to come here.

Remembered that the killer was still at large.

Time to leave . . .

Rune slipped the clipping into her bag and stood. She looked at the door, then at the window, and decided the fire escape was the choice of pros. She walked to the window and flung the curtain aside.

Jesus my Lord!

She stumbled backward as the man on the fire escape, his face a foot away from her, screamed.

Not a gasp or shout but a gut-shaking scream. She'd scared the hell out of him. He'd been standing outside on the fire escape, peering cautiously through the window. Now he backed away slowly, nearly paralyzed with terror, it seemed, easing step by step up the peeling black-enameled metal. Then he turned and sprinted up toward the third floor.

She guessed he was in his late sixties. He was balding, with a face that was tough and pocked and gray. Not the kind of face that should be screaming.

Her heart was pounding from the shock of the surprise. Her legs felt rubbery. She stood up slowly and pushed her head out the window.

Squinting, she watched him—his fat belly taut above hammy pumping legs—as he climbed through the window directly above Kelly's apartment. She heard his footsteps walking heavily and quickly overhead. She heard a door slam.

Rune hesitated, then walked to the front door, knelt down, and looked out through the crack. Coming down the stairs: scuffed shoes, baggy fat-man's pants, and suit jacket tight around the arms. Then his tough, pocked face, under a brown hat.

Yes, it was him, the man from the fire escape. He walked very quietly. He didn't want to be heard.

He's leaving, thank you, God. . . .

His face was the color of cooked pork; sweat glistening on his forehead.

. . . thank you, thank you, thank—

Then he stopped and looked at the door to Mr. Kelly's apartment for a long while. No, it's okay. He thinks I've left. He won't try to come inside.

Thank . . .

The man stepped closer. No . . . It's all right, she

told herself again. He thinks that once he went upstairs I climbed out onto the fire escape and got away through the alley.

. . . *you.*

Another step, as cautious as Don Johnson closing in on a dozen drug dealers in *Miami Vice.* The man paused, a foot away.

Rune was afraid to lock the dead bolt or put the chain on; he'd hear her. She pressed her palms against the door, pushing as hard as she could. The man walked directly to it, then stopped, inches away. The thin wood—hell, she'd whacked right through it herself—was all that protected her. Rune's small muscles trembled as she pressed against the door.

Which is when the screwdriver slid out of her pocket. In horror, she watched it fall—as if it were in slow motion. It was a scene from a Brian DePalma movie. She grabbed at the tool, caught it, then fumbled it . . . *No!*

She reached down fast and managed to snag the screwdriver an inch above the oak slats of the floor.

Thank you . . .

Frozen in position, like the game of statue she played as a kid, Rune listened to the man's labored breathing. He hadn't heard anything.

He'd *have* to know she left. He'd *have* to!

She slipped the screwdriver back into her pocket, but as she did so, she brushed the claws of the hammer, which was hooked into the waistband of her pants. The tool fell straight to the floor, its head bouncing twice with echoing slams.

"No!" she shouted in a whisper. Planting her feet on the opposite wall, leaning hard into the door, Rune ducked her head, waiting for the fist that she knew would slam through the cheap wood, clawing for her hair, her eyes. She'd be dead. Just like Robert Kelly. It would only be a matter of minutes, seconds, and she would die.

But, no . . . He turned and ran down the stairs.

Finally Rune stood, staring at her shaking hands and remembering some movie she'd seen recently where the teenage hero had escaped from some killer and had stood frozen, gazing at his quivering hands; Rune had groaned at the cliché. But it wasn't a cliché at all. Her hands were trembling so badly she could hardly open the door. She peered out, hearing sounds of chatting voices and far-off TVs. Children's squeals.

Why had he run? she wondered. Who was he? A witness? The killer's accomplice?

The killer?

Rune—every muscle shaking—walked fast to the incinerator room, scooped up the diapers, and hurried down the stairs. Two women on the landing nodded at her, preoccupied with their conversation.

Rune started past them, head down. But then she paused and in an exasperated voice said, "People don't know how to behave anymore. They don't know a thing about it, do they?"

The women looked at her, smiling in polite curiosity.

"That guy a minute ago? He almost knocked me over."

"Me too," one woman said. Her gray hair was in pink curlers.

"Who is he?" Rune asked, breathing hard, leaning against the banister.

"That's Mr. Symington. In 3B. He crazy." The woman didn't elaborate.

So he lived here. Which meant he probably wasn't the killer. More likely a witness.

"Yeah," the woman's friend added, "move up there last month."

"What's his first name?"

"Victor, I think. Something like that. Never says hello or nothing."

"So what?" the curler woman said. "He's nobody you'd want to talk to anyway."

"I don't know," Rune said indignantly. "*I'd* have a couple things to tell him."

The curler woman pointed to the box of diapers. "Greatest invention ever was."

"After TV," her friend said.

Rune said, "Well, sure," and started down the stairs.

———

She ran into Amanda on the street corner.

"Look," the woman said. She'd been to Hallmark and had bought a fake silver picture frame. Inside she'd put a picture of her and Mr. Kelly. It was at Christmas and they were in front of a skinny pine tree decorated with a few lights and tinsel. There was still a smear of adhesive on the glass from the price tag.

"It's totally cool," Rune said, and started to cry once more.

"You have babies?" Amanda was looking at the diapers.

"Oh. Long story. You want them?"

A faint laugh. "Did that years and years ago."

Rune pitched them out. "I've got a question. What do you know about Victor Symington?"

"That guy live upstairs?"

"Yeah."

Amanda shrugged. "Not so much. He been in the building for maybe six weeks. A month. He never say hi, never say how you doing. I no like him so much. I mean, why not say good morning to people? What's so hard about that? You tell me what's so hard."

"You said Mr. Kelly never talked about his life much?"

"No, he didn't."

"Did he mention anything about a bank robbery? Or a movie called *Manhattan Is My Beat*?"

"You know, I think he say something about that movie. Yeah. A couple times. He was real happy he find it. But he never say anything about a bank robbery."

"Are you going to have a funeral for him? I talked to the police and they said you wanted to bury him."

The woman nodded. Rune thought: This is what you think of when somebody says a "handsome" woman. Amanda wasn't beautiful. But she was ageless and attractive. "He has no family," Amanda said. "I have a friend, he cuts grass at Forest Lawn. Maybe I can work something out with him to get Mr. Kelly buried there. That's a nice place. If I can stay here in the U.S., I mean. But I no think that going to happen."

Rune whispered to her, "Don't give up just yet."

"What?"

"I think Mr. Kelly was about to get a lot of money."

"Mr. Kelly?" Amanda laughed. "He never said anything about that to me."

"I can't say anything for certain. But I think I'm right. *And* I think this Symington knows something about it. If you see him, will you let me know? Don't say anything to him." She gave the woman the number of the video store. "Call me there."

"Sure, sure. I call you."

Rune watched the skepticism surface on her face.

"You don't believe me, do you?" she asked Amanda.

The woman shrugged. "Believe that Mr. Kelly was going to get some money?" She laughed again. "No, I no think so. But, hey, you find it, you let me know," she said. Looked at the picture once more. "You let me know."

Once upon a time . . .

Walking west toward Avenue A. Rune looked up and down the street for Symington. Gone.

The heat was bad. City heat, dense heat, wet heat. She didn't feel like hurrying but she also didn't want to get into a shouting match with Tony so she broke one of her personal rules and hurried to work.

Once upon a time, in a kingdom huge and powerful and filled with many wonders, there was a princess. A very small princess who no one took seriously. . . .

She continued along the sidewalk, feeling exhilarated. She'd met her first black knight—a pock-faced man in his sixties, wearing an ugly brown hat—and escaped from him without being broadsworded to death.

Oh, she was a beautiful princess though she was too short to be a model. A beautiful princess—and would be a lot more beautiful when her hair grew out. Then one day the princess became very sad because a terrible dragon killed a kind old man and stole his secret treasure. A secret treasure that he'd promised to give her part of and that'd also save the bacon of a friend of his who was getting hassled by the creeps at Immigration and Naturalization.

Third Avenue. Broadway. University Place.

So the beautiful princess herself set out to find the dragon. And she did and she slayed him, or slew him, or at least bagged his ass so he'd have to hang around Attica for twenty-five to thirty years. She got the treasure of gold, which she split with the friend and they both netted a cool half million.

Rune walked into the video store, watching Tony inhale the breath that would come out as "Where the fuck've you been?"

"Sorry." Rune held up her hands to pre-empt him. "It's been one of those mornings."

She stepped behind the counter and logged onto the register so fast that she didn't notice, across the street, the man she'd thought of as Pretty Boy, the one in the meter-reader jacket, slide into a booth in the coffee shop. He continued to watch her, just like he'd been watching her as he'd followed her from the building on Tenth Street where they'd hit the old man.

Rune grabbed a handful of tapes, started to reshelve them. Thinking:

And the princess lived happily ever after.

CHAPTER NINE

On the phone with Susan Edelman.

The pink-suited jogger, the one who'd been struck by the car in the alley beside Mr. Kelly's building, couldn't talk long. She was very groggy. "I'm being released, uhm . . . tomorrow. Can you . . . uhm, call me then?"

She gave Rune her phone number but it had only six digits, then tried again and couldn't remember the last four numbers.

Oh, she'll be a great witness, Rune thought sourly.

"I'll look it up in the phone book," Rune told her. "You listed?"

"Uhm, yeah."

"Feel better," Rune told her.

"I got hit by a car," Susan said, as if telling Rune for the first time what had happened.

Rune reshelved a few more tapes, then, as soon as

Tony left, she told Frankie she was going for coffee, then booked out of the store.

Outside, she looked around the streets of the city. Caught a glimpse of somebody who looked familiar—a young man with dark, curly hair—but she couldn't place him. His back was to her. Something familiar about the stance, his muscular build. Where'd she seen him?

Where?

But he stepped quickly into a deli, so she didn't think anything more about him. That was one thing about Greenwich Village. You were always running into people you knew. Everyone thought New York was a huge city but that wasn't true; it was a collection of small towns. A Yellow Cab cruised up the street and she flagged it down. She was in the New York Public Library in twenty minutes.

The books on general city history—there were hundreds—didn't help her much at all. The history of *crime* in New York . . . that was something else. One thing she learned was that in Manhattan there were more bank robberies per square mile than anywhere in the country—and most of them occurred on Friday. The traditional payday. So with that volume of heists, the Union Bank stickup didn't get much coverage. She found a few references to it. The only one that gave any details was in a book about the Mafia, which reported only that the Family probably wasn't involved.

The newspapers were better—though the robbery didn't get a lot of coverage because it hadn't occurred on a slow-news day. At the same time the hero cop was bargaining with the holdup man for the hostage's life, the rest of the world was following King Edward's abdication, which had filled all the city papers with features and sidebars. Rune couldn't help but read some of the articles; she decided it was the most romantic thing she'd ever heard. She studied the picture of Mrs. Simpson.

Would anybody give up a kingdom for me?

Would Richard?

She couldn't come up with a satisfactory answer to that question and turned back to the stories about the Union Bank robbery.

After the shootout was over: the robber was in the morgue and the million bucks was missing, though that didn't seem too important at first because the hostage was safe and Patrolman Samuel Davies was a hero. The only hiccup was that there was no satisfactory explanation as to how the robber passed the suitcase containing the money to his partner outside the bank before Davies started negotiating with him.

> An accomplice of the deceased robber, it is suspected, secreted himself outside the bank and, in a moment of confusion while Patrolman Davies was boldly approaching the bank, seized the ill-gotten loot and absconded.

A month later the question of what had happened to the money had been answered and the newspaper stories were very different.

> Hero Patrolman Indicted in Union Bank Theft— Boy Admits Hiding Cop's Loot in Mother's House—A "Shame and Disgrace," Says Commissioner.

Rune, sitting at the huge oak platform of a table, felt a queasy shiver for the cop. The story came out that he'd talked the robber into exchanging himself for the hostage, who fled from the bank. Then he'd convinced the thief to hand over his revolver.

What happened next was speculation: Davies claimed the robber had a change of mind and jumped him. There was a scuffle. The robber knocked down the cop and went for the gun. Davies tried to pull the pistol away from him. They fought. The gun went off. The robber was killed.

But a young shoeshine boy testified that he'd been hiding outside the bank, waiting for something to see, when a door above him opened and a man looked out. It was Davies, the cop.

> Yes, sir, I can identify him, sir. He looks just like that man right there, sir, only that day he was wearing a uniform.

He asked for the boy's address and then handed him a suitcase, told him to take it home.

> He says to me . . . he says that if I opened the bag, or I said anything about what happened, I'd go to reform school and get the tar beat out of me every day. I done what he said, sir.

Davies denied it all—murdering the robber, taking the money, breaking into the shoeshine boy's home in Brooklyn and stealing the suitcase, then hiding the loot somewhere. The policeman made a tearful defendant, the papers reported. But that didn't sway the jury. Davies got five to fifteen years. The Patrolmen's Benevolent Association claimed all along he was the victim of a frame-up and urged his parole. He served seven years of the sentence.

But controversy around Davies continued after his release. Only two days after he walked out the front door of Sing Sing in Ossining, New York, in 1942 he was tommy-gunned to death at the corner of Fifth Avenue and Ninth Street, in front of the gothic Fifth Avenue Hotel. No one knew who was behind the shooting, though it looked like a professional hit. The money was never recovered.

Nothing more about the crime appeared in the press until the tiny blurb about the movie *Manhattan Is My Beat*—the clipping Rune had found in Kelly's apartment.

A homeless man sat down next to her at the library table. She smelled foulness in the wake of the air around him. Like most derelicts, he managed to seem both harmless and scary at the same time. He whispered to himself, wrote on a piece of wrinkled paper in the tiniest handwriting she'd ever seen.

One of her watches seemed to be working. She glanced at it. Oh shit! It was after two. Her ten-minute break had stretched to longer than two hours. Tony could be back. She took a cab to the Village but, on impulse, had the cabbie stop at 24 Fifth Avenue, the site of the Fifth Avenue Hotel. She paced back and forth slowly, wondering where Samuel Davies was when he was gunned down—what he'd been doing, what went through his mind when he realized what was happening, if he'd seen the black gun muzzle pointed at him.

She walked in wide circles, weaving through the crowd, until a cop—a real-life cop, NYPD—who was leaning on a patrol car must have decided she was acting a little suspicious and started walking slowly in her direction. Rune looked at the menu taped in the window of the glitzy restaurant on the corner, frowned, and shook her head. She strolled toward University Place.

The cop lost interest.

Back at the store, Tony was waiting for her. He lectured her for a whole two minutes on promptness and she did her best to look contrite.

"What?" he grumbled. "Thought I'd be out all day, huh?"

Like you usually are? she thought. But said, "Sorry, sorry, sorry. Won't happen again. Cross my heart."

"I *know* it won't. This's your last chance. Late once more and you're outa here. I've got people lined up to get a job."

"Lined up?" She looked out the front door. "Where, Tony? Out back? In the alley?" She then realized she should be more contrite. "Sorry. Just a joke."

He glowered and handed her a pink While-You-Were-Out slip. "Another thing, this isn't message central. Now, go get coffee and make it up to me."

"You bet," she said cheerfully. He eyed her uncertainly.

The message was from Richard. It said, "Confirming our 'date.'" She liked the quotation marks. She folded the pink slip of paper and slipped it into her shirt pocket.

"Here," Tony grumbled. Handing her money for the coffee.

"Naw, that's okay," she said. "It's on me."

Perplexing the poor man no end.

———

"You're from Ohio?"

It was eight P.M. They were sitting in Rune's gazebo, listening to the Pachelbel Canon. Rune had eight different recordings of the piece. She'd liked it for years—even before it had caught on, the way *Greensleeves* and *Simple Gifts* had.

Richard continued. "I've never met anyone from Ohio."

She was wearing a black T-shirt, black stretch pants, and red-and-white-striped socks. She'd done this as a homage to Richard's costume the other night. He, however, was in baggy gray slacks, Keds, and a beige Texaco Service shirt with the name Ralph embroidered on the pocket.

This man is *pure* Downtown. I love him!

Rune sang, " 'What's round on the ends and high in

the middle? It's O-Hi-O!' That's it. One more syllable and Rodgers and Hammerstein could've written a musical about it."

"Ohio," Richard said thoughtfully. "There must be something in that. Solid, dependable. Working-class. Sort of metaphoric. You were there and now you're"—he waved his hand around the loft—"here."

"It's a nice state," she said defensively.

"I don't mean anything bad. But why'd you come here and not Chicago or L.A.? A job?"

"No."

"I know. Boyfriend."

"Nope."

"You moved to Manhattan by yourself?"

"To go on a real quest, you *have* to go by yourself. Remember *Lord of the Rings*?"

"Sort of. Refresh my memory."

Sort of? How could he not remember the best book of all time?

"All the hobbits and everybody started out together, but in the end it was Frodo who got to the fiery pit to destroy the ring of power. All by his little-old lonesome."

"Okay," he said, nodding. Not sure what the connection was. "But why Manhattan?"

Rune explained. "I didn't spend a lot of time at home in the afternoons. After school, I mean. My dad was pretty sick and my mom'd send my sister and me out to play a lot. She got the dates and boyfriends. I got the books."

"Books?"

"I'd hang out at the Shaker Heights Library. There was this book of pictures of Manhattan. I read it once and just *knew* I had to come here." Then she asked, "Well, how 'bout *you*?"

"Because of what Rimbaud says about the city."

"Uhm." Wait. She'd *seen* the movie and hated it. She

didn't know *Rambo*'d been a book. She thought of the cardboard cutout in Washington Square Video—of Stallone with his muscles and that stupid headband. "Not sure."

"Remember his poem about Paris?"

Poem? "Not exactly."

"Rimband wrote that the city was death without tears, our diligent daughter and servant, a desperate love, and a petty crime howling in the mud of the street."

Rune was silent. Trying hard to figure Richard out. Downtown weird *and* smart. She'd never met anyone like him. She was watching his eyes, the way his long fingers went through a precise ritual of pulling a beer can out of the plastic loops that held the six-pack, tapping the disk of the top to settle the foam, then slowly popping it open. Watching his lean legs, long feet, the texture of his eyes. She had a feeling that the posturing was just a facade. But what was underneath it?

And why was *she* so drawn to him? Because there was something she couldn't quite figure out about him?

Because of the mystery?

Richard said, "You're avoiding my question. Why did you come here?"

"This is the Magic Kingdom."

"You're not addressing Rimbaud's metaphor."

Addressing? Why did he have to talk that way?

Rune asked, "You ever read the Oz books?"

" 'Follow the yellow brick road,' " he sang in a squeaky voice.

"That's the movie. But Frank Baum—he was the author—he wrote a whole series of them. In his magic kingdom of Oz, there were lots of lands. All of them are different. Some people are made out of china, some have heads like pumpkins. They ride around on sawhorses. That's just what New York is like. Every other city I've ever been in is like a discount store. You know—clean, cheap, convenient. But what, basically? Unsatisfying, that's what. They're *literal*. There's no magic to them. Come here." She took his hand and led him to the window. "What do you see?"

"The Con Ed Building."

"Where?"

"Right there."

"I don't see a building." Rune turned to him, her eyes wide. "I see a mountain of marble carved by three giants a thousand years ago. They used magic tools, I'll bet. Crystal hammers and chisels made out of gold and lapis. I think one of them, I forget his name, built this castle we're in right now. And those lights, you see them over there? All around us? They're lanterns on the horns of oxen with golden hides circling around the kingdom. And the rivers, you know where they came from? They were gouged out of the earth by the gods' toes when they were dancing. And then . . . and then there're these pits underground, huge ones. You ever heard the rumblings underneath us? They're worms crawling at fifty miles an hour. Sometimes they get tired of living in the dark and they turn into dragons and go shooting off into the sky." She grabbed his arm urgently. "Look, there's one now!"

Richard watched the 727 making a slow approach to LaGuardia. He stared at it for a long time.

Rune said, "You think I'm crazy, don't you? That I live in a fairy story?"

"That's not bad. Not necessarily."

"I collect them, you know."

"Fairy stories?"

Rune walked to her bookshelves. She ran her finger across the spines of maybe fifty books. Hans Christian Andersen, the Brothers Grimm, *Perrault's Fairy Tales,* the Quiller-Couch Old French stories, Cavendish's book on Arthur and three or four volumes of his *Man, Myth and*

Magic. She held up one. "An original edition of Lady Gregory's *Story of the Tuatha Dé Danann and of the Fianna of Ireland.*" Handed it to him.

"Is it valuable?" Richard flipped through the old book with his gorgeous fingers.

"To me it is."

"Happily ever after . . ." He scanned pages.

Rune said, "That's not the way fairy stories end. Not all of them." She took the book from him and began thumbing past pages slowly. She stopped. "Here's the story of Diarmuid. He was one of the Fianna, the warrior guards of ancient Ireland. Diarmuid let an ugly hag sleep in his lodge and she turned into a beautiful woman from the Side, that's the other side, capital S—the land of magic."

"That's sounds pretty happy to me."

"But that wasn't the end." She turned away and stared past her dim reflection at the city. "He lost her. They both had to be true to their natures—he couldn't live in the Side and she couldn't live on earth. He had to return to the land of mortals. He lost her and never found love again. But he always remembered how he much he'd loved her. Isn't that a sad story?"

She thought, for some reason, of Robert Kelly.

She thought of her father.

Tears pricked her eyes.

"You sure have a lot of stories," he said, eyes on the spines of her books.

"I love stories." She turned to him. Couldn't keep her eyes off him. He was aware of it and looked away. "You were like him, coming after me. The other night, all dressed in black. I thought of Diarmuid when I first saw you. Like a knight errant on a quest." She scrunched her face up. "Accompanied by two tacky wenches."

Richard laughed. Then added, "I *was* on a quest. For you." He kissed her. "You're my Holy Grail."

She closed her eyes, kissed him back. Then said suddenly, "Let's eat."

The cutting board in the shape of a pig was her kitchen table. She cut open a round loaf of rye bread, spread mayonnaise on both sides. She noticed him watching her. "Watch closely. I told you I could cook."

"That's cooking?"

"I think I can really cook. I just haven't done it much. I have a bunch of cookbooks." She pointed to the bookcases again. "My mother gave them to me when I left home. I think she wanted to give me a diaphragm but lost her nerve at the last minute, so she gave me Fannie Farmer and Craig Claiborne instead. I can't use them much. Most recipes you need a stove for."

She poured cold Chinese food from the carton onto the sliced loaf and cut it in half. The cold pork poured out the sides when she sawed the dull knife through the bread, and she scooped up the food with her hands and spread it back between the domes of rye.

"Okay," he said dubiously. "Well. That's interesting."

But when she handed him the sandwich he ate enthusiastically. For a skinny boy he had quite an appetite. He looked *so* French. He really *had* to be François.

"So," he asked, "you going with anybody?"

"Not at the moment."

Or for any moments in the last four months three weeks.

"Half my friends are getting married," he said. He went through his beer-can ritual again, his long fingers beating out a hesitant rhythm on the top of the can, then opening it and pouring the beer while he held the glass at an angle.

"Marriage, hmm," she said noncommittally.

Where was all *this* headed?

But he was on to a new subject. "So what're your goals?"

She took a big bite of rye bread. "To eat dinner, I guess."

"I mean your life goals."

Rune blinked and looked away from him. She believed she'd never asked herself that question. "I don't know. Eat dinner." She laughed. "Eat breakfast. Dance. Work. Hang out . . . Have adventures!"

He leaned forward and kissed her on the mouth. "You taste like Hunan mayonnaise. Let's make love." His arms encircled her.

"No." Rune drained her second beer.

"You sure?"

No . . .

Yes . . .

She felt herself pulled forward, toward him, and she wasn't sure whether he was actually pulling her or she was moving by herself. Like a Ouija board pointer. He rolled on top of her. They kissed for five minutes. Growing aroused, that warm water sensation flowing up her calves into her thighs.

No . . . yes . . . no.

But she was saved from the debate by a voice shouting, "Home!" A woman's head appeared up the stairway. "Zip it up!"

A woman in her late twenties, wearing a black minidress and red stockings, climbed up the stairs. High heels. Her hair was cut short in a 1950s style and teased up. The hair was black and purple.

So the roomie's date hadn't turned out the way she'd hoped.

Rune muttered, "Sandra, Richard, Richard, Sandra."

Sandra examined him. She said nothing to him but to Rune: "You did okay." Then turned toward her half of the room, unzipping her dress as she walked, revealing a thick white strap of bra.

Rune whispered. "She's a jewelry designer. Or that's

what she wants to do. Days, she's a paralegal. But her hobby is collecting men. She's slept with fifty-eight of them so far. She has the score written down. Of course she's only come twenty-two times so there's some debate on what she can count. There's no *Robert's Rules of Order* for this sort of thing."

"I suppose not."

Richard's eyes followed a vague reflection of Sandra in the window. She was on the far side of the cloud wall, stripping slowly. She knew she was being watched. The bra came off last.

Rune laughed and took his chin in her hand. Kissed him. "Darling, don't even think about it. That woman is a time bomb. You get into bed with her, it's like a group grope with a hundred people you don't know where they've been. Christ . . ." Rune's voice grew soft. "I worry about her. I don't like her but she's on some kind of weird suicide thing, you ask me. A guy looks at her, and bang, it's in the sack."

Richard said, "There're ways to be safe. . . ."

Rune shook her head. "I knew a guy, a friend used to work at one of the restaurants I tended bar at. I watched his boyfriend get sick and die. Then I saw my friend get sick and die. I was at the hospital. I saw the tubes, the monitors, the needles. The color of his skin. Everything. I saw his eyes. I was there when he died."

An image of Robert Kelly's face came back to her, sitting in the chair in his apartment.

An image of her father's face . . .

Richard was silent and Rune knew she'd committed *the* New York City crime: being too emotional. She cleaned up the remnants of dinner, kissed Richard's ear, and said, "Let's watch a movie."

"A movie? Why?"

"Because I have to catch a killer."

CHAPTER TEN

She'd already seen *Manhattan Is My Beat* once but watching it this time was different.

Not because she was on a quote date unquote with Richard, not because they were lying side by side in the loft, with hazy stars visible overhead through the peaks of glass.

But because when she'd watched it before, it had just been a movie that a nice, quirky old man had rented. Now it was the rabbit hole—a doorway to an adventure.

The film was hokey, sure. Filled with those classic images from that whole cumbersome era she'd told Frankie Greek about—the baggy suits, stiff hair, the formalities of the dialogue. The young cop, twirling his billy club, would say, "Well, now, Mrs. McGrath, how are the Mister's corns this morning?"

But she paid little attention to the period costumes and the words. Mostly what she noticed, watching it this time, was the grit. The film left a sandy uneasiness in her heart. Shadows everywhere, the contrasty black and white, the unanticipated violence. The shootings—where the robber winged one of the hero's fellow cops and a bystander, for instance, or the scene where the cop died in front of the hotel—were very disturbing, even though there was no Sam Peckinpah slow-motion blood splattering, no special effects. It was like that great old Alan Ladd movie *Shane*—unlike modern thrillers, there'd been only a half dozen gunshots in the entire film but they were loud and shocking and you felt each one of them in your gut.

Manhattan Is My Beat also seemed pretty G-rated. But Rune felt the studio pulling a fast one in its portrayal of the cop's virginal girlfriend, played by—what a name—Ruby Dahl. It was so clear to Rune that the poor thing was lusting. You'd never know it from her lines ("Oh, I can't explain my feelings, Roy. I just worry about you so. There's so much . . . evil out there.") But if her dresses and sweaters were high-necked, Ruby's bosom was sharp and beneath the tame dialogue you knew she had the hots for Roy. *She* was the character that got the long camera shot when the judge announced that her fiancé was going to prison. She was the one Rune cried for.

At two A.M. Sandra threw a shoe at them and Rune shut off the VCR and the TV.

"Not bad once," Richard said. "Why'd we have to sit through it twice?" He himself had given up his own quest for the evening and had kept his hands off her for the past several hours.

"Because I didn't take notes the first time." She rewound the tape, the bootleg copy she'd made for Robert Kelly. She looked at the scrawl of notes she'd written on the back of a flier for a health club.

Richard stretched and went into some weird yoga position, like a push-up with his pelvis pressed into the floor, his head back at a crazy angle, staring at the stars above them. "Okay, I slept through most of it the second time, I have to be honest. Were you joking about the killer?"

"The movie is why that customer I told you about is dead."

"He saw it *three* times. He couldn't take it anymore. He killed himself."

"Don't joke." She was whispering and he missed the flare in her voice.

She pulled her bag toward her and handed him the clipping she'd found in Kelly's apartment. He looked at it but put it down before he could have read more than a couple of paragraphs. He closed his eyes. She frowned and took the yellow, brittle paper.

"What it is," she explained, "the movie was a true story. There really *was* a cop in the thirties who stole some robbery money and hid it. He denied the whole thing and nobody ever found the million dollars. He got out of Sing Sing and got gunned down a few days later. And supposedly he never had a chance to collect the money. It's just the way it happened in the film."

Richard yawned.

Rune, on her knees, crouched like a geisha, holding the clipping. "I think what happened was Mr. Kelly bought an old book at a secondhand store on St. Marks. . . . You know the book vendors near Cooper Union? There was this clipping in it. He read it—I think he was interested in New York history—so he got a kick out of it but didn't think too much about it. Then what happens?"

"What?"

"Then," she said, "last month he's walking past Washington Square Video and sees the poster for the film. He rents it, he watches it. And he gets the bug. You know what I mean? The bug." She waited. Richard seemed to be listening. She said, "That feeling that gets to you when you know there's something out there. But you don't know what. But you *have* to find out what the mystery is."

"Like you. You're mysterious."

She felt a trill of pleasure. "That's what my name means, you know."

"Rune? I thought a rune was a letter."

"It is. But it also means 'mystery' in Celtic."

"And what does 'Doris' mean?"

"Anyway," she said, ignoring him, "I think Mr. Kelly and I were a lot alike. Sort of like you and me."

She let that sit between them for a minute, and when he didn't respond she wondered, And what's *your* mystery, François Jean-Paul Vladmir Richard?

After a moment he said, "I'm awake. I'm listening."

Rune continued. "What Mr. Kelly did was decide he was going to find the money."

"What money?"

"The money the cop took! That was never recovered."

"The million dollars? Come on, Rune, the robbery was when, fifty years ago?"

"Sure, maybe somebody found it. Maybe it got burned up. . . . You can always find excuses to give up on your quest before you start. Besides, quests aren't just about finding money or grails or jewels. They're about adventures! Mr. Kelly'd been alone for years. No family, not many friends, living by himself. This was his chance for an adventure. What was his life? Just sitting by the window all day and watching pigeons and cars. Here was a chance for a treasure hunt." She started bouncing up and down, remembering something. "He told me, listen to this, *listen,* when he took me out to lunch, he told me when his ship came in, he was going to do something nice for me. Well, what was the ship? It was a million dollars."

Richard said, "I'm tired. I have to work tomorrow."

"On your novel?"

He hesitated for a minute. And she didn't think he was being completely honest when he said, "That's right."

First date. Too early to push. She asked, "Are you going to put me in it? In your novel?"

"Maybe I will."

"Will you make me a little taller and grow my hair out?"

"No. I like you just the way you are."

As he rolled over on his side she reread the old newspaper clipping.

"Now, remember, in the movie, what the cop did with the money?"

The groggy answer: "He snuck outside the bank and gave it to a shoeshine boy, who took it home. The cop broke into the kid's house and stole it. I was awake for that part."

"And there was that totally melodramatic struggle, all that loud music, and the boy's mother fell down a flight of stairs," Rune pointed out. "That was big in old-time movies. Old ladies falling down flights of stairs. That, and angelic kids getting the dread unnamed disease guaranteed to make them waste away slowly." She thought back to the film. "Okay, in the newspaper stories there *was* a shoeshine boy. The cop—his real name was Samuel Davies, not Roy—gave the kid the money and said take it home or, basically, I'll beat the crap out of you. That was the last anybody every heard of the money in real life. But in the movie the cop gets it back from the kid and buries it in a cemetery someplace. Who came up with that idea? Hiding the money in a graveyard?"

"The writer, who else? He made it up." Richard's eyes were closed.

The writer . . . Interesting . . .

Then her attention returned to the TV. She turned the VCR on again and fast-forwarded it to the scene where Dana Mitchell, playing the dark-haired, square-jawed cop, buries the suitcase in a city cemetery.

She hit the freeze-frame button on the VCR and advanced the tape one frame at a time.

As the images shuffled slowly past, Rune said, out loud but mostly to herself, "The answer's here. It's here someplace. He watched it eighteen times, eighteen, eighteen, eighteen. . . ." Chanting the word. "Mr. Kelly gets a clue, he finds out something. And then he figures out where the money is. Or, okay, maybe . . . he can't get it himself, he's getting old. He had arthritis, a limp. He can't go digging around in cemeteries alone. He needs help. He tells somebody. A friend, an acquaintance. Somebody younger—who can help him. Mr. Kelly tells this guy everything and then, what's he do? He gets the money and kills Mr. Kelly. Maybe he was the guy in the green car. . . ."

"What green car?"

She hesitated. Another good social rule: On a first date don't tell the guy that a killer just tried to run you over at a murder scene.

"The police mentioned the killer was driving a green car."

Richard pointed out, "In which case it's gone. The killer left town with his million dollars. So what can you do?"

"Find him is what I can do. He killed a friend of mine. Anyway, part of that money's mine. And there's this friend of my friend in the building who's going to get deported if she doesn't get some money."

He said, "Why don't you just go to the police?"

"Police?" She laughed. "They don't care."

"Why else?" He was looking at her closely now.

"All right," she admitted. "Because they'd keep the

money. . . . I know it's out there. I mean, it could be. What you said before . . . about the writer making it up. He must've researched the real crime, wouldn't you think?"

"I'd guess," Richard responded.

"I mean, isn't that what you do for your novels? Research?"

"Yeah, sure. Research. A lot of research."

Rune mused, "Maybe he knows something. . . . 'Course he wrote the script fifty years ago. Think he's still alive?"

"Who knows?"

"How could I find out?"

He shrugged. "Why don't you ask somebody at the film school at NYU or the New School?"

It was a good idea. She kissed his ear. "See, you like quests as much as I do."

"I don't think so. But I also have a feeling I can't talk you out of this, can I?"

"Nup. You never give up on a quest. Until you succeed or you . . ." Her voice trailed off, seeing once again the pale skin of Robert Kelly dotted with his own blood, the green car speeding toward her, Susan Edelman flying into the brick wall. "Well, until you succeed. That's all there is to it."

She looked at Richard's face, his eyes closed, lips parted slightly. She tried to decide which she liked better, his looking dreamy—he was real good at dreamy—or the intense paisley eyes gazing intensely back at her. Dreamy, she concluded. He wasn't a warrior knight—not an Arthur or Cuchulain or Percival de Gales. No, he was more of a poet-knight. Or a philosopher-knight.

She heard his breath, steady, slow. How nice, she thought, to feel the warm weight of somebody next to you in sleep. She wanted so badly to lie beside him, feeling him against her whole body.

But instead of stretching out, she pulled off her Wicked Witch socks and aimed the remote control at the VCR, then watched the movie one more time until the scripty words *The End* splashed up on the screen.

CHAPTER ELEVEN

A karate flick was on the monitor.

Oriental men in black silk trousers sailed through the air, fists hissing like jet planes. Every time somebody got hit, it sounded like a cracking board.

One of the Chinese actors stepped toward a couple of rivals and spoke in a southern drawl. "Okay, you two, back outa here real slow and you won't get hurt."

Rune leaned back on the stool in front of the register at Washington Square Video. Squinted at the monitor. "Hey, you hear that? That is completely wild! He sounds just like John Wayne."

Tony held his blue deli coffee cup and cigarette in one hand and flipped through the *Post* with the other. He looked up at the screen critically. "And he's going to beat the shit out of those guys in ten seconds flat."

It took closer to sixty and while he was doing it Rune mused, "You think that's easy? Dubbing, I mean. You think I could get a job doing that?"

Tony asked, "Don't tease me, Rune. You quitting? . . . Or you mean when you get fired?"

Rune spun her bracelets. "They don't have to memorize their lines, do they? They just sit in a studio and read the script. That'd be so cool—it'd be like being an actress without having to get up in front of people and memorize things."

Frankie Greek was combing out his shaggy hair with a pick. He rubbed the mustache he'd started a month ago; it looked like a faint smudge of dirt. He stared at the TV screen. "Shit, look at that! He kicked four guys at once." He turned to Rune. "You know, I just found this out. A lot of music in movies, they do it afterward. They add it on."

"What, you thought they had a band on set?" Rune shut off the VCR. Tony looked at the TV. "Hey, what're you doing?"

"It stinks," she said.

"It doesn't stink. It's great."

"The acting's ridiculous, the costumes are silly, there's no story . . ."

Frankie Greek said, "That's what makes it so, like, you know . . ." The end of his sentence got away from him, as they often did. He prowled through the racks to find another film.

Rune looked over the store: the stained gray industrial carpet, the black strings—left over from promotional cards—hanging down from the air-conditioning, the faded red-and-green holiday tinsel that was stuck to the walls with yellowing glue. "I was at a video store on the Upper East Side and it was a lot classier than here."

Tony looked around. "What do you want? We're like the subway. We serve a valuable function. Nobody gives a shit we're classy, not classy."

Rune checked out two movies to a young man, one of the Daytime People, she called them. They'd rent movies during the day; they worked at night—actors, waiters, bartenders, writers. At first she'd envied them their alternative lifestyles but after she got to thinking about it— how they were always bleary-eyed or hung over and seemed dazed, smelled like they hadn't brushed their teeth—she decided aimlessness like that depressed her. People would be better off going on quests, she concluded.

She returned to her previous topic and said to Tony, "That place uptown? The video store? They had all these foreign films and ballets and plays. I'd never heard of most of them. I mean, it's like you go in there ask for *Predator Cop*, this alarm goes off and they throw you out."

Tony didn't look up from *Dear Abby*. "Got news, babe: *Predator Cop* makes us money. *Master-fucking-piece Theatre* doesn't."

"Wait, is that a real movie?" Frankie said. "*Master . . .* What?"

"Jesus Christ," Tony muttered.

Rune said, "I just think we could doll the place up some. Get new carpet. Oh, maybe we could have a wine-and-cheese night."

Frankie Greek said, "Hey, I could get the band to come down. We could play. Some Friday night. And, like, how's this? You could put a camera on us, put some monitors in the front window. So people, the ones outside'd notice us and they'd come in. Cool. How's that?"

"It sucks, that's how it is."

"Just an idea." Frankie Greek slipped a new cassette into the VCR.

"Another one?" Rune said, watching the credits.

"No, no. This is different," Frankie said. He showed Tony the cover.

"Now you're talking." Tony folded up the newspaper and concentrated on the screen. Patient as a priest with a novitiate, he said, "Rune, you know who that is? It's

Bruce Lee. We're talking classic. In a hundred years people'll still be watching this."

"I'm going to lunch," she said.

"You don't know what you're missing."

"Bye."

"Be back in twenty."

"Okay," she called. Adding, once she was outside, "I'll try."

———

Richard's idea about the film school was a good one. But she didn't actually need to go to the film department itself.

She stopped at the Eighth Street Deli, which did a big business selling overpriced sandwiches to rich NYU students and professors.

She paused on her way inside, looked around. This was the deli where that guy with the curly hair—the one she sorta recognized/sorta didn't—had ducked into yesterday. She wondered again if he'd been checking her out.

Thinking, You've got yourself *more* secret admirers? First Richard, now him. Never rains but . . .

Get real, she reminded herself, and walked up to the counterman, who said, "Next . . . oh, hi."

"Hey there, Rickie," Rune said.

He was working his way through school. He was an NYU junior, a film major, and he could have been Robert Redford's younger brother. When Rune first started working at WSV, she'd spent a ton of money and many hours here, talking to Rickie about films—and hoping he'd ask her out. They'd remained good friends even after Rickie introduced her to his live-in boyfriend.

She lifted the cello-wrapped apple pie for him to see, opened it, began eating. He handed her usual—coffee with milk, no sugar. They talked about movies for five minutes, while he made tall sandwiches out of roast beef and turkey and tongue. Rickie knew a lot of heavy-duty stuff about movies and even though he always said "film" or "cinema," never "movies," he didn't get obnoxious about it. She finished the pie and he refilled her coffee.

"Rickie," Rune asked, "you know anything about a film called *Manhattan Is My Beat*?"

"Never heard of it."

"Came out in the late forties."

He shook his head. Then she asked, "Is there like an old film museum at your school?"

"We've got a library. Not a museum. The public library's got that arts branch up at Lincoln Center. MOMA's probably got an archive but I don't think they let just anybody in."

"Thanks, love," she said.

"Hey, I don't make the rules. Start working on a grant proposal or get a letter from your grad school adviser and they'll let you in. But that's pretty heady stuff. Experimental films. Indies. What do you need to know?"

"I need to find the screenwriter."

"What studio made it?"

"Metropolitan."

He nodded. "Good old Metro. Why don't you just call 'em up and ask?"

"They're still around?"

"Oh, they're like everybody else nowadays, owned by some big entertainment conglomerate. But, yeah, they're still around."

"And somebody there'd know where the writer is now?"

"Be your best bet. Screen Writers Guild probably won't give out any information about members. Hell, I were you, I wouldn't even call; I'd just go pay 'em a visit."

Rune paid. He charged her a nickel for the pie. She

winked her thanks. Then said, "Can't afford to fly out to
L.A."

"Take a subway, it's cheaper."

"You need a hell of a lot of transfers," Rune said.

"The Manhattan office, darling."

"Metro has an office here?"

"Sure. All the studios do. Oh, the East Coast office
wants to rip the throat out of the West Coast office and
vice versa but they're still part of the same company.
They're that big building on Central Park West. You
must've seen it."

"Oh, like I *ever* go uptown."

━━━━━

Awesome.

The corporate office building of the Entertainment
Corporation of America, proud owner of Metropolitan
Pictures.

Forty stories overlooking Central Park. A *single* company. Rune couldn't imagine having twenty stories of
fellow workers above you and twenty stories below. (She
tried to imagine forty stories of Washington Square
Video, filled with Tonys and Eddies and Frankie Greeks.
It was scary.)

She wondered if all the Metro employees ate together
in a single cafeteria? Did they all go on a company picnic,
taking over Central Park for the day?

Waiting for the guard to get off the phone, she also
wondered if someone would see her and think she was
an actress and maybe pull her onto a soundstage and
throw a script into her hand. . . .

Though as she flipped through the company's annual
report she realized that that probably wouldn't be happening because this wasn't the *filmmaking* part of the
studio. The New York office of Metro did only financing,
licensing, advertising, promotion, and public relations.

No casting or filming. But that was all right; her life was a little too busy just then for a career change that'd take her to Hollywood.

The guard handed her a pass and told her to take the express elevator to thirty-two.

"Express?" Rune said. Grinning. *Excellent!*

Her ears popped in the absolutely silent, carpeted elevator. In twenty seconds she was stepping off on the thirty-second floor, ignoring the receptionist and walking straight to the ceiling-to-floor window that offered an awesome view of Central Park, Harlem, the Bronx, Westchester, and the ends of the earth.

Rune was hypnotized.

"May I help you?" the receptionist asked three times before Rune turned around.

"If I worked here I'd never get any work done," Rune murmured.

"Then you wouldn't be working here very long."

Reluctantly she pried herself away from the window. "This is the view you'd have if you flew to work on a pterodactyl." The woman stared. Rune explained, "That's a flying dinosaur." Still silence. Try being adult, Rune warned herself. She smiled. "Hi. My name's Rune. I'm here to see Mr. Weinhoff."

The receptionist looked at a chart on a clipboard. "Follow me." She led her down a quiet corridor.

On the walls were posters of some of the studio's older movies. She paused to touch the crisp, wrinkled paper delicately. Farther down the hall were posters of newer films. The ads for movies hadn't changed much over the years. A sexy picture of the hero or heroine, the title, some really stupid line.

He was looking for peace, she was looking for escape. Together, they found the greatest adventure of their lives.

She'd seen the action movie *that* line referred to. And if the story had been their greatest adventure, well, then those characters'd been leading some totally bargain-basement lives.

Rune paused for one last aerial view of the Magic Kingdom, then followed the receptionist down a narrow hallway.

Betting herself that Mr. Weinhoff's would be one totally scandalous office. A corner one, looking north and west. With a bar and a couch. Maybe he'd be homesick for California so what he'd insisted they do to keep him happy was to put a lot of palm trees around the room. A marble desk. A leather couch. A bar, of course. Would he offer her a highball? What *was* a highball exactly?

They turned another corner.

She pictured Weinhoff fat and wearing a three-piece checkered suit, smoking cigars and talking like a baby to movie stars. What if Tom Cruise called while she was sitting in his office? Could she ask to say hello? Hell, yes, she'd ask. Or Robert Duvall! Sam Shepard? Oh, please, please, please . . .

They turned one more corner and stopped beside a battered Pepsi machine. The receptionist nodded. "There." She turned around.

"Where?" Rune asked, looking around. Confused.

The woman pointed to what Rune thought was a closet, and disappeared.

Rune stepped into the doorway, next to which a tiny sign said S. WEINHOFF.

The office, about ten feet by ten, had no windows. It wasn't even ten by ten really, because it was stacked around the perimeter with magazines and clippings and books and posters. The desk—chipped, cigarette-burned wood—was so cluttered and cheap that even the detective with the close-together eyes would've refused to work at it.

Weinhoff looked up from *Variety* and motioned her

in. "So, you're the student, what's the name again? I'm so bad with names."

"Rune."

"Nice name, I like it. Parents were hippies, right? Peace, Love, Sunshine, Aquarius. All that. Can you find a place to sit?"

Well, she got one thing right: he was fat. A ruddy nose and burst vessels in his huge cheeks. A great Santa Claus—if you could have a Jewish Santa. No checkered suit. No suit at all. Just a polyester shirt, white with brown stripes. A brown tie. Gray slacks.

Rune sat down.

"You want coffee? You're too young to drink coffee, you ask me. 'Course my granddaughter drinks coffee. She smokes too. God forbid that's all she does. I don't approve, but I sin, so how can I cast stones?"

"No, thanks."

"I'll get some, you don't mind." He stepped into the corridor and she saw him making instant coffee at a water dispenser.

So much for the highballs.

He sat back down at his desk and said to her, "So how'd you hear about me?"

"I called the public relations department here?" Her voice rose in a question. "See, I'm in this class—*The Roots of Film Noir,* it's called—and I'm writing this paper. I had some questions about a film and they said they had somebody on staff who'd been around for a while. . . ."

" 'Around for a while,' I like that. That's a euphemism is what that is."

"And here I am."

"Well, I'll tell you why they sent you to me. You want to know?"

"I—"

"I'll tell you. What I am is the unofficial studio historian at Metro. Meaning I've been here nearly forty years and if I were making real money or had anything to do with production they'd've fired my butt years ago. But I'm not and I don't so I'm not worth the trouble to boot me out. So I hang around here and answer questions from pretty young students. You don't mind, I say that?"

"Say it all you want."

"Good. Now the message said—do I believe it?— you've got some questions about *Manhattan Is My Beat*?"

"That's right."

"Well, that's interesting. You see a lot of students or reporters interested in Scorsese, Welles, Hitch. And you can always count on Fassbinder, Spielberg, Lucas, Coppola. Three, four years ago we got calls about Cimino. That *Heaven's Gate* thing. Oh, we got calls! But I don't think anybody's ever done anything about the director of *Manhattan Is My Beat*. Hal Reinhart. Anyway, I digress. What do you need to know?"

"The movie was true, wasn't it?"

Weinhoff's eyes crinkled. "*Nu*, that's the whole point. That's why it's such a big-deal movie. It wasn't shot on sets, it was based on a real crime, it didn't cast Gable, Tracy, Lana Turner, Bette Davis, Gary Cooper, or any of the other sure-draw stars. You understand? None of the actors that'd guarantee that a film, no matter it was a good film, it was a bad film, that a film *opened,* you know what I mean, *opened*?"

"Sure." Rune's pen sped across the pages of a notebook. She'd bought it a half hour before, had written *Film Noir 101* on the cover, then smeared the ink with her palm to age it, like a master forger. "It means people go to see it no matter what it's about."

"Right you are. Now, *Manhattan Is My Beat* was probably the first of the independents."

"Why don't you hear about it nowadays?"

"Because it was also the first of the *bad* independents. You've seen it?"

"Four times."

"What, you also tell your dentist to drill without no-vocaine? Well, if you saw it that many times, you know it didn't quite get away from the melodrama of the big studio crime stories of the thirties. The director, Rein-hart, couldn't resist the shoeshine boy's mother falling downstairs, the high camera angles, the score hitting you over the head you should miss a plot twist. So other films got remembered better. But it was a big turning point for movies."

His enthusiasm was infectious. She found herself nodding excitedly.

"You ever see *Boomerang*? Elia Kazan. He shot it on location. Not the greatest story in the world for a crime flick—I mean, there's not much secret who did it. But the point isn't what the story was but *how* it was told. That was about a real crime too. It was a—whatta you call it?—evolutionary step up from the studio-lot produc-tions Hollywood thought you had to do. *Manhattan Is My Beat* was of the same ilk.

"Oh, you gotta understand, the era had a lot to do with it too, I mean, shifting to movies like that. The War, it robbed the studios of people and materials. The big-production set pieces and epics—uh-uh, there was no way they could produce those. And it was damn good they did. You ask me—hey, who's asking me, right?—but I think movies like *Manhattan* helped move movies out of the world of plays and into their own world.

"*Boomerang. The House on 92nd Street.* Henry Hatha-way did that. Oh, he was a gentleman, Henry was. Quiet, polite. He made that film, I guess, in forty-seven. *Man-hattan Is My Beat* was in that movement. It's not a good film. But it's an important film."

"And they were *all* true, those films?" Rune asked.

"Well, they weren't documentaries. But, yeah, they

were accurate. Hathaway worked with the FBI to do *House*."

"So, then, if there was a scene in the movie, say the characters went someplace, then the real-life characters may have gone there?"

"Maybe."

"Did you know anyone who worked on *Manhattan*? I mean, know them personally?"

"Sure. Dana Mitchell."

"He played Roy, the cop."

"Right, right, right. Handsome man. We weren't close but we had dinner two, three times. Him and his second wife, I think it was. Charlotte Goodman we had signed here for a couple films in the fifties. I knew Hal of course. He was a contract director for us when studios still did that. He also did—"

"*West of Fort Laramie*. And *Bomber Patrol*."

"Hey, you know your films. Hal's still around, I haven't talked to him in twenty years, I guess."

"Is he in New York?"

"No, he's on the West Coast. Where, I have no idea. Dana and Charlotte are dead now. The exec producer on the project died about five years ago. Some of the other studio people may be alive but they aren't around here. This is no business for old men. I'm paraphrasing Yeats. You know your poetry? You studying poets in school?"

"Yeah, all of them, Yeats, Erica Jong, Stallone."

"Stallone?"

"Yeah, you know, *Rambo*."

"Your school teaches some strange things. But education, who understands it?"

Rune asked, "Isn't there anybody in New York who worked on the film?"

"Whoa, darling, the spirit is willing but the mind is weak." Weinhoff pulled out a film companion book. And looked up the movie. "Ah, here we go. Hey, here we go.

Manhattan Is My Beat, 1947. Oh, sure, Ruby Dahl, who could forget her? She played Roy's fiancée."

"And she lives in New York?"

"Ruby? Naw, she's gone. Same old story. Booze and pills. What a business we're in. What a business."

"What about the writer?"

Weinhoff turned back to the book. "Hey, here we go. Sure. Raoul Elliott. And if he was credited as the writer, then he really wrote it. All by himself. I know Raoul. He was an old-school screenwriter. None of this pro-wrestling for credits you see now." In a singsong voice Weinhoff said, " 'I polished sixty-seven pages of the tenth draft so I get the top credit in beer-belly extended type-face and that other hack only polished fifty-three pages so he gets his name in antleg condensed or no screen credit at all.' *Whine, whine, whine* . . . Naw, I know Raoul. If he got the credit he wrote the whole thing—first draft through the shooting script."

"Does he live in New York?"

"Ah, the poor man. He's got Alzheimer's. God forbid. He'd been in a home for actors and theatrical people for a while. But last year it got pretty bad; now he's in a nursing home out in Jersey."

"You know where?"

"Sure, but I don't think he'll tell you much of anything."

"I'd still like to talk to him."

Weinhoff wrote down the name and address for her. He shook his head. "Funny, you hear about students nowadays, they don't want to do this, they don't want to do that. You're—I pegged you right away, I don't mind saying—you're something else. Talking to an old yenta like me, going to all this trouble just for a school paper."

Rune stood up and shook the old man's hand. "Like, I think you get out of life what you put into it."

All right. I'm two hours late, she thought.

She wasn't just hurrying this time; she was sprinting. To get to work! This was something she'd never done that she could ever remember. Tony's voice echoing in her memory. *Back in twenty, back in twenty.*

Along Eighth Street. Past Fifth Avenue. To University Place. Dodging students and shoppers, running like a football player, like President Reagan in that old movie of his. The one without the monkey.

No big deal. Tony'll understand. I was on time this morning.

Them's the breaks.

He's not going to fire me for being a measly two hours late.

A hundred twenty minutes. The average running time for a film.

How could he possibly be upset? No way.

Rune pushed into the store and stopped cold. At the counter Tony was talking to the woman who was apparently her replacement, showing her how to use the cash register and credit card machine.

Oh, hell.

Tony looked up. "Hi, Rune, how you doin'? Oh, by the way, you're fired. Pack up your stuff and leave."

He was more cheerful than he'd been in months.

CHAPTER TWELVE

████████ The woman, an attractive redhead in her twenties, looked uncertainly at Rune. Then at Tony.

Rune said, "Look, Tony, I'm really, really sorry. I got . . ."

You only lie to people who can control you.

But I don't want to get fired. I don't, I don't, I don't.

". . . I got stuck on the subway. Power failure. Or somebody on the tracks. It was disgusting. No lights, it was smelly, it was hot. And I—"

"Rune, I've had it. Frankie Greek's sister went into labor just after you left and he had to take her to the hospital. And I *know* she did, 'cause I called her ob-gyn to check."

"You did *what*?" Rune asked.

Tony shrugged. "He coulda been faking. What'd I know? But whatta you want me to do when *you* give me some half-assed excuse about the subway? Call the head of the MTA? Ask him if the E train got stuck at Thirty-fourth Street?"

"Please don't fire me."

"I had to work by myself for two fucking hours, Rune."

"Jesus, Tony, it's not like a hot dog stand at Giants Stadium at halftime. How many customers did you have?"

"That's not the point. I missed lunch."

"I'll be better. I really—"

"Time out," the redhead said, shutting them both up. She added, "I'm not taking the job."

"What?" Tony was looking at her.

"I can't take somebody else's job."

"You're not. I fired her before I hired you. It's just that she didn't know."

"Tony," Rune said. Hated that she was pleading but she couldn't help it. What would Richard think if he heard she got canned? He already thought she was totally irresponsible.

"I'd feel too guilty," the redhead explained.

Tony: "You said you needed a job."

"I do. But I'll find something else."

"No, no, doll," Tony said, "don't worry."

But then she said in a stony voice, "You fire her, I'm leaving too."

Tony closed his eyes momentarily. "Jesus Christ." He then leaned forward and glared at Rune. "Okay. Frankie's only going to be working half-days until his sister's back home. You can fill out his schedule. But if you miss any more shifts, without a *real* excuse, that'll be it."

"Thank you, thank you, thank you."

Tony then smiled at the woman, probably thinking he'd scored some points with her for his generosity. He didn't notice that her expression, as she looked back at him, was the way you squint at a roach just before you squoosh it.

"Rune," Tony said, "this is Stephanie. Isn't she pretty? Great hair, don't you think? Why don't you show our beautiful new employee the ropes? I'm going to the health club."

He sucked his gut in, slung his backpack over his shoulder, and pushed out the door.

Isn't she pretty, got great hair . . .

Rune stepped on the jealousy long enough to say to Stephanie, "Thanks. I don't know what to say. I can't really afford to get fired right now."

"Oh, I've been there." Stephanie glanced at the door as Tony disappeared down the street. "So *he's* really in a health club?"

"You bet he is," Rune whispered.

Then said, "Burger King," at the same time Stephanie said, "McDonald's?" They burst into laughter.

━━━━━

"You don't want to get the straight and gay adult mixed up when you're putting them back," Rune was explaining.

"Right. You don't." The woman *did* have incredible hair—long red-blond strands that tumbled over her shoulders the way hair seems to do only in shampoo commercials.

"What's your name again?" Rune now asked her. It started with an S. But she had a lot of problems with S names. Susan, Sally, Suzanne . . .

"Stephanie."

Right. Rune stored it away in her brain and continued with the training session. "See, we don't have covers on the porn so people have to rent them by the titles. With some it's easy. *Soldier Boys, Cowboy Rubdown, Muscle Truckers,* you know? But some, you can't tell. We had one guy rent *Big Blonds,* only it turns out that blondes with an

E on the end is girl blondes and *without* the E is boy blonds. Did you know that? I didn't. Anyway, he got boys with big dicks and he wanted girls with big boobs. He wasn't happy. Hey, your hair *is* totally radical. Is that your real color?"

"For now it is." Stephanie examined Rune's arm. "Love your bracelets."

"Yeah?" Rune shook her arm. They jingled.

Stephanie said, "Someone wanted me to do a porn movie once. In L.A. This guy said he was a UCLA film grad. Came right up to me in a coffee shop—I was hanging, reading *Variety*—and asked me if I wanted to do skin flick."

"No kidding," Rune said. Nobody'd ever asked her to do a porn film. She was wondering if she should feel insulted.

Stephanie paused, looking at a poster for *Gaslight*. "Ingrid Bergman. She was beautiful."

"Even with short hair," Rune said. "Like in *For Whom the Bell Tolls*." She ran her fingers over her head. Patted the strands down again. Thought about a wig. "The porn, did you do it?"

"Naw. Just didn't seem right."

"I'd be scared to death of, you know, catching something."

Stephanie shrugged. "Where'd you get them? The bracelets?"

"Everywhere. I'll be walking down the street and then there's this feeling I get and it's a bracelet calling me. Next store I come to, bang, there's one in the window."

Stephanie looked at her skeptically.

"It happens. I swear to God."

"Tony said you were slacking off."

"Every minute I spend not making his life easier is his definition of slacking off. What it is, this friend of mine got murdered. And I'm trying to find out what happened."

"No!"

"Yeah."

Stephanie said, "I got carjacked in Hollywood. I was in a Honda. You wouldn't think anybody'd kill somebody for a Honda. But I thought they were going to shoot me. I let 'em take it. They just drove off. Stopped at a stop sign and signaled to make a right turn. Like nothing'd happened. Doesn't it seem weird they'd kill you for a car? Or even just a few hundred dollars?"

Or for a *million* dollars, Rune thought. Seeing in her mind's eye Robert Kelly, lying back in his chair. The bullet holes in his chest. And the one in the TV.

Stephanie added, "I took a self-defense course after that. But that doesn't do you any good against a guy with a gun."

Rune pushed the sad thoughts from her mind and walked through the shelves, putting the tapes back, gesturing Stephanie after her.

"You'll learn stuff, working here. About human nature. That's why I took the job. Of course I don't exactly know what to do with the human nature I learn. But it's still fun to watch people. I'm a voyeur, I think."

"What can you learn about people in a video store?"

"How's a for-instance? There's this guy, cute, a stockbroker, always smelled like garlic but I flirted with him anyway. He rents all these Charles Bronson films, Chuck Norris, Schwarzenegger. Then he shows up here one night and he's got this yuppie trendoid girl hanging on him like he's a trapeze, okay? Suddenly no more *Commando*. All he wants are things like *The Seventh Seal* and Fellini and a lot of the recent Woody Allen—you know, not *Bananas* but the relationship stuff. And things you'd see on PBS, right? That lasts for a month, then Miss Culture goes bye-bye and it's back to *Death Wish 8* for a

couple months. Then he comes in with some other girl
all in leather and studs. I know what you're thinking but
guess what she likes? Old musicals. Dorothy Lamour,
Bing Crosby, Bob Hope, Fred and Ginger. That's all he
rents for *two* months. Guy's going to develop a complex.
I mean, you've gotta be yourself, right?"

Stephanie was brushing her hair.

Rune continued. "Like, speaking of adult films . . .
Oh, don't call them dirty movies. Tony doesn't like that,
and besides, it's a mega-business. We make forty percent
of our gross on them even though they're only twelve
percent of inventory. . . . Well, what I was saying was
that now women rent almost as many as men. And they
don't rent all that much straight . . . mostly it's gay
male flicks."

"Yeah?" Stephanie's sullen eyes flashed with a splinter
of interest then the lids lowered again. The brush went
back into her purse. Rune decided Stephanie would be a
Washington Square Video employee for thirty days max.
She could get just as boring work in restaurants and the
pay would be three times as good. "Why would women
rent gay films?"

"Way I figure it," Rune said, "it's that the guys in gay
films look a lot better than guys in straight films, you
know, they're really hunks, cut. Work out, take care of
themselves. Straight films, you see a lot of flab . . . I've
heard."

Stephanie, glancing with boredom at the adult section, said, "Lesbians are out of luck, sounds like."

"Naw, naw, that's another good market. We've got,
let's see, *Girls on Girls, Lesbos Lovers, Sappho Express* . . .
But it's mostly men rent those. There're more girlfriends
over in the West Village. Not so many here."

Rune walked back to the counter, fluffed her hair out
with her fingers. Stephanie looked at it, said, "That's an
interesting effect, with the colors. How did you do it?"

"I don't know. It just kind of happened." Trying to figure if her comment was a compliment. Rune didn't think so. *Interesting.* That's a bitch of a word. *Interesting.*

"You have any freaks come in?"

Rune said, "Depends on what you mean. There's a guy knows every line—even the TV and radio broadcasts—in *Night of the Living Dead.* Then this lawyer told me he and his wife rent *Casablanca* after they have sex. And I can look up in the computer and tell you that they must be having problems. There's this one guy, Mad Max, he's real creepy and always rents slasher films. Those stupid things like *Halloween* and *Friday the 13th, Part 85,* you know."

"Sexist bastards," Stephanie said, "that's who makes those films."

"But turns out he's a social worker for a big hospital uptown and volunteers for Meals on Wheels, things like that."

"Seriously?"

"I keep telling you . . . a video store is a great education."

Stephanie said, "You have a boyfriend?"

"I'm not sure," Rune said. She decided this was a pretty accurate statement.

"Is Rune your real name?"

"For now it is."

A queue formed—and Rune walked Stephanie through the check-out procedure.

"I can't believe this is your first day. You're a born clerk," Rune told her.

"Thanks loads," Stephanie drawled. "Don't tell Tony, but what I'm hoping is I'll meet some producers or casting agents here. I want to be an actress. Just a dry spell right now. I haven't auditioned for a month."

"What about all those casting calls in L.A.?"

"A casting call doesn't mean you get the part. L.A. is yucky. New York's the only place to be."

"I *knew* I liked you," Rune said, and rented *The Seven Samurai, Sleeping Beauty,* and *Lust Orgy* to a pleasant, balding businessman.

CHAPTER THIRTEEN

The rivers are moats, the buildings are parapets . . .

Wait, is that right? What exactly is a parapet?

Anyway . . .

The buildings are parapets. The stone, pitted and stained with age and cloudy water. Dripping. Slick stalactites and stalagmites. Dark windows with bars on the dungeons. We're riding down, down, down . . . The hooves of our horses muted by the cold brick. Down into the secret entrance that leads under the moat, out of the Magic Kingdom, out of the Side.

Richard guided the old Dodge into the Holland Tunnel and headed for New Jersey.

"Isn't it wild?" Rune asked. The orange lights flashed by, the gassy sweet smell of exhaust flowing into the car.

"What?"

"There is probably a hundred feet of water and yuck on top of us right now. That's really something."

He looked dubiously up at the yellowing ceiling of the tunnel, above which the Hudson River was flowing into New York Harbor.

"Something," he said uneasily.

It was *his* car, the Dodge they were in. This was pretty odd. Richard lived in Manhattan and he actually owned a car. Anybody who did that had to have a pretty conventional side to them after all. Paying taxes and parking and registration fees. This bothered her some but she wasn't really complaining. It turned out that the nursing home where the writer of *Manhattan Is My Beat* lived was forty miles from the city and she couldn't afford to rent wheels for this part of her quest.

"What's the matter?" she asked.

"Nothing."

And they drove through the rest of the claustrophobic yellow tunnel in silence. Rune was careful; when men got moody, it could be a real pisser. Put them with their buddies, let 'em get drunk and snap their jocks and throw footballs or lecture you about Buñuel or how airplane wings work and they were fine. But, holy St. Peter, something serious comes up—especially with a woman involved—and they go all to pieces.

But after twenty minutes, when they were out of the tunnel, Richard seemed to relax. He put his hand on her leg. More sparks. How the hell does that happen? she wondered.

Rune looked around as they headed for the Turnpike. "Gross." The intersections were filled with stoplight poles and wires and mesh fences and gas stations. She looked for her favorite service station logo—Pegasus—and didn't see one. That's what they needed, a winged horse to fly them over this mess.

"How did you get off work?" Richard asked her.

It was Sunday and she'd told him that she'd been scheduled to work.

"Eddie covered for me. I called him last night. That's a first for me—doing something responsible."

He laughed. But there wasn't a lot of humor in his voice.

Richard removed his hand and gripped the wheel. He turned southwest. The fields—flat, like huge brown lawns—were on either side of the highway. Beyond were marshes and factories and tall metal scaffolding and towers. Lots filled with trailers from semi trucks, all stacked up and stretching for hundreds of yards.

"It's like a battlefield," Rune said. "Like those things—what do you suppose they are, refineries or something?—are spaceships from Alpha Centauri."

Richard looked in the rearview mirror. He didn't say anything. He accelerated and passed a chunky garbage truck. Rune pulled an imaginary air horn and the driver gave her two blasts on his real one.

"Tell me about yourself," she said. "I don't know all the details."

He shrugged. "Not much to tell."

Ugh. Did he have to be such a *man*?

She tried a cheerful "Tell me anyway!"

"Okay." He grew slightly animated; the hipster from the other night had partially returned. "He was born in Scarsdale, the son of pleasant suburban parents, and raised to become a doctor, lawyer, or other member of the elite destined to grind down the working class. He had an uneventful boyhood, distinguished by chess club, Latin club, and a complete inability to do any kind of sport. Rock and roll saved his ass, though, and he grew to maturity in the Mudd Club and Studio 54."

"Cool! I loved them!"

"Then, for some unknown reason, Fordham decided to give him a degree in philosophy after four years of driving the good fathers there to distraction with his contrarian ways. After that he took the opportunity to see the world."

Rune said, "So you *did* go to Paris. I've always wanted to see it. Rick and Ilsa . . . *Casablanca*. And that hunchback guy in the big church. I felt so sorry for him. I—"

"Didn't exactly get to France," Richard admitted. Then slipped back into his third-person narrative. "What he did was get as far as England and found out that working your way around the world was a lot different from *vacationing* around the world. Being a punch press operator in London—if you can get to be a punch press operator at all—isn't any better than being one in Trenton, New Jersey. So, the young adventurer came back to New York to be a chic unemployed philosopher, going to clubs, playing with getting his M.A. and Ph.D., going to clubs, picking up blondes without names and brunettes with pseudonyms, going to clubs, working day jobs, getting tired of clubs, waiting to reach a moment of intersubjectivity with a woman. Working away."

"On his novel."

"Right. On his novel."

So far he seemed to be pretty much on her wavelength—despite the car and the moods. She was into fairy stories and he was into philosophy. Which *seemed* different but, when she thought about it, Rune decided they were both really the same—two fields that could stimulate your mind and that were totally useless in the real world.

Somebody like Richard—maybe him, maybe not—but somebody like him was the only sort of person she could be truly in love with, Rune believed.

"I know what's the matter," she said.

"Why do you think something's the matter?"

"I just do."

"Well," he said, "what? Tell me."

"Remember that story I told you?"

"Which one? You've told me a lot of stories."

"About Diarmuid? I feel like we're a fairy king and queen who've left the Side—you know, the magic land." She turned around. Gasped. "Oh, you've got to look at it! Turn around, Richard, *look*!"

"I'm driving."

"Don't worry—I'll describe it. There're a hundred towers and battlements and they're all made out of silver. The sun is falling on the spires. Glowing and stealing all that energy from the sun—how much energy do you think the sun has? Well, it's all going right into the Magic Kingdom through the tops of the battlements . . ." She had a sudden feeling of dread, as if she'd caught his mood. A premonition or something. After a moment she said, "I don't know, I don't think I should be doing this. I shouldn't've crossed the moat, shouldn't've left the Side. I feel funny. I almost feel like we shouldn't be doing this."

"Leaving the Side," he repeated absently. "Maybe that's it." And looked in the rearview mirror again.

He might have meant it, might have been sarcastic. She couldn't tell.

Rune turned around, hooked her seat belt again. Then they swept around a long curve in the expressway and the country arrived. Hills, forests, fields. A panoramic view west. She was about to point out a large cloud, shaped like a perfect white chalice, a towering Holy Grail, but Rune decided she'd better keep quiet. The car accelerated and they drove the rest of the way to Berkeley Heights, New Jersey, in silence.

———

"He hasn't had a visitor for a month," the nurse was saying to Rune.

They stood on a grassy hill beside the administration

building of the nursing home. Richard was in the cafeteria. He'd brought a book with him.

"That's too bad. I know it's good for the guests," the nurse continued. "People coming to see them."

"How is he?"

"Some days he's almost normal, some days he's not so good. Today, he's in fair shape."

"Who was the visitor last month?" Rune asked.

She said, "An Irish name, I think. An older gentleman."

"Kelly, maybe?"

"Could have been. Yes, I think so."

Rune's heart beat a bit faster.

Had he come to ask about a million dollars? she wondered.

Rune held up a rose in a clear cellophane tube. "I brought this. Is it okay if I give it to him?"

"He'll probably forget you gave it to him right away. But, yes, of course you can. I'll go get him. You wait here."

■

"They don't come to see me much. Last time was, let me see, let me see, let me see . . . No, they don't come. We have this party on Sundays, I think it is. And what they do is, it's real nice, what they do is put, when the weather's nice, put a tablecloth on the picnic benches, and we eat eggs and olives and Ritz crackers." He asked Rune, "It's almost fall now, isn't it?"

The nurse said, in a voice aimed at a three-year-old, "You know it's spring, Mr. Elliott."

Rune looked at the old man's face and arms. It seemed like he'd lost weight recently and the gray flesh hung on his arms and neck like thick cloth. She handed him the flower. He looked at it curiously, then set it on his lap. He asked, "You're . . ."

"Rune."

He smiled in a way that was so sincere it almost hurt. He said, "I know. Of course I know your name." To the nurse: "Where's Bips? Where'd that dog get to?"

Rune started to look around but the nurse shook her head and Rune understood that Bips had been in puppy heaven for years.

"He's just playing, Mr. Elliott," the nurse said. "He'll be back soon. He's safe, don't you worry." They were on a small rise of grass underneath a huge oak tree. The nurse set the brakes on his wheelchair and walked away, saying, "I'll be back in ten minutes."

Rune nodded.

Raoul Elliott reached up and took her hand. His was soft and very dry. He squeezed it once, then again. Then released it like a boy testing the waters with a girl at a dance. He said, "Bips. You couldn't believe what they do to him, these boys and girls. They poke at him with sticks if he gets too close to the fence. You'd think they'd be brought up better than that. What day is it?"

"Sunday," Rune answered.

"I know that. I mean the date."

"June fifteenth."

"I know that." Elliott nodded. He fixed a gaze on an elderly couple strolling down the path.

The grounds were trimmed and clean. Couples, elderly and mostly of the same sex, walked slowly up the paved paths. There were no stairs, curbs, steps, low plants; nothing to trip up old feet.

"I saw one of your movies, Mr. Elliott."

Flies buzzed in, then shot away on the warm breeze. Big thick white clouds sent their sharp-edged shadows across the grass. Elliott said, "My movies."

"I thought it was wonderful. *Manhattan Is My Beat*."

His eyes crinkled with recognition. "I worked on that with . . . Ah, this memory of mine. Sometimes I think

I'm going loony. There were a couple of the boys. . . .
Who were they? We'd have a ball. I ever tell you about
Randy? No? Well, Randy was my age. A year or two older
maybe. We were all from New York. Some'd been news-
papermen, some were writing for the *Atlantic* or editing
for Scribner's or Condé Nast. But we were all from New
York. Oh, it was a different town in those days, a very
different town. The studio liked that, they liked men
from New York. Like Frank O'Hara. We were friends,
Frank and I. We used to go to this bar near Rockefeller
Center. It was called . . . Well, there were a lot we went
to. In Hollywood too. We'd hang out in Hollywood."

"You worked on a newspaper?"

"Sure I did."

"Which one?"

There was a pause and his eyes darted. "Well, there
were the usual ones, you know. It's all changed."

"Mr. Elliott, do you remember writing *Manhattan Is
My Beat*?"

"Sure I do. That was a few years ago. Charlie gave it a
good review. Frank said he liked it. He was a good boy.
Henry too. They were all good boys. We said we didn't
like reviews. We said, what we said was reviewers were
so low, you shouldn't even ignore them." He laughed at
that. Then his face grew somber. "But we did care, oh,
yes, ma'am. But your father can tell you that. Where is
he, is he around here?" The old head with its wave of dry
hair swiveled.

"My father?"

"Isn't Bobby Kelly your father?"

Rune saw no point in breaking the news about Mr.
Kelly's death to the old man. She said, "No. He's a
friend."

"Well, where is he? He was just here."

"He stepped away for a few minutes."

"Where's Bips?"

"He's off playing."

"I worry about the traffic with him. He gets too excited when there's cars about. And these boys. They poke sticks at him. Girls too." He was aware of the flower again and touched it. "Did I thank you for this?"

She said, "You bet you did." Rune sat down on the grass beside the wheelchair, cross-legged. "Mr. Elliott, did you do your own research for the movie? For *Manhattan Is My Beat?*"

"Research? We had people do our research. The studio paid for it. Pretty girls. Pretty like you."

"And they researched the story that the movie was based on? The cop who stole the money from Union Bank?"

"They aren't there anymore, I'll bet you. They went on to Time-Life a lot of them. Or *Newsweek*. The studio paid better but it was a wild sort of life some of them didn't want. Is Hal doing okay now? And how's Dana? Handsome man he was."

"Fine, they're both fine. Did you find out anything about the cop who stole the money? The cop in real life, I mean?"

"Sure I did."

"What?"

Elliott was looking at his wrist, where his watch probably should have been. "I've lost it again. Do you know when we'll be leaving? It'll be good to get home again. Between you and I, I mean, between you and *me,* I don't like to travel. I can't say anything to them though. You understand. Do you know when we're leaving?"

"I don't know, Mr. Elliott. I sure don't . . . So what did you find out about the cop who stole the money?"

"Cop?"

"In *Manhattan Is My Beat?*"

"I wrote the story. I tried to write a good story.

There's nothing like that, you know. Isn't that the best thing in the world? A good story."

"It was a wonderful story, Mr. Elliott." She got up on her knees. "I especially liked the part where Roy hid the money. He was digging like a madman, remember? In the movie it was hidden in a cemetery. In real life did you ever have any idea where the cop who stole the money hid it?"

"The money?" He looked at her for a second with eyes that seemed to click with understanding. "All that money."

And Rune felt a low jolt in her stomach, a kick. She whispered, "What *about* the money?"

His eyes glazed over again and he said, "What they do here—they'll do it when the weather's nice—they put paper on the tables, like tablecloths and we have picnics here. They put nuts in little paper cups. They're pink and look like tiny upside-down ballet dresses. I don't know where the tables are. I hope they do that again soon. . . . Where's Bips?"

Rune sank back down on her haunches. She smiled. "He's playing, Mr. Elliott, I'll look out for him." They sat in silence for a moment and she asked, "What did Robert Kelly want when he came to visit you a month ago?"

His head nodded toward her and his eyes had a sudden lucidity that startled her.

"Who, Bobby? Why, he was asking me questions about that damn movie." The old face broke into a smile. "Just like you've been doing all afternoon."

███

Rune, leaning forward, studying his face, the lines and gnarls. "What exactly did you talk about, you and Bobby Kelly?"

"Your father, Bobby? Oh, the usual. I worked on *Manhattan* with some of the boys."

"I know you did. What did Bobby ask you about it?"

"Stuff."

"Stuff?" she asked cheerfully.

Elliott frowned. "Somebody else did too. Somebody else was asking me things."

Her heart pounded a little faster. "When was that, Mr. Elliott? Do you remember?"

"Last month. No, no, just the other day. Wait, I remember—it was today, little while ago." He focused on her. "It was a girl. Boyish. Looked a lot like you. Wait, maybe it *was* you."

He squinted.

Rune felt that he was on the verge of something. She didn't say anything for a moment. Like the times she and her father would go fishing in rural Ohio, playing the heavy catfish with the frail Sears rods. You could lose them in a wink if you weren't careful.

"Bobby Kelly," she tried again. "When he came to visit, what did he ask you about the movie?"

The eyes dropped and the lids pressed together. "The usual, you know. Are you his daughter?"

"Just a friend."

"Where is he now?"

"He's busy, he couldn't make it. He wanted me to say hello to you and tell you that he had a great time talking to you last month. You talked, he told me you talked all about . . . what was it again?"

"That place."

"What place?"

"That place in New York. The place I sent him. He'd been looking for it for a long time is what he told me."

Rune's heart thudded hard. She turned her head and looked directly into his milky eyes.

"He was happy when I sent him there. You should have seen his face when I told him about it. Oh, he was real happy. Where's Bips?"

"Just playing, Mr. Elliott. I'm looking after him. Where did you send Bobby Kelly?"

"He was real anxious to find it and I told him right off, I'm sure I did."

"Do you remember now?"

"Oh, one of those places . . . there are lots of them, you know."

Rune was leaning forward. *Please try to remember,* she thought. *Please, pleasepleaseplease* . . . Didn't say anything.

Silence. The old man shook his head. He sensed the importance of her questions and there was frustration in his eyes. "I can't remember. I'm sorry." He rubbed his fingers together. "Sometimes I think I'm going loony. Just loony. I'm feeling pretty tired. I could use a nap."

"That's okay, Mr. Elliott." She tasted her disappointment. But she smiled and patted his arm, then moved away quickly when she felt how thin it was. Thought of her father. "Hey, don't worry about it."

Rune stood up, walked behind him and took the white plastic handles of the chair. Undid the brakes. She started to wheel the chair toward the sidewalk. Elliott said suddenly, "The Hotel Florence. Five fourteen West Forty-fourth. At Tenth Avenue."

Rune froze. She dropped into a crouch next to him, her hand on the frail bone of his arm. "That's where you sent him?"

"I . . . I think so. It just came to me."

"That's wonderful, Mr. Elliott. Thank you so much." She leaned forward and kissed his cheek. He touched the spot and seemed to blush.

Richard appeared and stepped up toward them, starting to speak. Rune held up her hand to him. He stopped.

Raoul Elliott said, "I want to take a nap now. Where's Bips?"

"He's playing, Mr. Elliott. He'll be here soon."

Elliott looked around. "Miss, can I tell you something?"

"Sure."

"I lied."

Rune hesitated. Then said, "Go ahead. Tell me."

"Bips's a little shit. I've been trying to give him away for years. You know somebody who wants a dog?"

Rune laughed. "I sure don't. Sorry."

Elliott looked at the flower, curious again, started to pull off the cellophane wrapping; it defeated him and he set it back on his lap. Rune took the flower from him and opened it up. He held it lightly in his hands. He said, "You'll come back sometime, won't you? We have this party when it's spring. We can talk about movies. I'd like that."

Rune said, "I'd love to."

"You'll say hi to your father for me."

"Sure, I will."

The nurse was approaching. The old man's head sagged against the side of the wheelchair. He breathed slowly. His eyes were not quite completely closed but he was asleep. He started to snore very softly.

Rune looked at him, thinking again how much he resembled her father toward the end of his life. Cancer or AIDS or old age . . . death's packaging is all so similar.

The nurse nodded to her and took the chair, wheeled it down the path. The flower fell to the sidewalk. The nurse picked it up and set it on his lap again.

A dense shadow of a cloud that Rune thought looked just like a dragon rearing up on its sturdy hind legs passed over them. She turned to Richard. "Let's get out of here. Let's get back to the Side."

CHAPTER FOURTEEN

▰▰▰ The Florence Hotel, near the Hudson River, was in Hell's Kitchen, west of Midtown.

Rune knew her New York history. At one point this had been one of the most dangerous areas in the city, the home of the Gophers and the Hudson Dusters, murderous gangs that made the Mafia look tame. Most of the dangerous elements had been urban-renewed away when the tunnel to New Jersey was built. But the dregs of some Irish and Latino gangs remained. It was, in short, not a neighborhood to be hanging out in alone at night.

Thanks tons, Richard, she thought.

He'd left her there after dropping her off in front of the Florence, a four-story flophouse with a scarred and peeling facade. She'd started to ask him again what the matter was but then some kind of radar kicked in and she decided it would be a bad move.

"Can't really hang around," he'd told her. "You'll be okay?"

"I'll be fine. Wonder Woman. That's me."

"Gotta meet some people tonight. Otherwise, I'd stay."

She hadn't asked who. Been dying to. But hadn't.

"No, that's fine. You go on."

"You sure?"

"Go on."

Some people . . .

She watched his car drive away. He gave her a formal wave. She hesitated only a moment before she stepped carefully around the bum who slept in front of the beer-can-filled flower box under the narrow front window. She pushed open the lobby door and stepped inside. The smells were of damp wallpaper, disinfectant, some vague, unpleasant animal scents. The sort of place that made you want to hold your breath.

The clerk looked up at her from behind a Plexiglas security barrier that distorted his features. A thin man, hair slicked back, wearing a dress shirt and rust-colored corduroy pants. The shirt had dark stains, the pants, light.

"Yeah?" he called.

"I'm a social worker from Brooklyn?" Rune said.

"You asking me?"

"I'm telling you who I am."

"Yeah, a social worker."

"I'm trying to find some information about a patient of mine, a man who stayed here for a month or so."

"Don't you call 'em clients?"

"What?"

"We get social workers here all the time. They don't have patients. They have clients."

"One of my clients," she corrected herself.

"You got a license?"

"A license? A driver's license? Look, I'm older than I—"

"No, a social work license."

A license?

"Oh, that. See, I was mugged last week when I was on assignment. In Bedford Stuyvesant. Visiting a client. They took my purse—my other purse, my good purse—and that had my license in it. I've applied for a new one but you know how long it takes to get a replacement?"

"Tell me."

"Worse than a passport. I'm talking *weeks*."

The man was grinning. "Where'd you go to social work school?"

"Harvard."

"No shit." The smile didn't leave his face. "If there's nothing else, I'm pretty busy." He picked up a *National Geographic* and flipped it open.

"Look, I have my job to do. I have to find out about this man. Robert Kelly."

The clerk glanced up from his magazine. He didn't say anything. But Rune, even through the scuffed plastic, could see caution in his eyes.

She continued. "I know he stayed here for a while. I think somebody named Raoul Elliott recommended that he come here."

"Raoul? Nobody's named Raoul."

Summoning patience, Rune asked, "Do you remember Mr. Kelly?"

He shrugged.

She continued. "Did he check anything here? A suitcase? Maybe a package in the safe?"

"Safe? We look like the kinda hotel's gotta safe?"

"It's important."

Again, the man didn't respond. Suddenly Rune understood. She'd seen enough movies. She lifted her purse slowly and opened it, reached in and took out five dollars. She slid it seductively toward him. Just like an actor in a movie she'd seen a month or so ago. Harrison Ford, she thought. Or Michael Douglas.

That actor'd gotten results; she got a laugh.

Rune gave the clerk another ten.

"Look, kid. The going rate's fifty for information. That's the way it is all over the city. It's like a union."

Fifty? Shit.

She handed him a twenty. "That's all I got."

He took the money. "I don't know nothing—"

"You bastard! I want my money back."

"—except one thing. About your *client* Kelly. This priest or minister, Father so-and-so, called, I don't know, a couple days ago. He said Kelly'd dropped off a suitcase for safekeeping. He couldn't get him at his apartment and had this as his only other number. This priest figured I might know where Kelly was. He didn't know what to do with the suitcase."

Yes! Rune thought. Remembering the scene in *Manhattan Is My Beat* where Roy buried the money in a cemetery next to a church!

"Excellent, that's great! You know where the church was? You have any idea?"

"I didn't write nothing down. But I think he said he was in Brooklyn."

"Brooklyn!" Rune's hands were up against the grimy Plexiglas. She leaned forward, bouncing on her toes. "This's awesome!"

The man slipped her money into his pocket. "Well, happy day." He opened the magazine again and began reading an article about penguins.

Outside, she found a pay phone and called Amanda LeClerc.

"Amanda, it's Rune. How are you?"

"Been better. Missing him, you know? Robert . . . Only knew him for a little while but I miss him more than some people I knew for years and years. I was thinking about it. And you know what I thought?"

"What's that?"

"That maybe because we weren't so young no more we got to be more closer faster. Sort of like there wasn't a lot of time ahead of us."

"I miss him too, Amanda," Rune said.

"Haven't heard nothing about Mr. Symington."

"He hasn't been back?"

"No. Nobody's seen him. I was asking around."

"Well, I've got good news." She told her about the church and the suitcase.

The woman didn't answer for a moment. "Rune, you really thinking there maybe's some money? They keep coming after me for the rent. I'm trying to find a job. But it's tough. Nobody hires old ladies like me."

"I think we're on the right track."

"Well, what do you want me to do?"

"Start calling churches in Brooklyn. See if Mr. Kelly left a suitcase there. You can go to the library and get a Brooklyn phone book. We've got one at the video store. I'll take A through L. You take M through Z."

"Z? Do any churches start with a Z?"

"I don't know. St. Zabar's?"

"Okay. I'ma start calling first thing in the morning."

Rune hung up. She looked around her. The sun was down now and in this part of the city the bleakness was wrenching. But what she felt was only partly the sorrow of the landscape; the rest was fear. She was vulnerable. Low buildings—a lot of them burned-out or in various stages of demolition—a few auto repair shops, an abandoned diner, a couple of parked cars. Nobody on the street who'd help her if she was attacked. A few kids in gang colors, sitting on steps, sharing a bottle of Colt .45 or a crack pipe. A hooker, a tall black woman on nosebleed-high heels, leaned against a chain-link fence, arms crossed. Some bums shoring on grates or in doorways.

She felt very disoriented. She was back in Manhattan but she still felt that something separated her from her element, from the Side.

Starting down the street, eyes on the filthy pavement, keeping close to the curb—away from the alleys and the buildings, where muggers and rapists lurk.

Thinking back to *Lord of the Rings*. Thinking how quests always start off in springtime, with nice weather, good friends around to see you off, hearty food and drink in your pack. But they end up in Mordor—the bleakest of kingdoms, a place full of fire and death and pain.

It seemed to her that someone was following, though when she looked back she could see nothing but shadows.

She worked her way to Midtown and caught a subway. An hour later she was back home, in the loft. No note from Richard. And Sandra was out—a date on Sunday? Totally unfair! Nobody ever had a date on Sunday. Hell. She slipped *Manhattan Is My Beat* in the VCR and started it once more. The movie was halfway through before she realized that she'd been reciting the dialogue along with the actors. She'd memorized it perfectly.

Damn scary, she thought. But kept the film running till its end.

███

Haarte was angry.

It was Monday morning and he was sitting in his town house. Zane had just called and told him that the one witness, Susan Edelman, was about to be released from the hospital and that the other girl, the one with the weird name, was investigating the case harder than the NYPD.

Angry.

Which was a difficult emotion in this business. Haarte wasn't *allowed* to be angry when he'd been a cop. There was nothing he could *do* with his anger as a soldier and mercenary. And now—as a professional killer—he found anger to be a liability. A serious risk.

But he *was* mad. Oh, he was furious.

He was in his town house. Thinking about how messy this fucking job had become. Killing a man ought to be simplicity itself. He and Zane had gotten drunk a month ago, sitting in the bar in the Plaza hotel. They'd both grown maudlin and philosophical. Their job, they decided, was better than most because it was simple. And pure. As they poured down Lagavulin Scotch, Haarte had derided advertising execs and lawyers and salesmen. "They've got complicated, bullshit lives."

Zane had countered, "But that's reality. And reality's complicated."

And he'd answered, "If that's reality you can have it. I want simplicity."

What he meant was that there was a weird kind of ethics at work here. Haarte really believed this. Someone paid him money and he did the job. Or he couldn't do it. In which case he gave the money back or he tried again. Simplicity. Either someone was dead or not.

But this hit wasn't simple anymore. There were too many loose ends. Too many questions. Too many directions it might take. He was at risk, Zane was at risk. And of course the people who'd hired them were at risk too.

The man in St. Louis didn't know exactly what was going on but if he found out he'd be enraged.

And that made Haarte all the angrier.

He wanted to do something. Yet he couldn't decide what. There was the witness in the hospital. . . . There was the weird girl, the one in the video store. . . . He needed to snip some of those loose ends. But, as he sipped his morning espresso, he couldn't decide exactly how to handle it. There are many ways to stop people who're a risk to you. You can kill them, of course. Which is the most efficient way in some cases. And sometimes killing witnesses and meddlers makes the case so much more difficult to investigate that the police put the matter low on their list of priorities. But sometimes killing people does the opposite. It gets the press involved. It galvanizes cops to work even harder.

Killing's one way. But you can also hurt people. Scare them. It doesn't take much physical pain at all to put somebody out of commission for a long, long time. Lose a limb or your eyesight . . . Often they get the message and develop amnesia about what they saw or what they know. And the cops can't even get you for murder.

You can also hurt or kill someone *close* to the person you want to stop, their friends or lovers. This works *very* well, he'd found.

What to do?

Haarte stood up and stretched. He looked at his expensive watch. He walked into his kitchen to make another cup of espresso. The thick coffee made Zane agitated. But Haarte found it calmed him, cleared his head.

Sipping the powerful brew.

Thinking: What was supposed to be simple had become complicated.

Thinking: Time to do something about that.

■

There she was, up ahead.

Haarte had waited for her there, an alley, for a half hour.

Walking down the street in her own little world.

He wondered about her. Haarte often wondered about the people he killed. And he wondered what there was about him that could study people carefully and learn about them for the sole purpose of ending their lives. This fact or that fact, which somebody might find interesting or cute or charming, could in fact be the linchpin of the entire job. A simple fact. Shopping at this store, driving this route to work, fucking this secretary, fishing in this lake.

A half-block away she paused and looked in a storefront window. Clothes. Did women always stop and look at clothes? Haarte himself was a good dresser and liked clothes. But when he went shopping it was because a suit had worn out or a shirt had ripped, not because he wanted to amuse himself by looking at a bunch of cloth hanging on racks in a stuffy store.

But this was a fact about her that he noted. She liked to shop—window-shop at least—and it was going to work out for the best. Because farther up the street, a block away from the store she was examining, he noticed a construction site.

He crossed the street and jogged past her. She didn't notice him. He looked over the site. The contractor had rigged a scaffolding around a five-story building that was about to be demolished. There were workmen in the building but they were on the other block and couldn't even see this street. Haarte walked underneath the scaffold and stepped into the open doorway. He looked at the jungle of wires and beams inside the chill, open area of what had been the lobby. The floor was littered with glass, conduit, nails, beer cans.

Not great but it would do.

He glanced up the street and saw the girl disappear into the clothing store.

Good.

He pulled latex gloves out of his pocket and found a piece of rope, cut a 20-foot length with the razor knife he always kept with him. Then he went to work with the rope and several lengths of pipe. Five minutes later, he was finished. He returned to the entryway of the building and hid in the shadows.

Long to wait? he wondered.

But, no, it turned out. Only four minutes.

Strolling down the street, happy with her new purchase, whatever it was, the girl was paying no attention to anything except the spring morning as she strolled along the sidewalk.

Twenty feet away, fifteen, ten . . .

She started under the scaffolding and when she was directly opposite him he said, "Oh, hey, miss!"

She stopped, gasped in fright. Took a deep breath. "Like, you scared me," she said angrily.

"Just wanted to say. Be careful where you're walking. It's dangerous 'round here."

He said nothing else. She squinted, wondering if she'd seen him before. Then she looked from his face to the rope he held in his hand. Her eyes followed the rope out the doorway along the sidewalk. To the Lally column she stood beside.

And she realized what was about to happen. "No! Please!"

But he did. Haarte yanked the rope hard, pulling the column out from underneath the first layer of scaffolding. He'd loosened the other columns and removed the wood blocks from under them. The one that the rope was tied to was the only column supporting the tons of steel and two-by-eights that rose for twenty feet above the girl.

As she cried in fear her hands went up, fingers splayed. But it was just an automatic gesture, pure animal reflex—as if she could ward off the terrible weight that now came crashing down on her. The commotion was so loud that Haarte never even heard her scream as the wood and metal—like huge spears—tumbled over her, sending huge clouds of dust into the air.

In ten seconds, the settling was over. Haarte ran to

the column and undid the rope. He tossed it into a
Dumpster. Then he pulled off the latex gloves and left the
construction site, careful to avoid the spreading pool of
blood migrating outward from the mound of debris in
the center of the sidewalk.

The man stood at the top of the stairs, turning three
hundred sixty degrees around the girl's loft.

Any notes? Any diaries? Any witnesses?

He was wearing a jacket with a name stitched on it,
Hank. Below the name he himself had stenciled *Dept. of
Public Works. Meter Reading Service.*

The Meter Man turned back to the loft. Walked along
the bookshelves, pulled out several books, and flipped
through them.

There had to be something here. She'd looked like a
scavenger. The sort who doesn't throw anything away.
And, fuck, it looked like she hadn't.

He got to work: Looking through all the books, papers, all the shit. Stuffed animals, scraps of notes, diaries . . . Shit, she wasn't the least bit organized. This
was gonna take forever. His urge was to fling everything
around the room, rip open the suitcases, cut open mat-
tresses. But he didn't. He worked slowly, methodically.
This was against his nature. If you're in a hurry, do it
slowly. Somebody told him that and he always remembered it. One of the guys he worked for, a guy now
dead—dead not because he got careless but dead because
they were in a business where you sometimes got dead
and that was all there was to it.

You're in a hurry, do it slowly.

Carefully looking through the cushions, boxes, bookcases.

A box stuffed into the futon was labeled MAGIC CRYS-
TALS. Inside were pieces of quartz. "Magic." He whispered

the word as if he'd never said it before, as if it were Japanese.

Jesus. I'm in outer fucking space.

He found a cassette labeled *Manhattan Is My Beat* and picked it up, set it down.

Then: footsteps.

Shit. Who the hell was *this*?

Giggling. A woman's voice: "Not here, come on. No, wait!"

He reached into his pocket and wrapped his hand around his pistol.

A twentyish woman, in a white bra and dress bunched around her waist, stopped at the top of the stairs. She looked at him. He looked at her tits.

"Who the fuck are you?" she demanded. Pulling the cloth halfheartedly up to her chest.

"Who're *you*?" he asked.

The way he asked it she said, "Sandra," immediately.

"You're her roommate?"

"Rune? Yeah, I guess."

He laughed. "You *guess*? How long you known her?"

"Not, you know, long."

He took in this information carefully, noted her body language. If she was dangerous, innocent. If she'd ever killed anyone. "How long is 'you know long'?"

"Huh?"

"How the fuck long've you known her?"

"A couple of months is all. What the hell're you doing here?"

A man, late twenties, blond, jockish, came up the stairs. He squinted, then stepped up beside Sandra.

The Meter Man ignored him.

She said, "Like, what're you doing here?"

He finished looking through the bookcase. Jesus, he didn't want to have to flip through every book. There must've been five hundred of them.

"Hey," the blond man called, "the lady asked you a question."

Sounded like a line from a really bad movie. The Meter Man loved movies. He lived alone and spent every Saturday afternoon at the Quadriplex near him.

He squinted. "What was it? The question?"

"What're you doing here?" she asked uneasily.

He pointed to his chest. "I read meters."

"You can't just come in here," the young man said. Sandra tried to shush him—not concerned so much about the words themselves as the attitude. But the boy waved her off. "You can't enter without permission. It's trespassing. That's actionable."

"Oh. Actionable. What's that mean?"

"That she can sue your ass."

"Oh. Actionable. Well, we had reports of a leak."

"Yeah, what leak?" Sandra asked. "Who reported it?"

The Meter Man grinned at her, looked at her chest again. Nice tits. And she wasn't ugly. Just needed some color and to get rid of that punky makeup. And why a white bra like old ladies wear? He shrugged. "I dunno. Somebody downstairs complained."

"Well, I don't see a leak," she said. "So why don't you leave?"

"You haven't had any water damage lately?"

"Why's a meter reader interested in repairs and leaks?" From Sandra's horny companion.

The Meter Man glanced out the window. It really was one fucking incredible view. He looked back. "When there's a leak you can tell by looking at the meter. That makes sense, don'tcha think?"

"Were you looking through Rune's stuff?"

"Naw, I was looking for the meter."

Sandra said, "Well, it's not up here. So why don't you leave?"

"Why don't you say please?"

The blond jock did it just like Redford or Steve Mc-Queen or Stallone would've. He stepped in front of Sandra. Crossed his arms in his Polo shirt and said, "The lady wants you to leave."

Professional or not? The meter man debated. *That* side gave in, the way it usually did. He said, "If she's a lady why's she fucking an asshole like you?"

The blond smiled, shaking his head, stepping forward. Tensing the muscles that came from the magic of Nautilus machines. "You're outa here."

It turned out not to be that much fun and the Meter Man decided it hadn't been worth the unprofessional part. Oh, mixing it up with a guy who knew what he was doing . . . that would've been one thing. Going a few rounds. Really getting a chance to trade knuckles. But this fucking yuppie . . . Christ.

They did a little scuffling, a little push-pull. Saying that stuff you said in street fights "Why, you mother-fucker . . ." That sort of thing.

Then the Meter Man got bored and decided he couldn't risk being there any longer, and who knew who this pair had called. He broke free and got Blondie once in the solar plexus, then once in the jaw.

Zap, that was it. Two silent punches. The guy went to his knees. More nauseated than hurt, which is what gut punches do. Probably the first fight the guy had been in ever.

Shit, he's going to—

The guy puked all over the floor.

"Jesus, Andy," Sandra said. "That's gross."

Meter Man helped Andy to his feet. Eased him down on the bed.

Okay, enough fun, he thought. Time to get professional again. He said to Sandra, "Here's the deal—I'm from a collection agency. Your friend owes a couple thousand on her credit card and she's been dodging us for a year. We're tired of it."

"That sounds like Rune, sure. Look, I don't know where she is. I haven't heard—"

He held up his hand. "You fucking tell anybody you saw me here, I'll do the same thing to you." He nodded at the young man, who lay on his back, moaning, his arm over his eyes.

Sandra shook her head. "I won't say anything."

As he walked out, Sandra said, "You fight good." She let the dress slip, revealing her breasts again. The Meter Man tugged the dress back up, smiled, said, "Tell your boyfriend he should always keep his left up. He's a defense kinda guy."

CHAPTER FIFTEEN

"Ms. Rune?"

She turned, paused, as she was walking through the door of Washington Square Video.

Rune, however, wasn't looking at the man who'd stopped her. It was the badge and the ID card in the battered wallet that got her attention. He was a U.S. marshal.

Neat, she thought before she decided she ought to be nervous.

"My name's Dixon."

He looked just like what a casting director would pick for a federal agent. Tall and craggy. He had a faint Queens accent. She thought about Detective Virgil Manelli and how he'd worn a suit. This guy was wearing jeans and sneakers, a black baseball jacket: bridge-and-tunnel clothes—meaning: from the outer boroughs. He wouldn't get into Area, her favorite after-hours club, wearing this kind of outfit. Trimmed brown hair. He looked like a contractor.

"It's just Rune. Not Ms."

He put the badge away and she caught a glimpse of a huge gun on his hip.

Awesome . . . That's a Schwarzenegger gun, she thought. Man, that would shoot through trucks.

Then remembered she should be nervous again.

He squinted, then gave a faint smile. "You don't remember me."

She shook her head. Let the door swing shut.

"I saw you the other day—in the apartment on Tenth Street. I was part of the homicide team."

"In Mr. Kelly's apartment?"

"Right."

She nodded. Thinking back to that terrible morning. But she didn't remember anything except Manelli's close-together eyes.

The shot-out TV.

Mr. Kelly's face.

The blood on his chest.

Dixon looked at a notebook, put it back in his pocket. He asked, "Have you been in touch with a Susan Edelman recently?"

"Susan . . . Oh, the other witness." The yuppie with the designer jogging outfit. "I called her yesterday, the day before. She was still in the hospital."

"I see. Can I ask why you called her?"

Because somebody's got to find the killer, and the cops couldn't care less. But she told Dixon, "Just to see how she's doing. Why?"

Dixon paused for a moment. She didn't like the way he was looking at her face. Assessing her. He said, "Ms. Edelman was killed an hour ago."

"What?" she gasped. "No!"

"I'm afraid so."

"What happened?"

Dixon continued. "She was walking past a construction site. A scaffolding collapsed. It might have been an accident but, of course, we don't think so."

"Oh, no . . ."

"Has anyone threatened you? Or have you noticed anything suspicious since the killing on Tenth Street?"

"No." She looked down for a moment, uneasy, then back to the marshal.

Dixon examined her face closely. His expression gave away nothing. He said, "For your sake, for a lot of people's sake, I need you to tell me what your involvement with this whole thing is."

"There's no—"

"This's real serious, miss. It might've seemed like a game at first. But it isn't. Now, I can have you put into protective custody and we'll sort it out later. . . . I really don't think you'd like to spend a week in Women's Detention? Now, what's the story?"

There was something about his voice that sounded as if he was really concerned. Sure, he was threatening her in a way but that just seemed to be his style. It probably went with the job. And she felt that he was really worried that she might end up like Kelly or Susan Edelman.

So she told him a few things. About the movie, the stolen bank loot, about the connection between Mr. Kelly and the robbery. Nothing about Symington. Nothing about churches or suitcases. Nothing about Amanda LeClerc.

Dixon nodded slowly and she couldn't tell what he was thinking. The only thing that seemed to interest him was the old robbery.

Why'd he lift his eyebrow at that? she wondered.

Dixon asked, "Where do you live?"

She gave him the address.

"Phone number?"

"No phone. You can call here, the video store, leave a message."

Dixon thought for a moment. "I don't think you're in danger."

"I didn't see anything, I really didn't. Just this green car. That's all I remember. No faces, no license plates. There's no *reason* to kill me."

This seemed to amuse him. "Well, that's not really the issue, miss. The reason you're not dead is that somebody doesn't want you dead. Not yet. If they did, you'd be gone. If I were you, though, I'd forget about this bank robbery money. Maybe that's what was behind Mr. Kelly's shooting. You're probably safe for now but if you keep poking around . . . who knows what could happen?"

"I was just—"

Suddenly his face softened and he smiled. "You're a pretty woman. You're smart. You're tough, I can see that. I just wouldn't want anything to happen to you."

Rune said, "Thanks. I'll keep that in mind." Though she was really only thinking two things: That Dixon wasn't wearing a wedding ring. And that he was a hell of a lot cuter than she'd thought at first.

━━━━━

"What was that all about? Did that guy have a *badge*?" Stephanie sounded breathless.

Rune walked behind the counter at Washington Square Video, joining Stephanie at the register. She answered, "He was a U.S. marshal. . . ." Then she shook her head. "The other witness—to Mr. Kelly's murder?— she was killed."

"No!"

"It might've been an accident. Maybe not." Rune stared at the monitor. There was no movie in the VCR and she was looking at silent snow. "Probably not," she whispered.

"Are you, uhm, safe?" Stephanie asked.

"He thinks so."

"*Thinks?*"

"But there's one thing funny."

"What?"

"He was a U.S. marshal?"

"You said that."

"Why would he be involved in a murder of somebody in the East Village?"

"What do you mean?"

Rune was thinking. "I saw this movie on Dillinger. You know John Dillinger?"

"Not personally."

"Ha. He robbed banks. Which is, like, a federal offense—so it wasn't the *city* cops who were after him. It was the G-men."

"G-men?"

"Federal agents. You know, *government* men. Like the FBI. Like U.S. Marshals."

"Oh, wait, you're not thinking he's investigating that bank robbery you were telling me about. The one fifty years ago?"

Rune shrugged. "He didn't say anything but it's kind of a coincidence, don't you think? He seemed real interested when I said something to him about it."

Stephanie turned back to *Variety*. "Little far-fetched."

But what's far-fetched in the whole scheme of things—as Richard might have asked.

Rune found the Brooklyn Yellow Pages. She opened it to Churches. Seemed funny you could find escort services, Roto-Rooter companies, and churches in the same directory.

She flipped through the pages. Man, there were a lot of pages.

She started to make calls.

A half hour later Stephanie asked Rune, "You think I'll get the part?"

"What part?" Rune asked absently, phone tucked between her ear and her shoulder. She was on hold. (It also seemed weird to call a church and be put on hold.)

"Didn't I tell you? I'm auditioning next week. It's only a commercial. But still . . . They pay great. I've *got* to get it. It's totally important."

Rune stiffened suddenly as the minister came on the line.

"Hello?"

"Reverend, Father, sir . . . I'm trying to find some information about my grandfather? Robert Kelly? About seventy. Do you know if he spent any time at your parish?"

"Robert Kelly? No, miss, I sure don't."

"Okay, Father. Thank you. Oh, and have a nice day." She set the receiver in the cradle, pushed aside the Yellow Pages, and asked Stephanie, "Do you say that to priests?"

"What?"

" 'Have a nice day?' I mean, shouldn't you say something more meaningful? More spiritual?"

"Say whatever you want." Stephanie put *Variety* away, began reshelving cassettes in the stacks. She said, "If I don't get the job I'll just die. It's a whole commercial. Thirty seconds. I'd play a young wife with PMS and I can't enjoy my anniversary dinner until I take some pills."

"What pills?"

"I don't know. 'Cramp-Away.' "

"What?"

"Well, something *like* that. Then I take them and my husband and I waltz off happily. I get to wear a long white dress. That's so disgusting when they do that, wear white in menstrual commercials. I'm also worried 'cause I can't waltz. Dancing isn't exactly my strong suit. And I can't—just between you and me—I can't sing too good either. It's a real pain in the ass getting jobs when you can't sing and dance."

"You've got a great body and great hair."

And you're tall, Goddammit.

Flipping through more pages, ignoring the synagogues and mosques. "Amanda's calling too. . . . I feel sorry for her. Poor woman. Imagine—her friend's killed *and* they're kicking her out of the country."

"By the way, I don't think they're all parishes," Stephanie said.

"You think I was pissing them off by calling them parishes?" Rune was frowning.

"I think they get pissed when you worship Satan and cast spells. I don't think they care what you call their churches. I'm just telling you for your own, you know, edification."

Rune picked up the phone and then put it down again. She glanced at the door as a thin young woman, dark-complected, entered. The woman had a proper pageboy cut and was wearing a navy-blue suit, carrying a heavy, law- or accounting-firm briefcase in one hand. Rune swiftly sized her up, whispered to Stephanie, "A dollar says it's Richard Gere."

Stephanie waited until the woman moved to the comedy section and pulled *The Sting* off the shelf before reaching into her pocket and slipping four quarters onto the countertop. Rune put a dollar bill next to them. Stephanie murmured, "Think you're getting to be hot shit, huh? You can spot 'em?"

"I can spot 'em," Rune said.

The woman wandered around the aisles, not sensing Rune and Stephanie watching her while they pretended to work. She came up to the counter and set the

Newman-Redford movie on the rubber change mat beside the cash register. "I'll take that." She handed Rune her membership card. Stephanie, smiling, reached for the money. The woman hesitated and then said, "Oh, maybe I'll get another one too." Stepping away to the drama section.

She set *Power* next to *The Sting*. Richard Gere's bedroom eyes gazed out from the cover. Stephanie pushed the two dollars toward Rune and rang up the rental. The woman snagged the cassettes and left the store.

"How'd you know?" Stephanie asked Rune.

"Look." She typed in the woman's membership number into the computer and called up a history of all the movies she'd rented.

"That's cheating."

"Don't bet if you don't know the odds."

"I don't know, Rune," Stephanie said. "You think Mr. Kelly was into hidden treasure or something, but look, here's this woman rents Richard Gere films ten times in six months. That's just as weird as Kelly."

Rune shook her head. "Naw, you know why she does that? She's having an affair with him. You know the way it is now, sex is dangerous. You have to take matters into your own hands. So to speak. Makes sense to me."

"Funny, you seem like more of a risk-taker—tracking down hidden treasure and murderers. But you won't go to bed with a guy."

"I'll sleep with somebody. I just want to make sure it's the right somebody."

"'Right'?" Stephanie snorted. "You *do* like your impossible quests, don't you."

Rune slipped the bootleg *Manhattan Is My Beat* into the VCR. A few minutes later she mused, "Wasn't she beautiful?" On the screen Ruby Dahl, with the bobbed blond hair, was walking hand in hand with Dana Mitchell, playing her fiancé, Roy, the cop. The Brooklyn Bridge loomed in the background. It was before the robbery. Roy had been called in by his captain and told what a good job he was doing. But the young patrolman was worrying because he was broke. He had to support his sick mother. He didn't know when he and Ruby'd be able to get married. Maybe he'd leave the force—go to work for a steel company.

"But you're so good at what you do, Roy, darling. I would think they'd want you to be commissioner. Why, if I were in charge that's what I'd make you."

Handsome Dana Mitchell walked beside her solemnly. He told her she was a swell gal. He told her what a lucky stiff he was. The camera backed away from them and the two people became insignificant dots in a shadowy black-and-white city.

Rune glanced down at the countertop. "Ohmygod!"

"What?" Stephanie asked, alarmed.

"It's a phone message."

"So?"

"Where's Frankie? Dammit. I'm going to kick his butt. . . ."

"What?"

"He took the message but he just left it here under these receipts." She held it up. "Look, look! It's from Richard. I haven't heard from him since yesterday. He dropped me off on the West Side." Rune grimaced. "Kissed me on the cheek good-bye."

"Ouch. A cheek-kiss only?"

"Yeah. And after he'd seen me topless."

Stephanie shook her head. "That's not good."

"Tell me about it."

The message read:

Rune—Richard asked you over for dinner tomorrow, at seven, hes cooking. He has a surprise for

    you and he also said why the hell don't you get a
    phone. Ha ha but he was kidding

"Yes! I thought he'd given up on me after we went to the
nursing home on Sunday."

"Nursing home? Rune, you gotta pick more romantic
places for dates."

"Oh, I'm going to! I've got this totally excellent junkyard I go to—"

"No, no, no."

"It's really neat." She fluffed her hair out again. "What
should I wear? I have this polka-dot tank top I just got at
Second-Hand Rose. And this tiger-skin skirt that's about
eight inches wide . . . What?"

"Tiger skin?"

"Oh, like, it's not *real*. . . . If you're into rain forests
and stuff like that. I mean, it was made in New Jersey—"

"Rune, the problem isn't endangered species."

"Well, what *is* the problem?"

Stephanie was examining her closely. "Are those
glow-in-the-dark earrings?"

"I got them last Halloween," she said defensively,
touching the skulls. "Why are you looking at me that
way?"

"You like fairy stories, right?"

"Sure."

"You remember Cinderella?"

"Oh, it's the *best*. Did you know in the real story, the
Brothers Grimm story, the mother cut the ugly sisters'
heels off with a knife so their feet would fit into the—"

"Rune." Stephanie said it patiently.

"What?"

"Let's think about the Disney version for a minute."
Rune looked at her cautiously. "Okay."

"You remember it?"

"Yeah."

Stephanie walked around Rune slowly, examining her. "You understand what I'm getting at?"

"Oh . . . a makeover?"

Stephanie smiled. "Don't take it personal. But I think you need a fairy godmother."

CHAPTER SIXTEEN

███████ Rune wanted slinky.

Stephanie reluctantly indulged her but the expedition to stores that specialized in svelte was a failure. Rune spent a half hour in tiny, hot changing rooms trying on long black dresses and playing with her hair, trying to look like Audrey Hepburn, trying to look slinky. But then the word *frumpy* crept into her mind and, even though she could strip and look at her flat stomach and thin legs and pretty face, once she thought *frump,* that killed it. No long dresses today.

"You win," she muttered to Stephanie.

"Thank you" was the abrupt reply. "Now let's get to work."

They walked south, out of the Village.

"Richard likes long and slinky," Rune explained.

"Of course he does," Stephanie replied. "He's a man. He probably likes red and black bustiers and garters too." But she went on to explain patiently that a woman should never buy clothes for a man. She should buy clothes for herself, which will in turn make the man respect and desire her more.

"You think?"

"I *know*."

"Radical," Rune said.

Stephanie rolled her eyes and said, "We'll go for European."

"Richard's very French-looking. I'd like to get him to change his name."

"To what?"

"It *was* François. Now I'm leaning toward Jean-Paul."

"What does he think about that?"

"Haven't told him. I'm going to wait a few weeks."

"Wise."

SoHo, the former warehouse and manufacturing district adjoining Greenwich Village, was just becoming chic. The area used to be a bastion of artists-in-residence—working painters and sculptors, who were the only people who could legally live in the neighborhood under the city zoning code. But while the city granted permits only to certified artists, it did nothing about controlling the cost of the huge lofts, and as the galleries and wine bars and boutiques moved into the commercial buildings, the residential prices skyrocketed into the hundreds of thousands. . . . It was funny how many lawyers and bankers suddenly found they had talent to paint and sculpt.

They passed one clothing store, painted stark white inside. Rune stopped abruptly and gazed at a black silk blouse.

"Love it."

"So do I," Stephanie agreed.

"Can we get it?"

"No."

"Why not? What's wrong with it?"

"See that tag? That's not the order number. That's the price."

"Four hundred and fifty dollars!"

"Come on, follow me. I know a little Spanish place up the street."

They turned off West Broadway onto Spring and walked into a store that Rune loved immediately because a large white bird sitting on a perch by the door said, "Hello, sucker," to them when they entered.

Rune looked around. She said, "I'm game. But it's not funky. It's not New Wave."

"It's not supposed to be."

After twenty minutes of careful assembly, Stephanie examined Rune with approval and only then allowed her to look in a mirror.

"Awesome," Rune whispered. "You're a magician."

The maroon skirt *was* long though it was more billowy than slinky. On top she wore a low-cut black T-shirt and over that a lacy see-through blouse. Stephanie picked out some dangly earrings in orange plastic.

"It's not the old me but it's definitely a *sort of* me."

"I think you're evolving," Stephanie told her.

As the clerk wrapped up the clothes Rune said, "You know the story of the little red hen?"

"Was it on *Sesame Street*?"

"I don't think so. She was the one who was baking bread, and nobody helped her, except this one animal. I forget what it was. Duck, rabbit. Who knows? Anyway, when the bread was done all the other animals came to the hen and said they wanted some. But she said, 'Haul ass, creeps.' And she only shared it with the one that helped her. Well, when I find the bank money I'm going to share it with you."

"Me?"

"You believe me. Richard doesn't. The police don't."

Stephanie didn't say anything. They stepped outside

and returned to West Broadway. "You don't have to do that, Rune," she said finally.

"But I want to. Maybe you can quit the stupid video store and audition full-time."

"Really . . ."

"No." The Hungarian accent was back. "Don't argue with peasant woman. Very pigheaded . . . Oh, wait." Rune glanced at a store across the street. "Richard said he's got a surprise for me. I want to get him something."

They ran across Broadway, dodging traffic. Rune stopped, caught her breath, looked in the window. "What do men like?" she asked.

Stephanie said, "Themselves." And they walked inside.

———

The store seemed futuristic but it may actually have been antique, Rune reasoned, since it reminded her of how her mother described the sixties—gaudy and filled with weird glowing lights and spaceships and planets and a confusion of incense smells: musk, patchouli, rose, sandalwood.

Rune looked at a black-lit poster of a ship sailing in the sky and said, "Highly retro."

Stephanie looked around, bored.

In the display cases: geodes, crystals, stones, opals, silver and gold, magic wands of quartz wrapped with silver wire, headdresses, meteorites, NASA memorabilia, electronic music tapes, optical illusions. Colored lights broken apart by spinning prisms crawled up and down the walls.

"It's going to make me epileptic," Stephanie groused.

"This is the most radical store ever, don't you think? Isn't it fantastic?" Rune picked up two dinosaurs and made them dance.

"The jewelry's nice." Stephanie was leaning over a counter.

"What do you think he'd like?"

"This stuff is too expensive. A rip-off."

Rune spun a kaleidoscope. "He's not really into toys, I don't think."

The clerk, a thin black man with a round, handsome face framed by Rastafarian dreadlocks, said to Rune in a deep musical voice, "What you see in there?"

"Nirvana. Look." She handed the heavy tube to him.

He played along, peering inside. "Ah, nirvana, there she is. Special today on kaleidoscopes that show you enlightenment. Half price."

Rune shook her head. "Doesn't seem right you should pay for enlightenment."

"This is New York," he said. "Whatchu want?"

Stephanie said, "I'm hungry."

Then Rune saw the bracelets. In a huge glass pyramid, a dozen silver bracelets. She walked to the end of the counter, staring at them, her mouth slightly open. Exhaling an *Oh*.

"You like them, do you?" the clerk asked.

"Can I see that one, there?"

Rune took the thin bracelet, held it up to her face. Turned it over and over. The silver grew thicker and thinner and the ends were like two hands clasped together.

The Rastafarian grinned. "She look nice. She look nice on your arm but . . ."

" 'She'?" Stephanie asked.

The clerk was studying Rune's face. "Mebbe you thinkin' 'bout givin' her away to someone. Mebbe you thinkin' that?" He held the bracelet in his long, sensuous fingers, studied it carefully. Rune thought of Richard's hands slowly opening a beer can. The clerk looked up. "To some man friend of yours."

Rune didn't pay attention to his words. "How did you know that?" Stephanie asked him.

He grinned, silent. Then said, "He's a nice man, I think."

Stephanie looked at him uneasily. "How did you *know*?"

And Rune, who wasn't surprised at all by the clerk's words, said, "I'll take it."

"It's too expensive."

The Rastafarian frowned. "Hey, I offer you satori, I offer you love, and you say that be too expensive?"

"Bargain with him," Stephanie commanded.

Rune said, "Wrap it for a present."

The Rastafarian hesitated. "You sure?"

"Sure I'm sure. Why?"

"Oh, jus' this bracelet, she be important in your life, I got this feelin'. Be very important." He fingered the metal hoop. "Don't be too fast to give her away. No, no, don't be too fast to do that."

"Can we eat now?" Stephanie asked. "I'm hungry."

As they walked to the door the clerk called to Rune, "You hear me?"

Rune turned. Looked into his eyes. "I hear you."

———

" 'I'll go in, sir,' "

Rune handed Stephanie a hot dog she'd bought from the vendor in front of Trinity Church downtown, near Wall Street. She continued speaking. " 'I'll go in, sir' is what Roy the cop—Dana Mitchell—says to his captain. They're all standing around the front of the bank with their bullhorns and guns. 'I'll go in, sir.' And it's a big surprise because he's just a beat cop and a young guy. Nobody'd been paying any attention to him. But he's the one who volunteers to rescue the hostage."

Rune took her own hot dog from the man. They sat

down beside the wrought-iron fence in front of the cemetery. Thousands of people were walking past on Broadway, some disappearing down Wall Street into the curving, solemn griminess of the buildings.

Stephanie ate thoughtfully, looking at the hot dog uncertainly after each bite.

"Then Roy goes, 'Let me try it, sir. I can talk him out. I know I can.'"

"Uh-huh." Stephanie was gazing straight ahead; the hordes of passing crowds were mesmerizing.

"So the lieutenant goes, 'All right, officer, if you want to go, I won't stop you.'"

Rune threw out her half-eaten hot dog. Stood up. "'But it's dangerous.'" She sounded as melodramatic as the character in the film itself. "That was another cop, a friend of his, said that. And Dana—remember that dreamy kind of look he had?—Dana says, 'I'm not letting anyone get killed on *my* beat.' His jaw was all firm and he pulled his hat straight and handed his nightstick to his friend then walked across the street and climbed in the side window." Rune started pacing. "Come on, let's go. I want to see the real bank."

Stephanie glanced at the last inch of hot dog, then pitched it into a garbage can. She wiped her hands and mouth with a thin napkin.

They descended into Wall Street. A white luminescence shone through the milky clouds, but the Street, with its narrow, packed rows of dark office buildings, was gloomy.

Rune said, "They shot the movie at the old Union Bank Building itself—that's were the actual robbery took place. The bank went bust years ago and the building was sold. It's been a bunch of things since then. Last year some company bought it and made a restaurant out of the ground floor."

Stephanie said, "Can we get some coffee there? I need some coffee."

Rune was excited, walking ahead of her, then slowing and falling back into step. "Isn't this too much? Walking the same streets the actors did forty years ago? Maybe Dana Mitchell stopped right here and put his foot up on that fire hydrant to tie his shoe."

"Maybe."

"Oh, look!" Rune gripped her arm. "There, the corner! That's where the robber fired a shot as the cops were closing in after the alarm went off. It's a great scene." She ran toward the corner, dodged past a young woman in a pink suit, and pressed back against the marble as if she were under fire. "Stephanie! Get down! Get under cover!"

"You're crazy," Stephanie said, walking slowly to the wall.

Rune reached forward. "You want to get shot? Get down!"

She pulled Stephanie, laughing, into a crouch. Several passersby had heard her. They looked around, cautious. Stephanie, pretending she didn't know Rune, whispered, "You're out of your mind!" Looking at the crowd, speaking louder: "She's out of her mind."

Rune's eyes were bright. "Can you imagine it? The bank's around the corner. And . . . Listen!" A jackhammer sounded in the distance. "A machine gun! The robber's got a machine gun, an old tommy gun. He's blasting away at us. Okay, it's right around the corner and he's got a hostage and a million dollars. I've got to save him!"

Stephanie laughed and tugged at Rune's arm. Playing along now. "No, no don't go, it's too dangerous."

Rune adjusted an invisible hat, eased her shoulders back. "Nobody gets killed on my beat." And turned the corner.

Just in time to see a bulldozer shovel what had been

one of the floors of the Union Bank Building into a huge Dumpster.

"No . . ." Rune stopped in the middle of the congested sidewalk. Several businesspeople bumped into her before she stepped back. "Oh, no." Her hand went to her mouth.

The demolition company had taken down most of the building already. Only part of one wall remained. The stubby dozer was shoveling up masses of shattered stone and wood and metal.

Rune said, "How could they do it?"

"What?"

"They tore it down. It's gone."

Rune stepped away from Stephanie, her eyes on the men who worked the clanking jackhammers. They stood on the edge of the remaining wall, forty feet up, and dug apart the masonry at their feet. She glanced up the street, then walked slowly across it, to the plywood barricade that shut out pedestrians from the demolition site.

She couldn't look through the peepholes cut by the workers; they were at a six-footer's level. So she walked into the site itself through the open chain-link gate. A huge ramp of earth led down to the foundation where the truck holding the Dumpster idled. There was a resounding crash as the tons of rubble dropped into the steel vessel.

Stephanie caught up with her. "Hey, I don't think we're supposed to be here."

"I feel weird," Rune told her.

"Why?"

"They just destroyed the whole place. And it was so . . . familiar. I knew it so well from the movie and now it's gone. How could they do it?"

Below them, a second bulldozer lifted a huge steel-mesh blanket and set it on top of a piece of exposed rock. There was a painful hoot of a steam whistle above their heads. The bulldozer backed away. Then two whistles. A minute later the explosives were detonated. A jarring slam under their feet. Smoke. The metal blanket shifted a few feet. Three whistle blasts—the all-clear—sounded.

Rune blinked. Tears formed. "It's not the way it should be."

She stooped and picked up a bit of broken marble from the bank's facade—pinkish and gray, the colors of a trout, smooth on one side. She looked at it for a long time, then put it in her pocket.

"It's not the way it should be at all," she repeated.

"Let's go," Stephanie urged.

The bulldozer lifted the mesh away and began to dig out mouthfuls of the shattered rock.

CHAPTER SEVENTEEN

███████ She'd wrapped it up, the bracelet.

But then walking up to Third Avenue—past the discount clothing stores, the Hallmark shop, the delis— she'd decided the wrapping paper was too feminine. It had a viney pattern that wasn't anything sissier than you'd see in the old *Arabian Nights* illustrations. But Richard might think they were flowers.

So halfway to his apartment she slipped her hand, with its newly polished nails—pink, not green or blue, for a change—into her bag and tore off the paper and ribbon.

Then, waiting for the light on Twenty-third Street, Rune started to worry about the box. Giving him something in a box, something supposed to be, what was the word?, spontaneous, seemed too formal. Men got scared, you gave them something that was too premeditated.

Goddamn men.

The nails went to work again and opened the box,

which joined the crumpled Arabian paper in the bottom of the leopard-skin purse. She held the bracelet up in the light.

Wait. Was it too feminine?

Did it matter? He was a *philosopher* knight, remember, not the kind killing peasants with a broadsword. Anyway there *definitely* was something androgynous about him—like Hermaphroditus. And now that she thought about it, Rune decided that was one of the reasons they were so compatible. The male-female, yin-yang was in flux for both of them.

She put the bracelet in her pocket.

See, what it is, I was buying one for me—remember I told you I love bracelets, so what I did was I saw this one, and it looked too masculine for me and I thought, well, it just occurred to me you might . . .

Rune stopped for the light. She was in front of an Indian store, sitar music and the smell of incense flooded out into the street. The light changed.

See, I got this special deal at a jewelry store I go to. Two for one. Yeah, no shit. Amazing. And I thought: who do I know who'd like a bracelet? And, guess what? You won . . .

Crossing the street.

Then she saw his apartment building a block ahead. She tried to be objective. But was still disappointed. It was a boxish high-rise, squatting in a nest of boxish high-rises, a little bit of suburbia in Manhattan. She couldn't picture her black-clad knight living among tiny widows and salesmen and nurses and med students from NYU.

Oh, well . . . She continued along the sidewalk and stopped outside his building.

Hey, Richard, would you like a bracelet? If not, no big deal, I could give it to my mother, sister, roommate . . . But if you'd like it . . . It's a pretty radical design, don'tcha think?—take a look at it.

Rune stepped away from the building and looked at her reflection in the window.

Oh, a bracelet? Rune, it's fantastic! Put it on me. I'll never take it off.

She polished the silver on her sleeve then dropped it into her pocket again.

Oh, a bracelet. Well, the thing is, I never wear them. . . .

Well, the thing is my girlfriend gave me a bracelet just like this the day she killed herself. . . .

Well, the thing is I'm allergic to silver. . . .

Goddamn men.

───────

Seeing him, with that dark hair and the long French face, that crazy electricity hit her again. She knew her voice was going to shake, and she thought, goddammit, get this under control.

What's best? Flirty, surprised? Seductive? She opted for a neutral "Hi." She stood in his doorway. Neither of them moved.

He gave her one of those scary we're-just-friends looks. He almost seemed surprised to see her. "Rune, hey, how you doing?"

"Great, good. . . . You?"

Hey, how you doing?

"Okay." He nodded and she saw he was definitely uncomfortable. Though he kept the smile on his face. There were major explosions in her. Wanting to vaporize away, wanting to ease her arms around him and never leave. Mostly she wondered what the hell was wrong.

Silence, as an elderly lady with a jutting, sour mouth walked her cairn terrier past, glancing disdainfully at them. Richard said, "So how's the video business?" He looked her up and down. Didn't say a word about the new outfit. Glanced at the earrings. Didn't say anything about them either.

"Good. Okay."

"Well, why don't you come on in."

She followed him inside.

Wait, she thought, looking him over. What's going on? He was wearing a baby-blue button-down shirt, tan chino slacks, and Top-Siders. Ohmygod, Top-Siders! Nothing black, nothing chic. He looked like a yuppie from the Upper East Side.

Then she glanced around his apartment. She couldn't figure it—that somebody who wore black leather and tapped the tops of his beer cans with such elegant fingers could live in a place with white Conran furniture, rock and roll posters on the wall, and a metal sea gull statue.

A copper sea gull?

"Just let me check on something."

He disappeared into the kitchen. Whatever he was cooking smelled great. None of her girlfriends could get that kind of smell out of a kitchen. Lord knew, *she* never had.

She was examining his bookshelves. Mostly technical books about things she didn't understand. College paperbacks. Stacks of the *New York Times* and the *Atlantic Monthly*.

He came back into the room. Stood with his arms crossed. "So." Skittish now.

"Uh-huh. So." She couldn't think of anything to say for a moment. Then she blurted out, "I thought, maybe, after dinner, you might want to go for a ride. I found a great place. It's in Queens, a junkyard. I know the owner. He lets me in. It's really radical, like a huge dinosaur graveyard. You can sit up on some of the wrecks—it's not gross dirty, you know, like garbage—and watch the sunset over the city. It's really wild. It's your mega junk-

yard. . . . Okay, Richard, come on. Tell me what I did
to fuck up tonight."

"The thing is—"

"Hi," came the woman's voice from the door.

Rune turned to see a tall woman with long, blond
hair walk through the open door. The woman was wearing a gray pin-striped suit and black pumps. She gave
Rune a friendly glance, then walked up to Richard and
hugged him.

"Rune, this is Karen."

"Uhm, hi," Rune said. Then to Richard, "Your message? About dinner?"

Karen lifted a perfect eyebrow knowingly, took a bottle of wine out of a paper bag, and disappeared tactfully
into the kitchen.

"Actually," Richard said delicately, "that was supposed to be Thursday."

"Wait. The message said tomorrow. And the date on
it was yesterday."

He shrugged. "I told the guy I talked to—Frankie
somebody—I told him Thursday."

She nodded. "And he thought *today* was Thursday.
Goddamn heavy metal. It's destroyed his brain cells . . .
Shit, shit, shit."

Yo, Fairy Godmother! Yo! Wave your magic wand
and get me the hell out of here.

"Listen, you want to stay? Have some wine?"

That'd be a pretty picture, she thought. The three of
us sipping wine while he's waiting for me to leave so he
can put the Tantra moves on too-tall Karen.

"No, think I'll go."

"Sure. I'll walk you to the elevator."

Oh, don't argue *too* hard now.

Richard continued. "Oh, wait, let me get you what I
have for you."

"My surprise?"

"Right. I think you'll like it."

"So, Rune, how do you know Richard?" Karen was calling from the kitchen.

Yeah. He picked me up the other night and's been trying to fuck me ever since.

"Met in a video store. We talk about movies some."

"I *love* movies," Karen called. "Maybe we could all go sometime.

"Maybe."

Richard appeared from his bedroom. He was carrying a white envelope.

That's my present?

"Be right back," he said to Karen.

"This sauce is *so* good," she called from the kitchen. She stuck her pert head into the doorway. "Nice meeting you. Oh, love the earrings!"

As they walked to the elevator Richard said, "Karen's a friend. We work together."

Rune wondered: How does somebody work *with* you when you write novels?

They got four doors down the corridor before he said, "This's a little awkward but she and I *really* are just friends."

"We *are* going out, aren't we? You and me, I mean."

"Sure, we're going out. I mean, we aren't going out all the time though, right? We *can* have other friends."

"Sure. That's the way it has to work."

"Right."

I am absolutely going to murder Frankie Greek. . . .

He pushed the down button.

Aren't we in a hurry.

"Oh, here." He thrust the envelope at her.

She opened it. Inside was an application to the New School, over on Fifth Avenue.

A joke. It had to be a joke.

"I've got a buddy works for admissions," Richard explained. "He told me they're starting this new program. Retail management. You don't even need to get a degree. You get a certificate."

She felt sick. "Wait. You're giving me career counseling?"

"Rune, you're so smart, you've got so much energy, you're so creative. . . . I'm worried about you wasting your life."

She stared, numb, at the paper in her hand.

Richard said, "You could work your way up in the video store business. Become a manager. Then maybe you could buy a store. Or even a chain. You could really be on a hell of a vertical track."

She laughed bitterly. "But . . . that's not *me*, Richard. I'm not a vertical-track kind of person. Look, I've worked in that diner I told you about, in a bike repair shop, a deli, a shoe store. I've sold jewelry on the street, done paste-ups and mechanicals for a magazine, sold men's colognes at Macy's, and worked in a film lab. And that's just in the couple years I've been here. Before I die I'm going to do a lot more than that. I'm not going to devote my life to being manager of a video store. Or any other one thing."

"Don't you want a career?"

She felt utterly betrayed. More so than if she'd found Karen and Richard in bed, an event that was probably only minutes away.

When she didn't answer he said, "You should think about it."

Rune said, "Sometimes I get this idea I should go to school. Get a degree. Law school, maybe business school like my sister. Something. But then, you know what happens? I have this image. Of myself in ten years at a cocktail party. And somebody asks me what I do. And—this is the scary part—I have an answer for them." She smiled at him.

"Which is . . . ?"

He didn't get it. "*That's* the point. It doesn't matter; the scary part is that I *have* an answer. I say, 'I'm a lawyer, an accountant, a hoosey-whatsis maker.' Bang, there I am. Defined in one or two words. That scares the hell out of me."

"Why're you so afraid of reality?"

"My life is real. It's just not, apparently, *your* kind of reality."

He said harshly, "No, it's *not* real. Look at this game of yours . . ."

"What game?"

"Find-the-hidden-treasure."

"What's wrong with that?"

"Do you understand that a man was killed? Did it ever occur to you that it wasn't a game to Robert Kelly? That you could get hurt? Or a friend of yours could get hurt? That *ever* occur to you?"

"It'll work out. You just need to believe . . ."

She gasped as he took her angrily by the shoulders and led her to a window at the end of the hallway. Pointed outside. Beneath them was a mass of highways and rail sidings and rusting equipment—huge turbines and metal parts. Beyond that was a small factory, surrounded by standing yellowish water. Mud. Filth.

"What's that?" he asked.

She shook her head. Not understanding.

"What *is* it?" His voice rose.

"What do you mean?" Her voice crackled.

"It's a factory, Rune. There's shit and pollution. It makes a living for people and they pay taxes and give money to charity and buy sneakers for their children. Who grow up to be lawyers or teachers or musicians or people who work in other factories. It's nothing more than that. It's not a spaceship, it's not a castle, it's not an entrance to the underworld. It's a *factory*."

She was completely still.

"I like you a lot, Rune. But going with you is like living in some movie."

She wiped her nose. The cars below whined past. "What's wrong with movies? I love movies."

"Nothing. As long as you remember they aren't real. You're going to find out I'm not a knight and that, okay, maybe there was some bank robbery money—which I think is the craziest frigging thing I've ever heard—but that it's spent or stolen or lost somewhere years ago and you'll never find it. And here you are pissing your life away in a video store, jumping from fantasy to fantasy, waiting for something you don't even know what it is."

"If that's your reality you can keep it," she snapped, wiping her nose.

"Fairy stories aren't going to get you by in life."

"I told you they don't all have happy endings!"

"But even if they don't, Rune, you close the book, you put it on your shelf and you go on with your life. They. Aren't. Real. And if you live your life like you're in one you're going to get hurt. Or somebody around you's going to get hurt."

"So why're you the expert on reality? You write novels."

He sighed, looked away from her. "I don't write novels. I was trying to impress you. I don't even *read* novels. I write audiovisual scripts for companies. 'Hello, I'm John Jones, your CEO, welcome to Sales-Fest '88. . . .' It's not weird. It's not fun. But it pays the bills."

"But you . . . you're just like me. The clubs, the dancing, the magic . . . we like the same things."

"It's an act, Rune. Just like it is for everybody who lives that way. Except for you. Nobody can sustain your kind of weirdness. When you're frivolous, when you're *irresponsible,* you miss trains and buses and dinner dates. You—"

"But," she interrupted, "there'll *always* be a next train." She wiped her eyes and saw the mascara had run. Shit. She must look pathetic. She said softly, "You lied to me."

The elevator arrived. She pulled away from him and stepped into the car.

"Rune . . ."

They stood three feet away, she inside, he out. It seemed to take forever before the doors started to close. As they slowly did she thought that Diarmuid, or any knight, wouldn't let her get away like this. He'd push in after her, shove the doors aside, hold her.

Tell her they could work out these differences.

But Richard just turned and walked down the corridor.

"There'll always be another train," she whispered as the doors closed.

███

" 'Your stepsisters keep you in tatters like`this? No, no, no, dear, that will never do. How can you be the fairest one at the ball in these rags? Now, let me see what I can do. Yes, oh, my, that should be just right. . . .'

"And closing her eyes, she waved her magic wand three times. There appeared as if from thin air a gown of silk and lace, stitched with golden and silver thread. And for her feet . . ."

Rune recited this from memory as she walked along University Place. She paused, crumpled up the New School application, and three-pointed it into a trash basket.

She glanced at herself in a mirror hanging in a wig shop. The lipstick was fine and the blusher on the cheekbones was fun to do and easy. Thank you, Stephanie. The eyes had been okay—at least before the tears'd turned her into a raccoon.

Rune took another sip of Miller—from her third can—wrapped in a paper bag. She'd bought a six-pack at a deli up the street but had somehow managed to drop three cans within the past two blocks.

A couple holding hands walked past.

Rune couldn't help staring at them. They didn't notice. They were in love.

" 'Oh, dear,' Cinderella's fairy godmother said, 'coachmen. What's the good of turning a pumpkin into a coach if you have no coachmen to drive you? Ah-ha, mice . . .' "

Rune turned back to the mirror, teased her hair with her fingers, and stepped back to look at the results.

She thought: I don't look like Cinderella at all. I look like a short whore.

Her shoulders sagged and she dug into her bag. Found a Kleenex and scrubbed the rest of the makeup off her face, combed her hair back into place.

She pulled off the orange earrings, which Karen the girls' basketball champ had loved so much, and dropped them into her purse.

What was wrong? Why was it so hard to get men interested in her?

She considered everything.

I'm not tall and blond, true.

I'm not beautiful. But I'm not dog-ugly either.

Maybe she was a lesbian.

Rune considered this.

It seemed possible. And it explained a lot. Like why she got hit on by men but never proposed to—they could sense her orientation probably. (Not that she wanted to get married necessarily—but she *did* want the chance to say, "Lemme think about it.")

No, she just wasn't the sort men went for. That was

probably all part of it, maybe the way the Gods made you the way you were. They might make you short and cute, a little like Audrey Hepburn, but not enough to make men—real men, chivalrous men, Cary Grant men, knights errant—fall for you. The Gods are just letting you down easy. Saying: if they'd meant you to have somebody like Richard, they'd have made you four inches taller and a thirty-six C, or B at least, and given you blond hair.

But being gay . . . this was something to think about. Could she deal with it? It'd be hard to own up to but maybe she'd have to admit it. Some things you can't run from.

Admitting it, she felt relief flood through her. It explained why she was reluctant to sleep with a man right away—she probably didn't really *like* sex with men. And if Richard turned her on like an electric current it was probably just because of what she'd realized before—that there was something feminine about him. Sure, that made sense.

Telling Mother would be hard.

Maybe she should get a crew cut.

Maybe she should become a nun.

Maybe she should kill herself.

At the corner of Eighth Street, rather than turn toward the subway to get a train to the loft, she turned the other way, to return to the video store.

She knew what she wanted to do.

Get a movie. Maybe *It Happened One Night*. As long as I'm going to cry anyway, why not get a movie to go along with it? Ice cream, beer, and a movie. Can't lose with that combination.

How about *Gone With the Wind*?

How about *Lesbos Lovers*?

Ten minutes later she pushed inside Washington Square Video. Frankie Greek was behind the counter and he was looking totally sheepish.

Well, he damn well ought to. Fucking up when he took that message from Richard . . . She was going to give him hell. But, as she looked at him playing nervously with the VCR remote, it seemed there was something else on his mind. He *was* nervous but it wasn't because of her.

"Hello, Rune."

"What is it, Frankie? Your sister okay?"

"Yes, she's fine," he recited. "She had a baby."

"I know. You told us. What's the matter?"

"How are you tonight? Doing okay, I hope. Doing good." A wanna-be rock musician talking like Mister Rogers? Something was really wrong here. "What's with you?"

"Nothing, Rune. I heard it was kind of cold out there tonight." It was like he was in a bad skit on *Saturday Night Live.*

"Cold. What the hell are you—"

"Rune?" a man's deep voice asked.

She turned. Oh, it was that U.S. marshal. Dixon, she remembered.

"Hi," he said.

"Hey, Marshal Dixon."

He laughed. "You make it sound like a sheriff in a bad western. Call me Phillip."

She looked at Frankie, paler than Mick Jagger in February. "I saw his badge," Frankie said.

"He arrests people who screw up phone messages," Rune muttered.

"Huh?"

"Never mind."

"How you doing?" Dixon asked, smiling. Then he

frowned, looked at her face. "There's a little . . ." He pointed at her cheek.

She grabbed a paper towel and scrubbed away at a bit of eye makeup.

"That's got it," Dixon said, "Hey, love the outfit."

"Really?"

His eyes swept over it—and, sure enough, she felt a bit of that electric sizzle again. Not as high-voltage as with Richard, but still . . .

"I never do drugs," Frankie Greek said.

Dixon looked at him curiously.

"Some musicians do. I mean, you hear about it. But I never have. Some of my songs are about drugs. But that's, like, just something to write songs about. I stay away from them."

"Well, good for you."

Rune gave him an exasperated look then said to the marshal, "Anything more on the case?"

"Naw." Then he seemed to think he shouldn't be talking quite so blue-collar and added, "No. No evidence in the Edelman death." He shrugged. "No prints at the scene. No witnesses. You haven't seen anything odd lately? Been followed?"

"No."

Dixon nodded. Looked at some videos. Picked one up. Put it down.

"So," he said.

Two "so's" from two different men in one night. Rune wondered what this one meant.

"Could I talk to you?" he asked, motioning her to the front of the store.

"Sure."

They stood by the window, next to a distracting cardboard cutout of Michael J. Fox.

"Just thought you'd like to know. I checked out that case you told me about. The Union Bank heist?"

"You did?"

He shook his head. "I didn't find anything. Technically, it's still open but nobody's been on the case since the fifties. They only keep murder cases open indefinitely. I tried to find the file but it looks like it was pitched out ten, twenty years ago."

"I thought maybe *you* were investigating it."

"The robbery? Me?" Dixon laughed again. He had a nice smile. Richard, she was thinking, had that mysteriousness about him. Something going on under the surface—you couldn't quite believe his smile. Dixon's seemed totally genuine.

He took off his baseball cap, rubbed his hair in a boyish way, put the hat back on.

She said, "I mean, it was kind of a coincidence you were asking about Mr. Kelly and everything."

"Bank robbery'd be the FBI, not the Marshals. I'm involved only 'cause the killer used the kind of bullets a lot of hit men use. We check stuff like that out."

"Teflon," Rune said.

"Oh, you know about that?"

"The police told me. But if you don't care about the robbery then why'd you look up the case?"

He shrugged, looked away. "I dunno. Seemed important to you."

A little tingle. Nothing as high-voltage as with Richard. But it *was* something. Besides, Richard, who she thought she was in love with, had just been giving her crap about her life, while this guy, almost a stranger, had gone to the trouble to help her with her quest.

Little red hen . . .

She gave him a coy look, a Scarlett O'Hara look. "That's the only reason you came all the way down here? To tell me about a fifty-year-old case?"

He shrugged, avoided her eyes. "I stopped by your place and you weren't there and I called here and they said sometimes you just hang out and talk about movies with people." He said this as if he'd practiced it. Like a shy boy rehearsing his lines to ask a girl out on a date. Embarrassed. He crossed his arms.

"So you took the chance I'd be here?"

"Right." After a moment he said, "And I'll bet you want to know why."

"Yeah," she said. "I do."

"Well." He swallowed. How could somebody with such a big gun be so nervous? He continued. "I guess I wanted to ask you out. I mean, if you don't want to, forget it, but—"

"Rune," Frankie called, "phone!"

"Wait right there," Rune told Dixon, then added emphatically, "Don't go away."

"Sure. Sure. I won't go anywhere."

She picked up the phone. It was Amanda LeClerc. "Rune, I thought you want to know," the woman said quickly, her accent more pronounced because of her excitement. "Victor Symington's daughter, she over here. I mean, right now. You want to see her?"

Rune glanced at Dixon, who was looking at video boxes. He glanced at the X-rated section, blushed, and looked away quickly.

Rune, debating furious—what should she do?

A man who wanted to ask her out versus the quest.

This was totally unfair.

"Rune?" Amanda said. "I don't think she going to stay too long."

Eyes on Dixon.

Eyes on the Brooklyn Yellow Pages.

Oh, shit.

Into the phone she blurted out, "I'll be right over."

CHAPTER EIGHTEEN

"You had the baby?"

Rune looked up from the building directory, so thick with graffiti she couldn't find the number of Amanda LeClerc's apartment.

Her surprised eyes rested on the surprised face of the young man who'd let her into the apartment building two days before—when she'd been extremely pregnant. Now, she let him open the door for her again and she walked inside.

"I did, thanks," Rune said. "Courtney Madonna Brittany. Six pounds, four ounces."

"Congratulations," he said. He couldn't help but stare down at her belly. "You, uh, feeling okay?"

"Feeling great," Rune assured him. "I just ran out for a minute and forgot my keys."

"Where's your little girl?" he asked.

When you lie, lie with confidence. "She's upstairs. Watching TV."

"Watching TV?"

"Well, she's with her father and *he's* watching TV. They both like sitcoms. . . . Say, which apartment is Amanda LeClerc in again?"

"Oh, Amanda? On the second floor?"

"Yeah."

"I think 2F."

"Right, right, right." Rune started up the stairs two at a time.

"Don't you think you should take it a little easy?"

"Peasant stock," she called back cheerily.

On the second-floor landing she noticed that there was a piece of plywood over the hole in Mr. Kelly's door. There was also a large padlock on it. The police tape had been replaced. She walked past it.

It'd been hard to turn down Phillip Dixon (*he,* unlike Richard, was somebody who had no problem with either the word or the concept of "date").

"Rain check?" he'd asked.

"You bet. Hey, you like junkyards?" she'd asked him on her way out the door of the video store.

He hadn't missed a beat. "Love 'em."

Rune now knocked on Amanda's door and the woman called, "Who's there?"

"Me, Rune."

The door opened. "Good. She's upstairs. I talk her inta staying to see you. Didn't want to but she is."

"Has she heard anything from her father?"

"I don't know. I didn't ask her. I just said you were looking for him and it was important."

"What apartment is he in again?"

"Three B."

Rune remembered that Symington lived directly above Mr. Kelly.

Rune climbed the stairs. Amanda's and Mr. Kelly's floor had smelled like onions; this one smelled like bacon. She paused in the hallway. The door to 3B was six inches open.

Rune eased forward, seeing first the hem of a skirt, then two thin legs in dark stockings. They were crossed in a way that suggested confidence. Rune started to knock but then just pushed the door open all the way. The woman on the bed turned to her. She was looking through a stack of papers.

She had high cheekbones, a face glossy with makeup, frosted hair forced into place with a ton of spray. She looks like my mother, Rune thought, and guessed she was in her early forties. The woman wore a plaid suit and she smoked a long, dark brown cigarette. She gazed at Rune then said, "That woman downstairs . . . she said somebody was looking for my father. Is that you?"

"Yes."

The woman turned away slowly, stubbed out the cigarette, pressing it into an ashtray. It died with a faint crushing sound. She looked Rune up and down. "My, they're getting younger and younger."

"Like, excuse me?"

"How old are you?"

"Twenty. What's that got to do with anything? I just want to ask you a few—"

"What did he promise you? A car? He did that a lot. He was *always* giving away cars. Or saying he would. Porsches, Mercedes, Cadillacs. Of course then there'd be problems with the dealer. Or the registration. Or something."

"Cars? I don't even—"

"And then it came down to money. But that's life, isn't it? He'd promise a thousand and end up giving them a couple of hundred."

"What are you talking about?" Rune asked.

Another examination. The woman got as far as Rune's striped stockings and clunky red shoes before her face revealed her dismay. She shook her head. "You couldn't . . . forgive me, but you couldn't've charged all that much. What *was* your price? For the night?"

"You think I'm a hooker?"

"My father called them girlfriends. He actually brought one to Thanksgiving dinner once. At my house! In Westchester. Lynda with a y. You can imagine *that* scene. With my husband and children?"

"I don't even know your father."

The woman frowned, wondering if Rune might be telling the truth. "Maybe there's some misunderstanding here."

"I'll say there is."

"You're not . . ."

"No," Rune said. "I'm not."

A faint laugh. "I'm sorry . . ." The woman extended her hand. "My name's Emily Richter."

"I'm Rune." She reluctantly shook it.

"First name?"

"And last."

"Actress?"

"Sometimes."

"So, Rune, you really don't know my father?"

"No."

"And you're not here for any money?"

Not exactly, she thought. She shook her head.

Emily continued. "What do you want to see me about?"

"Do you know where he is?"

"That's what I'm trying to find out. He just vanished."

"I know he did."

Emily examined Rune's face carefully. The woman had probing eyes and Rune looked away. Emily said, "And I have a feeling you know *why*."

"Maybe."

"Which is?"

"I think he witnessed a murder."

"That man who was killed in the building?" Emily asked. "I heard about that. It was downstairs, wasn't it?"

"Right."

"And you think Father saw it happen?"

Rune walked farther into the apartment. She sat down on a cheap dining room chair. She glanced around the place. It was very different from Mr. Kelly's. She couldn't figure out why at first. Then she realized. This was like a hotel room, furnished by one phone call to a store that sold everything: pictures, furniture, carpet. A lot of light wood and metallic colors and laminate. Coordinated. Suburban tack.

What did it remind her of? Ohmygod, Richard's place . . .

Emily lit another cigarette.

Rune glanced into the kitchen. She saw enough food to last through a siege. Like her mother's pantry, she thought. With its provisions of flour, yellowing boxes of raisins and oatmeal and cornstarch. The colored cans. Green, Del Monte. Red, Campbell's. Only here, the difference was that everything was new. Just like the furniture.

Emily's voice was softer as she said, "I didn't mean to suggest anything. What I said before. Ever since our mother died, Father's been, well, a little unstable. He's had a series of young friends. At least he waited until she died to turn adolescent again." She shook her head. "But a murder . . . So maybe he's in danger." The cigarette paused halfway to her mouth, then lowered.

Rune told her, "I guess he's okay. I mean, I don't know that he isn't. He sure didn't hang around for very long after the man downstairs was killed."

"What happened?"

Rune told her about Robert Kelly's death.

"Why do you think my father saw it happen?"

"What it was, I came back here to pick up something after Mr. Kelly was killed. And I was in the apartment downstairs—"

"How did you know him, this Mr. Kelly?"

"He was a customer at the store where I work. We were sorta friends. Anyway, I saw your father. And he saw me in the apartment. He was terrified. That was weird—*me* scaring anybody." She laughed. "But the way I figure it, the day Mr. Kelly was killed your father was hanging out on his fire escape. He saw the killer come out of the apartment after he killed Mr. Kelly. I think your father got a look at the killer."

Emily shook her head. "But why would he run, just seeing you?"

"I don't know. Maybe he couldn't see me too clearly and thought I was the killer who'd come back to destroy some evidence or something."

Emily was looking down at the fake Oriental carpet. "But the police haven't called me"—she nodded again—"which must mean you haven't told them about him."

"No."

"Why not?"

Rune's eyes drifted away. "The thing is, I don't like police."

Emily watched her carefully for a moment more. Then said probingly, "But that's not exactly *the* thing, is it? There's something else."

Rune looked away. Trying to be cool and poised. It wasn't taking.

"Well, all I know is that I'm worried about my father," Emily said. "He can be exasperating at times but I still love him. I want to find him. And it sounds like you do too. Why won't you tell me?"

Then, from somewhere, Rune managed to find an adult gaze. She slapped it on her face and gave Emily a woman-to-woman smile. "I have this feeling you're not telling me everything either."

The woman hesitated. She inhaled and blew a fat stream of smoke away from them. "Maybe I'm not."

"I'll show you mine if you . . ."

Emily didn't want to smile. But she did. "Okay, the truth?" She looked around the apartment. "I've never been here before. This is the first time. I haven't been in *any* of his apartments for the past year. . . . Isn't that an awful thing to say?"

Rune said nothing. Emily sighed. She was looking much *less* adult than she had. "We had a fight. Last summer. A bad one."

There was silence.

Then she smiled at Rune. A bleak lifting of her mouth. Trying to make light. The smile faded. "He ran away from home. Isn't that silly?"

"Your father ran away from home? Like, that's radical."

Emily asked, "Are your parents still alive?"

"My mother is. She's in Ohio. My father died a few years ago."

"Did you get along with them when you were at home?"

"Pretty good, I guess. My mom is a sweetheart. My dad . . . I was sort of his favorite. But don't tell my sister I said that. He was really, really cool."

Emily looked at her with a cocked head. "You're lucky. My father and I fought a lot. We always have. Even when I was young. I'd have a boyfriend and Dad wouldn't like him. He wasn't from the right kind of family, he didn't make enough money, he was Jewish, he was Catholic . . . I fought back some but he was my father and fathers have authority. But then I grew up and after my mother died a few years ago, something odd happened. The roles switched. *He* became the child. He'd

retired, didn't have much money. I'd married a business-
man and I was rich. He needed a place to stay and he
moved in with us.

"But I didn't do it right. Suddenly *I* had the power, *I*
could dictate. Just the opposite of the way it was when I
lived at home. I handled it badly. Last summer we were
arguing and I said some terrible things. I didn't mean
them, I really didn't. They weren't even true. I thought
Dad'd just fight back or ignore them. Well, he didn't.
What he did was he took some things and disappeared."
Her voice quaked.

Emily fell silent. She held her cigarette in an unsteady
hand. "I've been trying to find him ever since. He stayed
at the Y for a while, he stayed at a hotel in Queens. He
had an apartment in the West Village. I don't know when
he moved here. I've been calling people he knows—some
of his old co-workers, his doctors—trying to find him.
Finally a receptionist at his doctor's office broke down
and gave me this address."

Emily smoothed her skirt. It was a long skirt, expensive silk. Slinky was the only way to describe it, Rune
decided. "Now I've missed him again," Emily told her.

"Didn't you just call and apologize?"

"I tried a few months ago. But he hung up on me."

"Why don't you just give it time? Maybe he'll calm
down. He's not that old, is he? In his sixties."

A look at the carpet again. "The thing is, he's sick. He
doesn't have much longer. That's why the doctor's receptionist agreed to tell me where he was. He has cancer.
Terminal."

Rune thought of her father. And now she recognized
Symington's gray face, the sweaty skin.

She thought too: He'd better not die before she herself had a chance to find him and ask him about Mr.
Kelly and the stolen money. Feeling guilty. But thinking
it anyway.

"So what is it *you're* not telling *me*?" The adult Emily had returned. "Time to show me *yours*."

"I'm not sure he's just a witness," Rune said.

"What do you mean?"

"Okay, if you really want to know. I think your father might be the murderer."

CHAPTER NINETEEN

██████ "Impossible."

Rune said, "I think Mr. Kelly found some money and your father found out about it. I think your father stole the money and killed him."

Emily was shaking her head. "Never. Dad'd never hurt anybody."

Once again Rune thought of Symington's face—how terrified he'd seemed. "Well, maybe he had a partner who killed him."

Emily started to shake her head. But then she paused.

"What?" Rune asked. "Tell me."

"Dad wouldn't kill anybody. I *know* that."

"But . . . ? I see something in your face. Keep talking." A good adult line to say. Right out of a Cary Grant movie, she believed. The sort Audrey Hepburn had said a million times.

"But," the woman said slowly, "the last time I talked to him I asked if he needed money and he said—he was really angry—but he said that he was about to get more money than I could imagine and he'd never take another damn penny from me or Hank ever again."

"He said that?" Rune asked excitedly.

Emily nodded.

"We've got to find him," Rune said.

"Will you turn him in to the police?" Emily asked.

Rune was going to say no. But she stopped herself. *You only lie to people who can control you.*

"I don't know. I think I believe he didn't kill Mr. Kelly. I want to talk to him first. But where is he? How can we find him?"

Emily said, "If I knew I wouldn't be here now."

"Is there anything there?" Rune nodded toward the mail Emily had been looking through.

"No, it's mostly just Dear Occupant. . . . The only lead I've got is the name of his bank. I tried calling them to see if they had an address but they wouldn't talk to me."

Rune was thinking about another movie she'd seen a few years ago. Who was in it? De Niro? Harvey Keitel? The actor—a private eye—had bluffed his way into a bank and gotten information.

Maybe it was Sean Connery.

"Look, you don't understand . . . The man is dying! For God's sake, give me his address. Here's his account number."

"Sir, I can't. It's against policy."

"Hell with your policy. A man's life is at stake."

"You have the account number?" she asked Emily.

"No."

"Well, how about the branch?"

"I've got that."

"That should be all we need."

"I don't think they'll give you any information."

"You'd be surprised. I can be extremely persuasive."

Rune wiped her eyes—thinking how Stephanie, the only real actress she knew—would do it.

"I'm sorry. But it's really, really important."

The young man was a vice president of the bank but he looked young enough to be a clerk at a McDonald's, what with that wimp mustache and baby-smooth cheeks.

It was the next morning, nine-thirty, and the branch had just opened. The lobby surrounding them was deserted.

The vice president seemed uncomfortable with this young woman sitting in front of his desk, crying. He scanned his desktop helplessly then looked back at Rune. "He's not getting his bank statements? Any of them?"

"None. He's very upset. Grandfather's such a tense man. I'm sure that was the reason for the stroke. He's very . . . what's the word? You know."

"Fastidious?" the young man offered. "Meticulous?"

"That's it. And when he realized he's not getting the statements, Jesus, he really had a fit."

"What's his account number?"

Rune was digging in her purse. One minute. Two. She heard Muzak pumping through the glossy white marble lobby. She stared into the pit of her purse. "I can't seem to find it. Anyway, we probably couldn't read it. He tried to write it down for me but he can't control his right hand too well and that frustrates him, and I didn't want to upset him unnecessarily."

"I can't do anything without his account—"

"His face was all red and his eyes were bulging. I thought he was going to burst a—"

"What's his name?" the man asked quickly. The mustache got an anemic swipe and he leaned toward his computer.

"Vic Symington. Well, Victor."

He typed. The young man frowned. He typed some more, his fingers flying across the keys. He read, frowned again. "I don't understand. You mean that your grandfather wants another copy of his *final* statement?"

"Final statement? He's moved, see, and the statement hasn't come to his new address. What do you have listed as the new address?"

"We've got a problem, miss." The hamburger-slinging vice president looked up.

Rune felt herself start to sweat, her stomach churning. She'd blown it now. He was probably pushing one of those secret buttons that alerts the guards. Shit. She asked, "Problem?"

"Someone closed out your grandfather's account two days ago. If he thinks he's still got money in this bank, something's wrong."

"How could he have gotten here to close his account? The poor man can't even eat by himself."

"He didn't do it in person. It says 'POA' next to the withdrawal. He issued a power of attorney and the attorney-in-fact closed the account."

"Mother! She didn't!" Rune's hands went to her face. "She's always said that she'd rob Grandfather blind. How could she've done it?" Rune was sobbing again, dry tears pouring into her hands. "Tell me! You have to! Was it Mother? I have to know."

"I'm sorry, miss, it's against our policy to give out information on customers witout written permission."

Oh, this sounded familiar. Remembering the movie.

She leaned forward. "To hell with your policy. A man's *life* is at stake."

"His life?" the vice president asked placidly, sitting back. "Why?"

"Well, because . . ." (In the De Niro or Keitel or Connery movie the bank officer had just caved.)

"Because why?" the man asked. He wasn't really suspicious. He was just curious.

"The stroke. If Mother stole his money . . . It could be the end for him. Another stroke, a heart attack. I'm *really* worried about him."

The young man sighed. Another mustache swipe. Another sigh. He looked at the computer screen. "The check was drawn to Ralph Stein, Esquire. He's a lawyer. . . ."

"Oh, thank God," Rune exclaimed. "That's Grandfather's lawyer. S-t-i-n-e, right?"

"E-i-n."

"Oh, sure. We call him Uncle Ralph. He's a sweetheart." Rune stood up. "Here in Manhattan, right?"

"Citicorp Building."

"That's the one."

The vice president, tapping computer keys like a travel agent, said, "But does your grandfather think he still has an account here?"

Rune walked toward the exit. "The poor man, he's really like a child, you know?"

███████

The man placed his fingers together. They were pudgy fingers and Rune imagined that he would leave good fat fingerprints on whatever he touched, just like a clumsy felon. His nails were dirty too.

The office where they sat was large, yellow-painted, filled with boxes and dusty legal books. A dead plant sat in the greasy window. Diplomas from schools she'd never heard of hung on one wall, next to a clock.

It was two in the afternoon—it had taken her this long to track down Attorney Stein. She had to be at work at four but there was still plenty of time. Don't panic, she told herself.

The lawyer looked at her with a cool gaze. *Neutral*

was the word that came to mind. He seemed to be the sort of man who wanted to find some weakness about you and notice it and let you know he noticed it even though he'd never mention it.

He wore a suit that fit very closely, and monogrammed cuffs that protruded. The sausages of fingers pressed together.

"How do you know Victor?" His voice was soft and neutral and that surprised her because she expected lawyers would ask questions with gruff voices, sneery and mean.

Rune swallowed and realized suddenly she couldn't be Symington's granddaughter. Stein might have done the man's will; he'd know all the relatives by heart. Then she remembered who his daughter, Emily, thought she was at first. She smiled and said, "I'm a *friend*." Putting special emphasis on the word.

He nodded. Neutrally. "From where?"

"We used to live near each other. The East Village. I'd come and visit him sometimes."

"Ah. And how did you know about me?"

"He mentioned you. He said good things about you."

"So, you'd *visit* him." The lawyer looked her up and down with a whisper of lechery on his face.

"Once a week. Sometimes twice. For an old guy he was pretty . . . well, energetic. So can you tell me where he is?" Rune asked.

"No."

She swallowed again and was mad that this man was making her swallow and be nervous. Sometimes it was so hard to be adult. She cleared her throat and sat forward. "Why not?"

The lawyer shrugged. "Client confidentiality. Why do you want to see him?"

"He left in such a hurry. I wanted to talk to him is all

and I didn't get a chance to. One day he was on Tenth Street and the next he was gone."

"How old are you?"

"Isn't that some kind of crime to ask how old someone is?"

"I'm not discriminating against you on the basis of your age. I just want to know how old you are."

Rune said, "Twenty. How old are you?"

"I assume you don't really want to *talk* to him. Do you? I assume your relationship or whatever you want to call it wasn't based on talking. Now—"

"Five hundred," she blurted out. "He owed me five hundred."

"For one night?" Stein looked her up and down again.

"For one *hour*," Rune said.

"One hour," he responded.

"I'm very good."

"Not that good," the lawyer said. "One client of mine paid four thousand for two hours."

Four thousand? What'd that involve? She thought of several best-selling tapes at Washington Square Video: *Mistress Q* and *House of Pain*.

Sick world out there.

The lawyer's neutral voice asked, "And if I were to give you that five hundred dollars, would you forget about Mr. Symington? Would you forget that he left in a hurry? Would you forget everything about him?"

"No," Rune said abruptly. The man blinked. Got a rise out of him there. She tried on her adult persona again. "But I will for two thousand."

Which got an even bigger rise and he actually gave her a smile. It was—naturally—neutral but it was a smile nonetheless. He said, "Fifteen hundred."

"Deal." She started to extend her hand to shake but apparently this wasn't done in matters of this sort.

He pulled a pad toward him. "Where should I send the check?"

"Here." Rune held her hand forward, palm out.

Another smile. Irritated, less neutral this time. She was supposed to be stupid and intimidated. But here she was, staring back into his eyes, looking, more or less, adult. Finally he rose. "I'll just be a minute. Payable to cash, I assume?"

"That'll work."

He walked silently out of the office, buttoning his jacket as he left. He was gone longer than Rune thought he'd be—thinking he'd just tell his secretary to cut a check—but no, he was gone for a full five minutes.

Which was more than enough time for Rune to lean forward and flip through Stein's Rolodex and find Victor Symington's card. The address had been crossed out several times and a new one written in.

In Brooklyn. The address was in Brooklyn. She recited it several times softly out loud. Closed her eyes. She tested herself and found she'd memorized it. She flipped the Rolodex back to where it had been.

Rune fell back into her slouch in the chair and looked at the lawyer's wall, wondering if there were some special kinds of frames you were supposed to use for diplomas. Mr. Go-to-School-and-Lead-a-Productive-Life Richard didn't have *any* goddamn diplomas on *his* ugly beige suburban walls.

Phillip Dixon, the U.S. marshal, hadn't even gone to college, she bet. He seemed perfectly happy. But before she could play her game of making up an elaborate life for him, starting with his partner being tragically gunned and dying in his amrs, Lawyer Stein returned.

He had an envelope and a sheet of paper. Handed her both. She scanned the document quickly but it was full of *whereases* and words like *indemnity* and *waiver*. She gave up after the first paragraph.

"That's a receipt for the money. You agree that if you don't keep your bargain we can sue you for all this money back plus costs and attorney's fees, and . . ."

Rune was staring at the check.

". . . punitive damages."

What*ever*.

Rune signed the paper, put the check in her bag.

"So Mr. Symington doesn't exist, right?"

"Mr. who?"

CHAPTER TWENTY

██████████ "So how was the date?" Stephanie asked.

"With Richard?" Rune responded.

"Who else?" the redhead replied.

Rune considered the question for a moment. Then asked. "You ever see *Rodan*?"

They were at the counter of Washington Square Video.

"You mean his sculpture?"

Who? This was like Stallone's poetry. "No, I mean the flying dinosaur that destroyed Tokyo. Or maybe New York. Or someplace. A movie from the fifties."

"Missed that."

"Anyway, *that* was my date. A disaster. Not even a Spielberg disaster movie. A B-movie disaster."

She told Stephanie about Karen.

"Shit. That's bad. Other-woman stuff. Hard to get around them."

Them's the breaks . . .

Rune said, "Here." She reached into her purse and handed Steph the orange earrings.

"No," the woman protested. "You keep them."

"Nope. I'm off high fashion. Listen, do me a favor, please?"

"What?"

"I've got to go to Brooklyn. Can you work for me?"

"I guess. But won't Tony be pissed?"

"Just tell him . . . I don't know. I had to go someplace. To visit Frankie's sister in the hospital."

"She's home. With the baby."

"Well, I went to see her at home."

"Tony'd call and check."

Rune nodded. "You're right. Just make up something. I don't care."

"What're you gonna do in Brooklyn?"

"The money. I've got a lead to the money."

"Not that stolen bank money?"

"Yep. And don't forget the story of the Little Red Hen."

Stephanie smiled. "I'm not quitting my day job just yet."

"Probably a good idea." Rune slung her leopard-skin purse over her shoulder and headed out the door. "But keep the faith. I'm getting close."

██████████

Ten minutes later she was en route to Brooklyn. In search of Victor Symington.

On the subway, the riders were silent, subdued. One woman whispered to herself. A young couple had their precious new TV on the seat next to them, bundled in thick string, a receipt from a Crazy Eddie store taped to the box. A Latino man stood leaning forward, staring absently at the MTA map; he didn't seem to care much where he was headed. Almost everyone in the car, bathed in green fluorescence, was slumped and sullen as the car lurched into the last station in Manhattan before the descent beneath the East River.

Uneasy again.

Leaving the Side, leaving *her* territory.

Just before the doors eased shut, a man walked stiffly onto the train. He was white but had a dark yellowish tan. She couldn't guess his age. The car wasn't full but he sat directly across from Rune. He was wearing dusty clothes. Coming home from a construction job or hard day labor, tired, spent. He was very thin and she wondered if he was sick. He fell asleep immediately and Rune couldn't help but stare at him. His head bobbed and swayed, eyes closed, his head rolled. Keeping his blind focus on Rune.

She thought: He's Death.

She felt it deep inside her. With a chill. Death, Hades, a Horseman of the Apocalypse. The dark angel who'd fluttered into her father's hospital room to take him away. The spirit who wrapped his ghostly arms around Mr. Kelly and held him helpless in the musty armchair while someone fired those terrible bullets into his chest.

The lights flickered as the train switched tracks and then slowed as it rolled into one station. Then they were on their way again. Five minutes later the train lurched and they stopped again. The doors rumbled open. Waking him up. As his eyes opened he was staring directly into Rune's. She shuddered and sat back but couldn't look away. He glanced out the window, stood up quickly. "Shit, missed my stop. Missed my stop." He walked out of the car.

And because she kept staring at him shuffling along the platform as the train pulled out, Rune saw the man who'd been following her.

As her gaze eased to the right she glanced into the car

behind her. And saw the young man, compact, Italian-looking.

She blinked, not sure why she remembered him, and then recalled that she'd seen somebody who looked a lot like him someplace else. The loft? No, in the East Village, near Mr. Kelly's apartment . . .

Outside Mr. Kelly's apartment the day she'd broken in. Yes, that was it! And it was the same guy who'd ducked into the deli when she'd been on the street in front of Washington Square Video.

Pretty Boy, wearing the utility jacket. Sitting on the doorstep, smoking and reading the *Post*.

Or was it?

It *looked* like him. But she wasn't sure. No Con Ed jackets today.

The man wasn't looking her way, didn't even seem to know she was there. Reading a book or magazine, engrossed in it.

No, it couldn't be him.

Paranoid, that's what she was. Seeing the man with the yellow eyes, seeing Death, had made her paranoid.

It was just life in a city of madmen, dirty screeching subways, fifteen hundred homicides a year, a thousand police detectives with close-together eyes. U.S. marshals who like to flirt.

Paranoia. What else could it be?

Hell, she thought, get real: it could be because of a million dollars.

It could be because of a murder.

That's what else it could be.

The lights went out again as the train clattered through another switch. She leapt up, heart pounding, ready to run, sure that Pretty Boy'd come pushing through the door and strangle her.

But when the lights came back on the man was gone,

was probably standing in a cluster of people by the door, about to get off at the next stop.

See, just paranoia.

She sat down and breathed deeply to calm herself. When the crowd got off he wasn't in the car any longer.

Two stops later, at Bay Ridge, Rune slipped out of the car, looking around. No sign of any Pretty-Boy meter readers. She pushed through the turnstile, climbed to the sidewalk.

Glancing up and down the street, trying to orient herself.

And saw him. Walking out of the other subway exit a half-block away. Looking around—trying to find *her*. Jesus . . .

He *had* been following her.

She looked away, trying to stay calm. Don't let him know you spotted him. He pushed roughly through crowds of exiting passengers and passersby, aiming in her direction.

Trying to look nonchalant, strolling along the street, pretending to gaze at what was displayed in store windows but actually hoping to see the reflection of an approaching taxi. Pretty Boy was getting closer. He must've shoved somebody out of the way: she heard a macho exchange of "fuck you, no, fuck *you*." Any minute he'd start sprinting toward her. Any minute he'd pull out the gun and shoot her dead with those Teflon bullets.

Then, reflected in a drugstore window, she saw a bright yellow cab cruising down the street. Rune spun around, leapt in front of a pregnant woman, and flung the door open before the driver even had a chance to stop.

In a thick Middle-Eastern accent the driver cried, "What the hell you doing?"

"Drive!"

The cabbie was shaking his head. "No, uh-uh,

no. . . . ." He pointed to the off-duty lights on the top of
the yellow Chevy.

"Yes," she shouted. "Drive, drive, drive!"

Rune saw that Pretty Boy'd stopped, surprised, not
sure what to do. He stood, cigarette in his hand, then
began taking cautious steps forward toward them, maybe
worried that the scene at the cab would attract some
cops.

Then he must have decided it didn't matter. He
started to run toward her.

Rune begged the driver, "Please! Only a few blocks!"
She gave him an address on Fort Hamilton Parkway.

"No, no, uh-uh."

"Twenty dollars."

"Twenty? No, uh-uh."

She looked behind her. Pretty Boy was only a few
doors away, hand inside his jacket.

"Thirty? Please, please, please?"

He debated. "Well, okay, thirty."

"Drive, drive, drive!" shouted Rune.

"Why you in a hurry?" the driver asked.

"Forty fucking dollars. Drive!"

"Forty?" The driver floored the accelerator and the
car spun away, leaving a cloud of blue-white tire smoke
between the Chevy and Pretty Boy.

Rune sat huddled down in the vinyl, stained rear
seat. "Goddammit," she whispered bitterly as her heart
slowed. She wiped sweat from her palms.

Who was he? Symington's accomplice? Probably.
She'd bet he was the one who'd killed Mr. Kelly. The
triggerman—as the cops in *Manhattan Is My Beat* had
called the thug who'd machine-gunned down Roy in
front of the hotel on Fifth Avenue.

And, from the look in his dark eyes, she could tell he
intended to kill *her* too.

Time for the police? she wondered. Call Manelli. Call

Phillip Dixon . . . It made sense. It was the *only* thing that made sense at this point.

But then there was the matter of the million dollars . . . She thought of Amanda. Thought of her own perilous career. Thought of how she'd like to pull up in front of Richard and Karen in a stretch limo.

And decided: No police. Not yet.

A few minutes later the cab stopped in front of a light-green-and-brick two-story row house.

The driver said, "That's forty dollars. And don't worry about no tip."

███

She stood on the sidewalk, hidden behind some anemic evergreens, looking at the row house that was, according to his lawyer's Rolodex, Victor Symington's current residence. A pink flamingo stood on one wire leg on the front lawn. A brown Christmas wreath lay next to a croquet mallet beside the stairs. An iron jockey with black features painted Caucasian held a ring for hitching a horse.

"Let's do it," she muttered to herself. Not much time. Pretty Boy would be looking for a pay phone just then to call Symington and tell him that he couldn't stop her and that she was on her way there. It wouldn't be long before Pretty Boy himself'd show up.

She thought she could handle Symington by himself. But with his strong-arm partner, probably a hothead, there'd be trouble.

She rang the doorbell. She had her story ready and it was a good one, she thought. Rune would tell him that she knew what he and Pretty Boy had done and that she'd given a letter to *her* lawyer, explaining everything and mentioning their names. If anything happened to her, she'd tell him, the letter would be sent to the police.

Only one flaw. Symington wasn't home. Goddammit. She hadn't counted on that.

She banged on the door with her fist.

No answer. She turned the knob. It was bolted shut.

Glancing up and down the street. No Pretty Boy yet. She clumped down the gray-painted stairs and walked around to the back door. She passed a quorum of the Seven Dwarfs, in plaster, planted along the side of the building, then found the gate in a cheap mesh fence around the backyard.

At the back door Rune pressed her face against the glass, hands shrouding out the light. It was dark inside. She couldn't see much of anything.

Part of her said Pretty Boy could be there at any minute.

The other part of her broke out a small windowpane with her elbow. She reached in and opened the door. She tossed the broken glass into the backyard, which was overgrown with thick bright grass. She stepped inside.

She walked through to the living room. "Like, minimal," she muttered. In the bedroom were one bed, a dresser, a floor lamp. The kitchen had one table and two chairs. Two glasses sat on the retro Formica counter, spattered like a Jackson Pollock painting. A few chipped dishes and silverware. In the living room was a single folding chair. Nothing else.

Rune paused in front of the bathroom. There was a stained glass window in the door. "Oooo, classy poddy," she muttered. Somebody's initials on the door. "W.C." The guy who built the house, she guessed.

She looked through the closets—all of them except the one in the bedroom, which was fastened with a big, new glistening lock. Under the squeaky bed were two suitcases. Heavy, battered leather ones. She pulled them out, starting to sweat in the heat of the close, stale apartment. She stood up and tried to open a window. It was nailed shut. Why? she wondered.

She went back to the suitcases and opened the first one. Clothes. Old, frayed at the cuffs and collar points. The browns going light, the whites going yellow. She closed it and slid it back. In the second suitcase: a razor, an old double-edged Gillette, a tube of shave cream like toothpaste; a Swiss Army knife; keys; a small metal container of cuff links; nail scissors, toothbrush.

She dug down through the layers.

And found a small, battered brown accordion folder with a rubber band around it. It was very heavy. She opened it. She found a letter—from Weissman, Burkow, Stein & Rubin, P.C.—describing how his savings, about fifty-five thousand, had been transferred to an account in the Cayman Islands. A plane ticket, one-way coach, to Georgetown on Grand Cayman. The flight was leaving day after tomorrow.

Next to it, she found his passport. She'd never seen one before. It was old and limp and stained. There were dozens of official-looking stamps in the back.

She didn't even look at the name until she was about to put it back.

Wait. Who the hell was Vincent Spinello?

Oh, shit! At Stein's law firm, when she'd looked through the lawyer's Rolodex, she'd been so nervous she'd misread the name. She'd seen *Vincent Spinello* and thought *Victor Symington*. Oh, Christ, she'd gotten it all wrong. And she'd even broken the poor man's window!

All a waste. She couldn't believe it. The danger, the risk, Pretty Boy . . . all a waste.

"Goddamn," she whispered harshly.

Only, wait . . . The letter.

She opened the letter again. It *was* addressed to Symington and at *this* address. So what was he doing with Vincent Spinello's passport?

But as she looked at the passport again, the condensed, grim little picture, there was no doubt. *Spinello* was the man she'd seen at Robert Kelly's apartment. Who was he?

She dug to the bottom of the folder and found out. What made it so heavy was something that was wrapped in a piece of newspaper—a pistol. With it was a small box of cheap cardboard, flecked brown-green. The box, too, was heavy. On the side was printing in what she thought was German. She could make out only one word. *Teflon.*

Oh, God . . .

Symington—or Spinello—was the man who'd killed Robert Kelly. He and Pretty Boy *had* found the Union Bank robbery money. They'd stolen it and killed him! And the loot was in the closet!

Rune dropped to her knees and looked at the padlock on the closet. Leaned close, squinting. Pulled it, rattled the solid lock.

Then she froze. At the sound of a door opening then closing.

Was it the front or the back door? She couldn't tell. But she knew one thing. It was either Pretty Boy or Symington. And she knew something else: they both wanted her dead.

Rune gave one last tug at the closet door. It didn't move a millimeter.

Footsteps inside now. Nearby. If he finds me here, he'll kill me! She stuffed the accordion envelope into her bag and slung it over her shoulder.

A creak of floorboards

No, no . . .

She thought they were in the front of the apartment. In the living room, which wasn't visible from where she was. She could probably get out the back without being

seen. She glanced into the corridor fast, then ducked
back into the bedroom. Yep, it was empty.

Rune took a breath and ran from the bedroom.

She slammed right into Victor Symington's chest.

He gasped in terror, stepped back, the ugly hat falling
from his head. In reflex he lunged out and slugged her
hard in the stomach, doubling her over. "Oh, God," she
wheezed. A huge pain shot through her chest and jaw.
Rune tried to scream but her voice was only a whisper.
She dropped to the floor, unable to breathe.

Symington, furious, grabbed her by the hair and
spun her around. Dropped to his knees. His hands
smelled of garlic and tobacco. He began to search her
roughly.

"Are you with them?" he gasped. "Who the fuck are
you?"

She couldn't answer.

"You are, aren't you? You're working for them!" He
lifted his fist. Rune lifted an arm over her face.

"Who?" she managed to ask.

He asked, "How did you . . ."

He stopped speaking. Struggling to catch her breath,
Rune looked up. Symington was staring at the doorway.
Someone stood there. Pretty Boy? Rune blinked, rolled to
her knees.

No . . . Thank you, thank you, thank you . . . It
was his daughter, Emily.

Rune was so grateful to see the woman that it wasn't
until a second later that she wondered: How'd Emily find
the place? Had she *followed* me here?

Wait, something is wrong.

Symington let go of Rune, backed up.

Emily said, "How did we find you, you were going to
ask? Haarte has some good contacts."

Haart? Rune wondered. "Who's Heart?" she asked.

"Oh, no, it's Haarte?" Symington whispered. Then he nodded hopelessly. "I should've guessed."

"What's going on?" Rune demanded.

Symington was looking at Emily with an imploring expression on his face. "Please . . ."

Emily didn't respond.

He continued. "Would it do any good to say I have a lot of money?"

"The money!" Rune said. "He killed Mr. Kelly and stole his money!"

Both Symington and Emily ignored her.

"Is there *anything* I can do?" Symington pleaded.

"No," Emily said. And took a pistol from her pocket. She shot him in the chest.

CHAPTER TWENTY-ONE

The way he fell is what saved Rune.

The gun was small but the impact knocked Symington backward and he slammed into the pole of the floor lamp, which fell against the bathroom door, sending a shower of glass into the hallway.

Emily danced out of the way of the splinters, which gave Rune a chance to sprint into the bedroom. But the woman recovered fast. She fired the gun again and Rune heard a terrible stereo sound of noises: the blasts of the gun behind her, the crash of the bullets slamming into the plaster wall inches from her head.

Then—with another punch of breathtaking pain—she dove through the bedroom window.

Hands covering her face, shards of glass flying around her, trailing the window shade, she rolled onto more sad evergreens and dropped onto the grass, coming to rest against one of the plaster dwarfs. Panting, she lay on the lawn. The smell of dirt and damp grass enveloped her. She could hear birds squabbling in the trees overhead.

And then the air around her exploded. A dwarf's face
disintegrated into white splinters and dust. On the street,
fifty feet away, Rune caught a glimpse of a man with
shotgun. She couldn't see his face but she knew it was
Pretty Boy—Heart probably, the one Symington mentioned. Or Heart's partner. He and Emily were working
together. . . . She didn't know who they were exactly
or why they wanted to kill Symington but she didn't
pause to consider those questions. She rolled under another plant, then scrabbled to her feet. Clutching her
purse, she sprinted into the backyard. Then clambered
over the chain-link fence.

And then she ran.

Behind her, from Symington's yard, came a shout. A
second shotgun blast. She heard the hiss of something
over her head. It missed and she turned, down an alley.
Kept running.

Running until her vision blurred. Running until her
chest ignited and she couldn't breathe another ounce of
air.

Finally, miles away it seemed, Rune stopped, gasping. She doubled over. Sure she was going to be sick. But
she spit into the grass a few times and remained motionless until the nausea and pain went away. She trotted
another block but pulled up with a cramp in her side.
She slipped into another backyard—behind a house with
boarded-up windows. She crawled into a nest of grass
between a smiling Bambi and another set of the Seven
Dwarfs, then lay her head on her purse, thinking she'd
rest for ten, fifteen minutes.

When she opened her eyes a huge garbage truck was
making its mournful, behemoth sounds five feet away
from her. And it was dawn.

They'd be watching for her.

Maybe at the Midtown Tunnel, maybe at a subway stop. Emily and Pretty Boy. And not just them. A dozen others. She saw them *all* now—Them with a capital T. Walking down the streets of Brooklyn on this clear, cool spring morning. Faces glancing at her, knowing that she was a witness. Knowing that she and her friends were about to die—to be laid out like Robert Kelly, like Victor Symington.

They were all after her.

She was hitching her way back to Manhattan, back to the Side. She'd thumbed a ride with a delivery van, the driver a wild-eyed Puerto Rican with a wispy goatee who swore at the traffic with incredible passion and made it to the Brooklyn Bridge, a drive that should have taken three-fourths of an hour at this time of day, in fifteen minutes.

He apologized profusely that he couldn't take her into Manhattan itself.

And then she ran once more.

Over the wooden walkway of the Brooklyn Bridge, back into the city, which was just starting to come to life. Traffic hissed beneath her; the muted horns of the taxis sounded like animals lowing. She paused halfway across to rest, leaning against the railing. The young professionals walked past—wearing running shoes with their suits and dresses—on their way to Wall Street from Brooklyn Heights.

What the hell had she been thinking of?

Quests? Adventures?

Knights and wizards and damsels?

No, she thought bitterly. *These* were the people who lived in the Magic Kingdom: lawyers and secretaries and accountants and deliverymen. It wasn't a magic place at all; it was just a big, teeming city filled with good people and bad people.

That's all. Just a city. Just people.

It's a factory, Rune. There's shit and pollution. It makes a living for people and they pay taxes and give money to charity and buy sneakers for their children. Who grow up to be lawyers or teachers or musicians or people who work in other factories. It's nothing more than that.

Once over the bridge she walked north toward the courthouses, past City Hall, staring up at the twisty gothic building—the north face made of cheap stone, not marble, because no one ever thought the city would spread north of the Wall Street district. Then into Chinatown and up through SoHo to Washington Square Park.

Which, even this early, was a zoo. A medieval carnival. Jugglers, unicyclists, skateboard acrobats, kids slamming on guitars so cheap they were just rhythm instruments. She sat down on a bench, ignoring a tall Senegalese selling knockoff Rolexes, ignoring a beefy white teenager chanting, "*Hash, hash, sens, sens, smoke it up, sens.*" Women in designer jogging outfits rolled their expensive buggies of infant lawyers-to-be past dealers and stoned-out vets. It was Greenwich Village.

Rune sat for an hour. Once, some vague resolve coalesced in her and she stood up. But it vanished swiftly and she sat down again, closed her eyes, and let the hot sun fall on her face.

Who *were* they? Emily? Pretty Boy?

Where was the money?

She fell asleep again—until a Frisbee skimmed her head and startled her awake. She looked around, in panic, struggling to remember where she was, how she'd gotten there. She asked a woman the time. Noon. It seemed that a dozen people were staring at her suspiciously. She stood and walked quickly through the grass, north through the white, stone arch, a miniature Arc de Triomphe.

━━━━━━

They were old films, both of them.

One was *She Wore a Yellow Ribbon,* the John Wayne cavalry flick. It was playing now. Rune didn't notice what the other one was. Maybe *The Searcher* or *Red River.* *Yellow Ribbon* was showing when she sat down. The seats in the old theater on Twelfth Street were stiff—thin padding under crushed fabric upholstery. There were only fifteen or so people in the revival house, which didn't surprise her—the only time this place had ever been crowded was on Saturday night and when they were showing selections from the New York Erotic Film Festival.

Watching the screen.

She knew the old John Ford-directed western cold. She'd seen it six times. But today, it seemed to her to be just a series of disjointed images. Salty old Victor McLaglen, the distinguished graying Wayne, the intensified hues of the forty-year-old Technicolor film, the shoulder-punching innocent humor of the blue-bloused horse soldiers . . .

But today the movie made no sense to her. It was disconnected images of men and women walking around on a huge rectangle of white screen, fifty feet in front of her. They spoke funny words, they wore odd clothing, they played into staged climaxes. It was all choreographed and it was all fake.

Her anger built. Anger at the two dimensions of the film. The falsity, the illusion. She felt betrayed. Not only by Emily Symington or whoever she was, not only by what had happened in Brooklyn, but by something else. Something more fundamental about how she lived her life, about how the things she believed in had turned on her.

She stood and left the theater. Outside, she bought a pair of thick-rimmed dark glasses from a street vendor and put them on. She turned the corner and walked down University Place to Washington Square Video.

———

Tony fired her, of course.

His words weren't cute or sarcastic or obnoxious like she'd thought he'd be. He just glanced up and said, "You missed two shifts and you didn't call. You're fired. This time for real."

But she didn't pay him much attention. She was staring at the newspaper on the counter, lying in front of Tony.

The headline: *Mafia Witness Hit.*

Which didn't get her attention as quickly as the photo did: a grainy flashlit shot of Victor Symington's town house in Brooklyn, the six surviving dwarfs, the shattered window. Rune grabbed the paper.

"Hey," Tony snapped. "I'm reading that." One look at her eyes, though, and he stopped protesting.

A convicted syndicate money launderer who had been a key witness in a series of Racketeering Influenced Corrupt Organizations (RICO) trials of midwest crime leaders earlier this year was shot to death yesterday in a gangland-style hit in Brooklyn.

Vincent Spinello, 70, was killed by gunshots to the chest. A witness, who asked not to be identified, reported that a young woman with short hair fled from the scene and is a primary suspect in the case.

Another witness in the same series of cases,

Arnold Gittleman, was murdered, along with two
U.S. marshals, in a St. Louis hotel last month.

The paper crumpled in her hands. Me! she thought.
That's me, the young woman with short hair.

She *used* me! Emily. The bitch used me. She knew all
along where Symington was and got me out there to
make it look like *I* killed him.

And, hell, my fingerprints're all over the place!

Primary suspect . . .

Tony snatched the newspaper away from her. "You
can pick up your check on Monday."

"Please, Tony," she said. "I need money now. Can't I
get cash?"

"No fucking way."

"I've got to get out of town."

"Monday," he said. Returned to his paper.

"Look, I've got a check for fifteen hundred bucks.
Give me a thousand and I'll sign it over to you."

"Yeah, like *you've* got a check that's going to clear. I'm
sure."

"Tony! It's payable to cash. From a law firm."

"Out."

Frankie Greek stuck his head out of the storeroom
and said, "Hey, Rune, like, you got a couple calls. This
cop, Manelli. And that U.S. marshal guy. Dixon. Oh, and
Stephanie too."

Tony barked, "But don't call 'em from here. Use the
pay phone outside."

Stephanie! Rune thought. If they'd been following
me, they've seen me with her.

Oh, Jesus Mary, she's in danger too.

She ran back to the counter and swept the phone off
the cradle. Tony started to say something but then
seemed to decide that it wasn't worth fighting the battle;
after all, he'd won the war. He turned on his worn heel

and retreated to the other counter, carrying the newspaper.

Stephanie's groggy voice finally answered.

"Rune! Where've you been? You missed work last night. Tony's really pissed—"

"Steph, listen to me." Her voice was raw. "They murdered that man I was trying to find, Symington, they're trying to make it look like I did it."

"What?"

"And they tried to kill me!"

"Who?"

"I don't know. They work for the Mafia or something. I think they might've seen you too."

"Rune, are you making this up? Is this one of your fantasies?"

"No! I'm serious."

Several customers glanced at her. She felt a shiver of fear. She cupped her hand over the receiver and lowered her voice. "Look on the front page of the *Post*. The story's there."

"You have to call the police."

"I *can't*. My fingerprints're all over the house where Symington got killed. I'm a suspect."

"Jesus, Rune. What a mess."

"I'm going back to Ohio."

"When? Now?"

"As soon as I can get some money. Tony won't pay me."

"Prick," Stephanie spat out. "I can lend you some."

"I can give you a check for fifteen hundred."

"Are you serious?"

"Yeah, it's payable to cash. You can have it. But, listen, you have to come with me!"

"Come with you?" Stephanie asked. "Where?"

"To Ohio."

"No way. I've got an audition next week."

"Stephanie . . ."

"I'll get you a couple of hundred. I'll stop at the bank. Where'll you be?"

"How 'bout Union Square Park? The subway entrance, southeast side."

"Okay. Good. A half hour."

"Is it safe?" Stephanie asked cautiously.

"Pretty safe."

A pause. "I don't want to get beat up or anything. I bruise real easy. And I can't be bruised for my audition."

█████████

As she stepped into the street, Rune heard the man's voice right beside her.

"You're a hard person to find."

Panicked, Rune spun around.

Richard was leaning on a parking meter. The yuppie in him had been exorcized; Mr. Downtown was back. He wore boots, black jeans, and a black T-shirt. He also wore a gold hoop in his ear. She noticed that it was a clip-on. He looked tired.

"You have," he continued, "as FDR said, a passion for anonymity. I called you at the store a couple of times. I was worried about you."

"I haven't been in for a while."

"There was this party last night. I thought you might want to go."

"You didn't ask . . . what's her name? Cathy the Amazon?"

"Karen." He held on to the parking meter and spiraled around it slowly. "We've only had dinner that once. Don't worry about her. We're not going out."

"That's your business. I don't care."

"Don't act so possessive."

"How can I be acting possessive if I tell you I don't care what you do with Cathy/Karen?"

"What's wrong?" He was frowning. Following her eyes to the short, dark-complected man with curly hair standing two doors away. His back was to them.

Rune inhaled with a frightened hiss. The man turned and walked past them. It wasn't Pretty Boy.

She turned back to Richard, trying to focus on him, though what she was seeing was the stupid grin of the plaster statue of Dopey or Sneezy as it disintegrated under the shotgun blast. The gun had been astonishingly loud. Sounded more like a bomb going off.

Richard took her by the shoulders. "Rune, aren't you listening to me? What's wrong?"

She backed away, eyes narrowing slowly. "Leave me alone."

"What?"

"Stay *away* from me. Do you want to get hurt? I'm poison. Stay away."

"What are you talking about?" He reached out and took her hand.

"No, no!" she shouted. The tears started. She hesitated, then hugged him. "Get away from me! Forget about me! Forget you ever met me!"

She turned and ran through the crowds of Greenwich Village toward Union Square.

━━━━━

Waiting under the art-deco steel entrance to the subway, Rune slouched against the cool tile.

She absently watched a crane, a lopsided T-shaped structure rising above an enormous new housing project on Union Square. It's just a crane, she told herself. That's all it was. Not a tool of the gods, not a huge skeleton of a magic animal. What she saw was just a construction crane. Moving slowly, under the control of a faceless union worker, lifting steel reinforcing rods for workmen in dusty jeans and jackets to install.

Magic . . . hell.

She thought again about calling Manelli or Dixon.

But why should they believe her? There was probably an all-points bulletin out on her already, just like there'd been for Roy the cop after he'd stolen the loot in *Manhattan Is My Beat*. At least she'd had the foresight to get rid of some of the evidence: When she'd stopped by her loft to pick up the check, she'd realized she still had Spinello's accordion envelope and thrown it into the trash. If the cops found her with *that,* it'd be a sure conviction.

No, she'd leave town, leave the Side, leave the Magic Kingdom. Go back home. Get a job. Go to school.

Well, it was damn well about time.

Time to grow up. Forget quests . . .

She saw Stephanie, her reddish hair glowing in the afternoon sun as she walked through the park. They waved at each other. It seemed ridiculously innocent, Rune thought, as if they were girlfriends meeting for drinks after work to complain about bosses and men and mothers.

Rune looked around, saw no one suspicious—well, no one *more* suspicious than you'd normally see in Union Square Park—then joined Stephanie.

"You're hurt." The woman glanced at her forehead, where Rune had been cut by a piece of glass or plaster.

"It's okay."

"What happened?"

Rune told her.

"God! You have to go to the police. You can talk to them. Tell them what happened."

"Yeah, right. They can place me at two different crime scenes. I'm the number one suspect."

"But won't the cops find you in Ohio?"

She gave a faint smile. "They might—if they knew my real name. Which they don't."

Stephanie smiled back. "True. Oh, here." She handed

Rune a wad of bills. "It's about three hundred. That enough?"

Rune hugged her. "I don't know what to say." She gave Stephanie the check.

"No, no, this is too much."

"Little Red Hen, remember? I just need enough to get home on. You keep the rest. Tony'll probably fire you too. Just for helping me."

"Come on," Stephanie told her. "I'll help you pack and take you to the airport." They started down into the subway. "You think it's safe to go back to your loft?"

"Emily and Pretty Boy don't know about it. Manelli and that U.S. marshal do, but we can sneak in through the construction site. Nobody'll see us. We can—"

A chill like ice down her back. She gasped.

Ten feet away Pretty Boy stepped out from behind a pillar, holding a black pistol. "Don't fucking move," he muttered to Rune.

Anger on his face, he moved forward toward Rune, not paying any attention to Stephanie. Apparently he didn't even think they were together.

Rune froze. But Stephanie didn't.

She stepped past him fast, which caught him completely off guard. Screaming "Rape, rape!" she shoved her palm, fingers stiff and splayed, into his face. His head snapped back and he staggered against the wall, blood pouring from his nose.

"Fuck," he cried.

Her self-defense class . . .

Stephanie stepped toward him again. It looked like she was going to kick him this time.

But Pretty Boy was good too; he knew what he was doing. He didn't try to fight back. He leapt to the side about three steps, out of range, wiped the blood from his mouth and started to raise the pistol toward her.

Then the arm closed around his neck.

A passenger—a huge black man—had heard Stephanie's cry and had come up behind their attacker and locked his muscular arm around Pretty Boy's throat. Choking, he dropped the gun and grabbed the man's forearm, trying futilely to break the grip.

The big man behind him seemed to be enjoying the whole thing. He said cheerfully to Pretty Boy, "H'okay, asshole, leave th'ladies 'lone. You hear me?"

They ran.

Stephanie in the lead.

She *must* have belonged to a health club—she was moving like a greyhound. If Pretty Boy was there, Rune figured, Emily must be nearby too. Besides, the token seller would've called the cops by then; Rune wanted to get as far away from the station as possible.

Gasping, running. Following Stephanie as best she could.

They were two blocks from the subway when it happened.

At Thirteenth and Broadway a taxi jumped a red light just before it changed.

Which was the exact moment Stephanie ran into the intersection between two double-parked trucks.

She didn't have a chance . . .

All she could do was roll onto the hood to keep from getting crushed under the wheels. The driver hit the brakes, which gave a low, wild scream, but still the cab hit her hard. Some part of her body—her face, Rune thought in despair—slammed into the windshield, which turned white with fractures. Stephanie cartwheeled onto the concrete, a swirl of floral cloth and red hair and white flesh.

"No!" Rune screamed.

Two women ran up and started tending to her. Rune

dropped to her knees beside them. She hardly heard the litany of the cabdriver: "She ran through light, it wasn't my fault, it wasn't my fault."

Rune cradled Stephanie's bloody head in her arms.

"You'll be okay," she whispered. "You'll be okay. You'll be okay."

But Stephanie couldn't hear.

CHAPTER TWENTY-TWO

Rune stood by the window of the hospital, looking out onto the park.

It was an old city park on First Avenue. More rocks and dirt than grass, most of the boulders painted with graffiti, tinted red and purple. They seemed to be oozing from the underbelly of the city itself like exposed organs.

She turned away.

A doctor walked by, not looking at her. None of them had looked at her—the doctors, the orderlies, the nurses, the candy stripers. She'd given up waiting for a kindly old man in a white jacket to come into the hallway, put his arm around her, and say, "About your friend, don't you worry, she'll be fine."

The way they do in movies.

But movies're fake.

Richard's words echoed: *They. Aren't. Real.*

No one had stopped to talk to her. If she wanted any information she had to ask the nurses. Again.

And she'd get the same look she'd gotten two dozen times before.

No news. We'll let you know.

She looked out the window once more. Watching for Pretty Boy. Thinking maybe he'd gotten away from the man in the subway and escaped from the cops. Followed the ambulance here.

Paranoia again.

But it's not paranoia if they're really after you.

Hoping that Stephanie had hurt Pretty Boy really bad when she'd hit him. A character in one of her fairy stories, a friendly witch, had told someone never to hope for harm to someone else. Hope for all the good you want but never wish harm on anyone. Because, the witch said, harm's like a wasp in a jar. Once you release it you never know who it's going to sting.

But now Rune hoped Stephanie had hurt the bastard real bad.

She wandered up to the nurses' station.

An older woman with a snake of a stethoscope around her neck finally looked up. "Oh. We just heard about your friend."

"What? Tell me!"

"They just took her to Radiology for more scans. She's still unconscious."

"*That's* what you were going to tell me? That you don't know anything?"

"I thought you'd want to know. She'll be back in ICU in forty minutes, an hour. Depending."

Useless, Rune thought.

"I'll be back. If she wakes up, tell her I'll be back."

█████████

Oh, please, Pan and Isis and Persephone, let her live.

Rune stood by the East River, watching the tugs sail upstream. The Circle Line tour boat too. A barge, three or four cabin cruisers. The water was ugly and ripe-smelling. The traffic from the FDR Drive rushed past with a moist, tearing sound, which set her on edge. It sounded like bandages being removed.

Just an adventure. That's all I wanted. An adventure.

Lancelot searching for the Grail. Psyche for her lost lover Eros. Like in the books, in the movies. And Rune would be the hero. She'd find Mr. Kelly's killer, she'd find the million dollars. She'd save Amanda and would live happily ever after with Richard.

O God of heavenly powers, who by the might of thy command, drivest away from men's bodies all sickness and infirmity, be present in thy goodness . . .

These were the words she'd said so often during the last week of her father's life that she'd memorized them without trying to.

Her father, a young man. A handsome man. Who played with Rune and her sister all the time, taught them to ride bicycles, who read them stories, who took them to plays as readily as to ball games. A man who always had time to talk to them, listen to their problems.

No, fairy stories didn't always have happy endings. But they always had endings that were just. People died and lost their fortunes in them because they were dishonest or careless or greedy. There was no justice in her father's death though. He'd lived a good life and he'd still died badly, slow and messy, in the Shaker Heights Garden Hospice.

No justice in Mr. Kelly's death.

No justice in Stephanie's getting hurt. None if she died.

Please . . .

Speaking out loud now. "With this thy servant Stephanie that her weakness may be banished and her strength recalled."

Her voice fell to a whisper and then she stopped praying.

Staring at the ugly river in front of her, Rune took off her silver bracelets one by one and tossed them into the water. They disappeared without any sound that she could hear and she took that as a good sign that the gods who oversaw this wonderful and terrible city were happy with her sacrifice.

Though when she got to last bracelet, the one that she'd bought for Richard, she paused, looking at the silver hands clasped together. She heard his voice again.

You're going to find out I'm not a knight and that, okay, maybe there was some bank robbery money—which I think is the craziest frigging thing I've ever heard—but that it's spent or stolen or lost somewhere years ago and you'll never find it . . .

She gripped the bracelet firmly, ready to throw it after the others. But then decided, no, she'd save this one—as a reminder to herself. About how adventures can get friends and family hurt and killed. How quests work only in books and in movies.

And here you are pissing your life away in a video store, jumping from fantasy to fantasy, waiting for something you don't even know what it is.

She slipped the last bracelet back on her wrist and slowly returned to the hospital.

Upstairs, the nurses had changed shifts and no one could find Stephanie. Rune had a terrible moment of panic as one nurse looked at a sheet of paper and found a black space where there should have been a list of patients from Adult Emergency Services who'd gone to Radiology. She felt her hands trembling. Then the nurse found an entry that said Stephanie was still upstairs.

"I'll let you know," the nurse promised.

Rune stood at the window for a long time again, then heard a voice asking for her.

She turned. Froze. The doctor was very young and he had a mournful expression on his face. It seemed that he hadn't slept in a week. Rune wondered if he'd ever told anyone before that a patient had died. Her breath came fast. She gripped the bracelet maniacally.

"You're a friend of the woman hit by the cab?" he asked.

Rune nodded.

He said, "She's transitioned from a deteriorating status."

Rune stared at him. He stared back, waiting for a response.

Finally he tried again. "She's in a stable situation."

"I—" She shook her head, his words not making sense to her.

"She'll be okay," the doctor said.

Rune started to cry.

He continued. "She has a concussion. But there isn't much blood loss. Some bad contusions."

"What's a contusion?"

"A bruise."

"Oh," Rune said softly.

Stephanie, who didn't want to get bruised for her audition.

She asked him, "Is she awake?"

"No. She won't be for a while."

"Thank you, doctor." She hugged him hard. He endured this for a moment then retreated wearily back through the swinging doors.

At the nurses' station Rune asked for a piece of paper and a pen.

Rune wrote:

Steph:
I'm leaving. Thanks for everything. Don't come near
me, don't try to contact me. I'll only get you hurt
again. Love,

R.

She handed the note to the nurse. "Please give this to her when she wakes up. Oh, and please tell her I'm sorry."

Running again.

Looking behind her, as often as she looked forward. Past garbage cans, litter on the street, puddles. Past the fake, gaudy gold of the Puck Building in SoHo, surrounded by the sour smell of the fringe of the Lower East Side. Running, running. Rune felt the trickle of sweat down her back and sides, the pain in her feet as they slammed on the concrete through the thin soles of her cheap boots.

Air flooded into her lungs and stung her chest.

A block from her loft Rune pressed against the side of a building and looked behind her. No one was following. It was just a peaceful, shabby street. She checked out the street in front of her loft: No police cars, even unmarked ones. Familiar shadows, familiar trash, the same broken-down blue van that had been there for days, plastered with parking tickets. She waited until her pounding heart calmed.

If Emily and Pretty Boy found out about her place, would they come here? Probably not. They'd know the police would be staking it out. Besides, they were probably gone themselves. She'd been the fall guy they needed; their job was done. They'd probably left town.

Which is what I'm going to do. Right now.

Round on the ends and hi in the middle, it's O-Hi-O.

Rune walked around the block then snuck through

the plywood fence of the construction site. Workers in hard hats came and went.

She walked past them quickly, into her building. She started up in the freight elevator, smelling the grease and paint and solvents. She was already sick—from exhaustion and fear—and the scents turned her stomach even more.

The elevator clanked to a stop at the top floor. She unhooked the chain guard and stepped out. No sounds from the loft upstairs. But there was a chance somebody was there. She called, "Rune? It's me. Are you home?" No response. "It's your friend Jennifer. Rune!"

Nothing.

Then up the stairs, slowly, peering out of the opening in the floor. The empty loft stretched out around her. She raced to her side of the loft, grabbed one of the old suitcases she used for a dresser, opened it. She walked around the room, trying to decide what to take.

No clothes. No jewelry—she didn't own much other than her bracelets. She picked some pictures of her family and the friends she'd met in New York. And her books—twenty or so of them, the ones she'd never be able to replace. She considered the videos—Disney, mostly. But she could get new copies of those.

Rune noticed the tape of *Manhattan Is My Beat*. She picked it up and flung it angrily across the room. It crashed into a table, shattering several glasses. The cassette itself broke apart too.

She found a pen and paper. She wrote:

Sandra, it's been radical rooming with you. I've got the chance to go to England for a couple years. So if anyone comes looking for me, you can tell them that's were I am. I'm not sure where but I think I'll be somewhere near London or Edinborow. Hope your jewelry makes it big, your designs are really super and if you ever sell it in London I'll buy some. Good lox, Rune.

She folded the paper, left it on Sandra's pillow, and picked up the heavy suitcase.

Which is when she heard the footsteps.

They were on the floor below.

Whoever it was hadn't come up via the elevator. They'd snuck up the stairs. So they wouldn't be heard.

The only exit was the stairway—the one the intruder was now coming up. She heard cautious feet, gritty.

She looked across the loft to her side of the room—at her suitcase and leopard-skin bag.

No time to get a weapon. No time for anything.

Nowhere to run.

She looked around her glass house.

Nowhere to hide.

CHAPTER TWENTY-THREE

He took the stairs one at a time, slowly, slowly. Pausing, listening.

And struggling to control his anger. Which throbbed like the pain in his face—from when that fucking redhead had nailed him in the subway. Listening above him and listening below. He was out of his uniform now—he'd ditched the meter reader's jacket a while ago, before he trailed the little short-haired bitch to Brooklyn—and downstairs some of the construction guys had given him some shit about just walking into the building. He'd just kept walking, giving them a fuck-you look and not even bothering to make up a cover story.

So, listening for somebody laying in wait for him upstairs, listening for somebody following.

But he heard no footsteps, no breathing, no guns being racked.

Pausing at the top of the stairs, head down.

Okay . . . go!

Walking fast into the loft, eyes taking in places he could go for cover.

Only he didn't have to worry. She wasn't there.

Shit. He'd been sure she'd come back. If only to get her stuff before she took off. Pointing the gun in front of him, he made a circuit of the loft. She'd been there—there was a suitcase half filled. There was that God-ugly purse of hers. But no sign of the bitch.

Maybe—

Then he heard it.

A click and a grind.

The elevator! He ran to the stairs, thinking she'd snuck out behind him. But, no, the cage was empty. It was going down. So, she *was* coming home. He'd gotten there before her.

He ducked behind a half-height wall of cinder block, out of view of the stairway, and waited for her to come to him.

■■■■

Rune was exactly eight feet away from Pretty Boy, standing in the steady stream of wind outside the loft, a hundred feet above the sidewalk.

Her boots perched on a thin ridge of metal that jutted out six inches from the lower edge of the building's facade. Most of her body was below the glass windows, and if she ducked, Pretty Boy couldn't see her.

Only she was compelled to look.

Because she'd heard the elevator start down. Somebody was coming up!

And Pretty Boy was going to kill them.

Her hands quivered, her legs were weak, as if her muscles were melting. The wind was cold up there, the smells different. Raw. She looked down again, at the cobblestone patches of the street coming through the asphalt. She closed her eyes and pressed her face against her arm for comfort.

Cobblestones—the final scene in *Manhattan Is My Beat*. Ruby Dahl, walking slowly down the wet street, crying for her tormented fiancé gunned down in Greenwich Village.

Roy, Roy, I would have loved you even if you were poor!

Rune looked back into the loft and saw Pretty Boy shift slightly, then cock his ear toward the doorway.

Who was coming up in the elevator? Sandra? Some of the construction guys?

Please, let it be the police—Manelli or Dixon. Coming to arrest her for the shooting in Brooklyn. They had guns. They'd at least have a chance against the killer.

Suddenly, Pretty Boy crouched and held the gun's muzzle up, his right index finger on the trigger. He looked around him, turning his head as though listening.

Whoever was there was calling out some words. Yes, she could vaguely hear a voice, "Rune? Rune? Are you here?" It was a man.

Richard ran up the stairs, shouting something.

No, no, no! she cried silently. Oh, not him. Please, don't hurt him!

She closed her eyes and tried to send him a message of danger. But when she looked again she saw that he'd walked farther into the loft. "Rune?"

Pretty Boy couldn't see him from the other side of the wall. But he was following Richard's steps with the gun. Rune saw him cock it with his long thumb and point it to the spot where Richard was about to appear.

Oh, no . . .

There was nothing else to do. She couldn't let anybody else get hurt because of her. She raised her right fist above the glass. She'd break the window, scream for Richard to run. Pretty Boy would panic and spin around, shoot her. But Richard might just have enough time to leap down the stairs and escape.

Okay, now! Do it.

But just as she started to bring her fist down on the window, Richard paused. He'd seen the note—the note she'd written to Sandra. He picked it up and read it. Then shook his head. He looked around the loft one more time and then started down the stairs.

Pretty Boy peeked out from behind the wall, slipped his gun into his belt. He stood.

Thank you, thank you . . .

Rune lowered her right arm and held on to the ledge again. Pretty Boy searched the loft again, looking for her, then started down the stairs. Rune's fingertips were numb, though her arm muscles ached and her legs were on fire with pain. But she stayed where she was until below her she saw Pretty Boy jog out of the building and disappear east.

She edged to the small access door and crawled inside. She lay on her bed for five minutes until the quivering in her muscles stopped.

Then she picked up the suitcase and purse and left the loft. Not even thinking to say good-bye to her castle in the sky.

On the streets of TriBeCa she paused.

Looking around.

There were construction workers, there were businessmen and businesswomen, there were messengers.

She'd thought Pretty Boy and Emily were gone, wouldn't bother with her. But she'd been wrong there. And that meant they might have other partners. Was it any one of these people?

Several faces glanced at her, and their expressions were dark and suspicious. She shrank back into an alley, hid behind a Dumpster. She'd wait until it was night—just hide there—then hike up to the bus station.

Then she saw a bum coming up the alley. Only he didn't look *quite* like a bum to her. He was dirty like a homeless man and he wore shabby clothes. But his eyes seemed too quick. They seemed dangerous. He looked up and saw her. Paused for just an instant too long. Lowered his head again and continued up the alley.

Ignoring her. But really trying too hard to ignore her.

He was one of them too!

Go, girl. Go! She slung her purse over her shoulder, grabbed the heavy suitcase, and bolted from behind the Dumpster.

The bum saw her, debated a moment, then started running too. Directly behind her.

Rune couldn't run fast, not with the suitcase. She struggled into Franklin Street and paused, gasping, trying to figure which way to go. The bum was getting closer.

Then a man's voice: "Rune!"

She spun around, heart hammering.

"Rune, over here!"

It was Phillip Dixon, the U.S. marshal. He was waving toward her. She started toward him instinctively, then stopped, remembering that he was one of the people who wanted to arrest her.

What should she do?

She was in the middle of the street—thirty feet from the subway. She heard a rumbling underground—a train was approaching. She could vault the turnstile and be on her way uptown in fifteen seconds.

Thirty feet from the bum, running toward her, anger on his face.

Thirty feet from Dixon.

"Rune!" the marshal called. "Come on. It's not safe here. They're around here somewhere. The killers."

"No! You're going to arrest me!"

"I know you didn't kill Symington," Dixon said.

But what else was he going to say? And after the cuffs were on, it'd be: *You have the right to remain silent* . . .

The bum was closer, staring at her with dark, cold eyes.

The train was almost in the station. *Run for it! Now!*

"I want to help you," Dixon shouted. "I've been worried about you." He started across the street but stopped when she turned away from him, started toward the subway.

He held up his hands. "Please! They're after you, Rune. We know what happened. They set you up! They hadn't figured on you getting away in Brooklyn. But we *know* you didn't do it. You were just at the wrong place at the wrong time."

Choose, she told herself. *Now!*

She started across the street tentatively toward Dixon. The bum was closer now, slowing.

"Please, Rune," the marshal said.

Beneath her feet, through the grating, the train eased into the station, brakes squealing.

Choose!

Come on, you've gotta trust *somebody*. . . .

She bolted toward Dixon, ran to his side. He put his arm around her. "It's okay," he said. "You'll be all right."

She blurted out, "There's a man after me. In the alley." And saw a car pulling up at the curb beside them.

The bum turned the corner. He stopped cold as Dixon drew that huge black gun of his.

"Shit," the bum said, holding up his hands. "Hey, man, I'm sorry. I just wanted her purse. No big deal. I'm just going to—"

Dixon fired once. The bullet slammed into the bum's chest. He flew backward.

"Jesus!" Rune cried. "What'd you do that for?"

"He saw my face," Phillip said matter-of-factly, lifting the suitcase and purse away from Rune.

From the car that had just driven up, a woman's voice said to Dixon, "Come on, Haarte, you're standing right out here in broad daylight. There could be cops any minute. Let's go!"

Rune stared at the woman; it was Emily. And the car she was driving was the green Pontiac that had tried to run her and the other witness down at Mr. Kelly's apartment.

Wrong place, wrong time . . .

Phillip—or Haarte—opened the back door of the Pontiac. He shoved Rune inside, tossed her purse and suitcase into the trunk. Haarte got into the backseat with Rune.

"Where to?" Emily asked.

"Better make it my place," he answered calmly. "It's the one with the basement. Quieter, you know."

CHAPTER TWENTY-FOUR

███████ Lost in a forest.

Hansel and Gretel.

Rune stared at the ceiling and wondered what time it was.

Thinking how fast she'd lost track of the hours.

Just like she'd lost track of her life over the past few days.

It reminded her of the time she was a little girl, visiting some relatives with her parents in rural Ohio. She'd wandered away from a picnic in a small state forest. Strolling for hours through the park, thinking she knew where she was going, where her family's picnic bench was. A little confused maybe but, with a child's confidence and preoccupation, never even considering that she was lost. Never knowing that hours had passed and she was miles away from her frantic family.

Now she *knew* how lost she was. And she knew, too, how impossible it was to get home again.

Welcome to reality, Richard would've told her.

The room was tiny. A storeroom in the cellar. It had only one window, a small one she couldn't possibly reach, barred with twisty bars of wrought iron. Part of the concrete floor was missing. The dirt beneath was overturned. When Haarte had shoved her into the room she'd noticed *that* right away: the dug-up dirt. She told herself it was just because he was doing some work down there. Replacing pipes, putting in a new concrete floor.

But she knew it was a grave.

Rune lay on her back and looked at the cold streetlight coming through the unreachable window.

Back-street light.

Light to die by.

There was a sudden metallic snap, and she jumped. A shuffle of feet outside the door.

A second lock clicked and the door opened. Haarte stood in the doorway. He was cautious. He looked around the room, maybe to see if she'd rigged any traps or found any weapons. Then, satisfied, he nodded for her to follow. Tears of fear pricked in her eyes but she wouldn't let them fall.

He led her up some rickety stairs.

Emily's attention was on her. She was amused, studying Rune like a real estate agent appraising an apartment. When Rune hesitated outside the doorway Haarte pushed her in. Emily didn't seem to like that but she didn't say anything.

No one spoke. Rune felt the tension in the air. Like the scene inside the bank in *Manhattan Is My Beat* where the cop is staring down the robber. His hand is out, not moving, saying over and over, "Give me the pistol, son. Give it to me." The lighting shadowy and stark, the camera moving in close on the muzzle of the .38.

Would the robber shoot or wouldn't he? You wanted to scream from the tension.

Haarte pushed Rune into a cheap dining-room chair, stared down at her. She whimpered, feeling not the least bit adult.

But then, from somewhere in her mind, an image came. An illustration from one of her fantasy books. Diarmuid. Then another: King Arthur.

She ripped his hand off her shoulder. "Don't touch me," she snarled.

He blinked.

Rune waited a moment, staring into his eyes, then walked slowly to the chair. She adjusted it so she was facing Emily and sat down, then said in a sly, tough, Joan Rivers voice, "Can we talk?"

Emily blinked then laughed. "Just what we had in mind."

Haarte pulled up a chair and sat down too.

Rune kept spinning the sole bracelet on her wrist, slipping it on and off. Trying to be tough, looking as hip and cynical as she could. The silver ring spun. She looked down and saw the hands clasped together. She tried not to think about Richard.

Emily said, "We need to know who you told about Spinello and about me."

Rune snapped, "You killed Robert Kelly. Why?"

Emily looked at Haarte. He said, "You could say that it was his fault."

"What?"

"He moved into the wrong apartment," Emily said. "We felt bad. I mean, it looks bad for us. To make a mistake like that. Felt bad for him, too, of course."

Rune exhaled in shock. "He was just . . . You killed him by mistake?"

Haarte continued. "After Spinello testified in the St. Louis RICO cases in January, the U.S. Marshals moved him to New York. Witness protection. They gave him a new identity—Victor Symington—and put him in a place uptown but, well, you saw he was pretty paranoid. He didn't stay where they'd set him up and got the apartment down in the Village. He moved into Apartment 2B. But then he heard there was a bigger apartment available on the third floor. So he moved upstairs. Your friend Kelly moved into Spinello's place."

"The information we had from the people hiring us," Emily said, "was that the hit lived in 2B."

"And, I mean, what can we say?" Haarte reflected. "I checked the directory down in the lobby, but it was so covered up with graffiti, I couldn't read a fucking thing. Besides, Kelly and Spinello looked a lot alike."

"They didn't look a *thing* alike!" Rune spat out.

"Well, they did to me. Hey, accidents happen."

Rune asked, "Then you came back and tore up his place just for the fun of it?"

Haarte looked insulted. "Of course not. We heard on the news that this Robert Kelly guy'd been killed. That wasn't the hit's new name. So we started to think we'd hit the wrong man. I mean, *you* interrupted me during the job. We didn't have time to verify it. I checked out the place later and found a picture of Kelly with his sister, letters. They looked legit."

Rune remembered the torn picture. Haarte had probably lost his temper when he'd realized his mistake then ripped up the photo in anger.

He continued. "Witness relocation doesn't do *that* thorough a job, faking old family pictures. So I figured we'd fucked up. We had to make it right."

Make it *right*? Rune thought.

"When you came to the store," Rune said, "when you pretended to be that U.S. marshal, Dixon, you said you were part of the homicide team at Mr. Kelly's apartment."

"Fuck, of *course* I wasn't there." Haarte laughed. "That's the trick to lying. Make the person you're lying to your partner in the lie. I suggested I was there and you just assumed I was."

Rune remembered Mr. Kelly's apartment, looking through his books, finding the clipping, the heat and the stuffiness of the apartment. The horrible bloodstained chair. The torn photo.

Rune closed her eyes. She left overwhelmed with hopelessness. Her big adventure—it was all because of a mistake. There was no stolen bank loot. Robert Kelly was just a bystander—a weird old man who happened to like a bad movie.

"So, honey, we need to know," Emily said impatiently, "who'd you tell about me?"

"Nobody."

"Boyfriends? Girlfriends? You've had plenty of time to talk to people after you ran out of our little party at Spinello's house in Brooklyn."

"You knew where Spinello was all along?" Rune asked. "And you were just using me?"

"Of course," Emily said, "I just had to lead you there, through the bank and the lawyer, so there'd be a trail the police could find. The cops'd see that you were tracking him down, then they'd find him and your body—we were going to make it look like he shot you after you shot him. They'd have their perp. End of investigation. The police're like everybody else. They prefer the least work possible. Once they've found *a* killer they stop looking for anybody else. On to other cases. You know. So, come on: Who'd you tell?"

"Why would I say anything to anybody?"

"Oh, come on," Haarte said. "You see somebody killed right in front of you and you don't tell the police?"

"How could I? My fingerprints were all over Spinello's apartment. I *knew* I was a suspect. I figured out what you were doing."

"No, you didn't," Haarte said. "You're not that smart."

Rune remained silent. At least one thing was good, Rune thought. They don't know about Stephanie.

Suddenly Haarte leapt up from the chair, grabbed Rune's hair, and jerked her head back so far she couldn't breathe. She was choking. His face was close to hers. "See, you think it's better to live. No matter what I do to you. But it isn't. The only way we could let you live—and we aren't really inclined to kill you—but the only way we'd *let* you live is if we make it so that you can't tell anybody about us. Pick us out of a lineup, say."

He moved a finger slowly down toward her eye. She closed the lid and a moment later felt increasing pain as he pressed hard on her eyeball.

"No!"

His fingers lifted off her face. "There's a *lot* we could do to you." His hand massaged the back of her neck. "We could make you a vegetable." He touched her breasts. "Or a boy." Between her legs. "Or . . ."

He released her hair so quickly that she screamed. Emily looked on without emotion.

Rune caught her breath. "Please let me go. I won't say anything."

"It's demeaning to beg," Emily said.

"I'll give you the million dollars," she said.

"What million?" Haarte asked. "From that old movie? That's bullshit."

"Oh," Emily said, laughing, "your secret treasure?"

"I will. I found it!"

Haarte asked cynically, "You did?"

"Sure. Where do you think I've been for the past twenty-four hours? After what happened in Brooklyn, you think I'm going to hang around town? Why didn't I just leave yesterday as soon as you killed Spinello? I didn't leave because I had a lead to the money."

Haarte considered this. Rune thought he was genuinely intrigued. Rune, hands together, was kneading her one remaining silver bracelet. "It's true, I promise."

He shook his head. "No, doesn't make sense."

"Mr. Kelly *did* have the money. I found it. It's in a locker at the bus station."

"That sounds like a scene out of a movie," Emily said slowly.

"Whatever it sounds like, it's true."

They were both sort of believing her now. Rune could tell.

Rune fiddled with the bracelet again. "A million dollars!"

Haarte said to Emily, "It's old money. How hard to move?"

"Not that hard," she said. "They're always finding old bills. Banks have to take 'em. And the good news is even if they took the serial numbers years ago, nobody's gonna have the records anymore."

"You know anybody who could take 'em?"

"A couple guys. We could probably get seventy, eighty points on the dollar."

But then Haarte shook his head again. "No, it's crazy."

"A million dollars," Rune repeated. "Aren't you getting tired of killing people for a living?"

There was a pause. Haarte and Emily avoided each other's eyes.

The room was sepia, gloomy, lit by two dim lamps. Rune looked out the window. Outside, it was very dark, with only that one cold streetlight nearby. She played nervously with her bracelet, squeezing it.

Haarte and Emily whispered to each other, their heads down. Emily finally nodded and looked up. "Okay, here's the deal. You give us the names of everyone you've told about me and hand over the money, we'll let you live. You don't tell us, I'll let Haarte here take you downstairs and do whatever he wants."

Rune thought for a moment. "What will you do with them? Whoever I told?"

Haarte said, "Nothing. As long as there are no police after us. But if there are then we might have to hurt them."

Rune squeezed the bracelet again several times. Hard. It snapped in half.

She looked up. "You're lying."

"Honey—" Emily began.

That's the trick to lying. Make the person you're lying to your partner in the lie.

"But that's all right," Rune said matter-of-factly. "Because I was too." And leapt out of the chair.

CHAPTER TWENTY-FIVE

███████ Emily laughed.

Because Rune might have run toward the front door of the town house or the rear. Or tried for a window. But she didn't do either. Instead, she rolled toward a small door in the living room.

"Rune," Emily said patiently, "what do you think you're doing? That's a closet."

And a locked one, at that, Rune learned, tugging on the glass knob.

Haarte looked at Emily. He shook his head at Rune's stupidity. There was no way out. She'd boxed herself in. Rune glanced back at them and saw with relief that they didn't have a clue what she really had in mind.

Until Rune jumped for the electric outlet she'd had her eye on for five minutes.

"No!" Emily shouted to Haarte. "She's going to—"

Rune pushed the two ends of the broken bracelet into the socket.

This bracelet, mon, she be important in your life, very important. Don't be too fast to give her away. . . .

There was a fierce white flash and a loud crack. Pure stinging fire poured through her thumb and finger. The lights throughout the town house went out as the fuse popped from the short circuit. She smelled the scorched-meat scent of the burn on her finger and thumb.

Instantly, ignoring the pain, she was on her feet and running. Emily and Haarte, blinded by the flash, were groping toward the doorway. Rune, who'd had her eyes closed when the spark arced, was already thirty feet ahead of them, running cautiously, crouched, toward the front door, her useless right arm cradled in her left hand.

She missed the two steps down, from the hallway to the entry foyer, and fell heavily forward. Her right arm shot out in front of her instinctively, and she felt the searing pain as the burned hand broke her fall. She couldn't stop the grunt of pain.

"There—she's over there," Emily called. "I'll get her."

Rune climbed to her feet, hearing the woman's high heels clattering after her. She couldn't see Haarte anywhere. Maybe he was down in the basement, changing the fuse.

Rune leapt toward the front door, chilled by panic from the thought of Emily, undoubtedly armed, moving close behind her.

She reached for the top latch on the door. Then stopped, stepped slowly, stepped back against the wall. No! Christ no!

There was a man outside. She couldn't see clearly through the lacy curtains but she knew it had to be Pretty Boy. Haarte's and Emily's partner. The halo of curly hair caught pale light from the street. He seemed to be looking in the window, wondering why the lights had gone off inside.

Rune turned and started toward the back of the house.

Slowly, listening for Emily's heels and Haarte's footsteps.

But there was no sound at all. Had they fled? Rune turned the corner and froze. There, only four or five feet away, was Emily, who inched forward, feeling her way along the wall, holding a gun. She'd kicked off her shoes, was silently barefoot.

Rune pressed against the wall. The woman's head turned, squinting into the gloom. Probably hearing Rune's shallow breathing. She had a vague image of the woman's silhouette lifting the gun. Pointing it toward Rune.

She'll hear my heart beating! She *has* to hear that.

And that it may please thee to preserve all who are in danger by reason of their labor.

The silenced gun fired with a loud clicking *pop*. There was a fierce slap as the bullet hit the plaster a foot away from Rune's head.

We beseech thee to hear us, good Lord.

Another shot, closer.

Rune struggled with all her will to remain silent.

Emily turned toward the front door. Rune's groping fingers grabbed the closest thing she could find—a heavy vase on a pedestal. She raised it and flung it hard toward the woman. It was a solid hit. Emily cried out in a high wail and fell to her knees. The gun disappeared into the shadows. The vase thudded, unbroken, onto the parquet.

"I can't find the fuses!" Haarte's voice shouted from very near. "Where the hell is she?"

"Help me!" Emily called.

Haarte walked forward. "I can't see a fucking thing."

Rune dodged out of his way.

"There!" Emily called. "Beside you!"

"What—" Haarte began, and Rune sprinted down the hallway, heading toward where the back door should be.

Yes! There it was. She could see it. And it didn't look like anybody was outside.

She heard Haarte's voice in the front of the house, calling to Emily.

And Rune knew then that it was going to be all right; she could escape. They were nowhere near her and Rune had to spring only twenty feet or so to get to the back door. She slammed the hallway door shut, wedged a chair under the knob, and kept running.

Haarte got to the door in a few seconds and tried to open it but it was tightly blocked.

Rune could see dim light coming through the lace curtains on the back door.

Nothing could stop her now. She'd get outside, into the alley, run like hell. Call 911 from the first phone she found.

Haarte slammed into the door and pushed it open slightly, but the chair still held.

Fifteen feet. Ten.

Another slam.

"Go around, through the kitchen," Haarte called to Emily.

But their voices were a world away. Rune was at the door. She was safe.

She undid the chain. Turned the latch and then the knob. She swung the door wide and stepped out onto the back porch.

And stopped cold.

Oh, no . . .

No more than two feet away from her was Pretty Boy. He was startled but not so startled he didn't lift his pistol like a quick-draw gunslinger and point it directly at her face.

No, no, no . . .

She leaned back against the doorjamb. Tears streaming down her face. Arms limp, shaking her head. Oh, no . . . It's over. It's over.

But then something odd happened, the sort of thing that happened in the Side, in the magic realm. Rune seemed to go out of her body. She felt as if she died and rose away into the air. Actually wondering—did he shoot me? Am I dead?

Floating away. Completely numb. Sailing up into the air.

And from there, from a cloud hovering over the Side, she looked down and saw:

Pretty Boy putting his arm around her and leading her away from the open back door of the town house, handing her off to another man behind him, a man in a blue jacket that said U.S. MARSHAL on the back, and from there to another man wearing what looked like a bullet-proof vest printed with the letters "NYPD." Passed along again until finally at the end of the line was Detective Manelli, with his close-together eyes, with his funny first name.

Virgil Manelli.

The detective held a finger to his lips to keep Rune quiet, then led her away from the house. She looked back at the line of men clustered around the door. Big men with stony faces, wearing suits of thick blue armor and carrying stubby machine guns.

On the sidewalk, Manelli handed her off one last time—to two medics, who put her on a cot and began hovering over her, pouring ice water on her burnt hand and then wrapping it with bandages.

Rune paid no attention. She kept her eyes on the men around the back door. Then Pretty Boy said into a microphone on his collar, "Subject is clear. Move in, move in, move in!"

Everyone on the stairs, all the knights, charged

into the building, shouting, "Police, police, federal agents . . ." Flashlights illuminated the interior of the town house.

Rune heard a funny sound. Laughter. She looked at the attendant. But he wasn't laughing. His partner wasn't either. She realized that the sound was coming from her.

Delicately, one of the medics asked, "What's so funny?"

But she didn't answer. Because from inside the town house came the sound of gunshots. Then calls of "Medic, medic!"

And the men in the ambulance left her while they ran toward the back door with their bags in hand, their stethoscopes flapping around their necks.

CHAPTER TWENTY-SIX

████████ She huddled away from him. From Pretty Boy.

"I want to see something. Some identification."

They were sitting in the back of a new-smelling Ford. Government issue. Manelli stood outside.

The NYPD detective rubbed his mustache and said, "He's legit."

"I want to *see* something!" Rune snapped.

Pretty Boy offered her his badge and an ID card.

She looked at the card three times before she actually read everything. His name was Salvatore Pistone.

"Call me Sal. Everybody does."

"You're, like, an FBI agent."

"You just insulted me. I'm a U.S. marshal." He was smiling. But his eyes were oddly cold.

"That's what Haarte said."

"Yeah, I found his fake badge and ID. He's used that identity before. Frosts me how often people don't fucking bother to read ID cards. You had, you woulda seen his was fake."

The medic stopped by the car. "Soak that hand in Betadine solution tonight before you go to bed. Tomorrow see your doctor. You know what Betadine is?"

She had no idea. She nodded yes.

Then, to Manelli, the man said, "Guy's dead."

Sal scoffed. "I shot him three times in the head. What the fuck else would he be?"

"Yeah, well. It's confirmed."

"Who?" Rune asked. "Haarte?"

Sal said, "Yeah. Haarte."

"The woman, she'll be okay?" Manelli asked.

"Hell of a bruise on her back. Don't have a clue how she got that—"

Rune remembered the vase. Wish she'd aimed for Emily's head.

"—but aside from that she'll be fine. The bitch'll *definitely* see the inside of a courtroom."

Manelli straightened up. "All right, miss, I'm handing you over to the feds. It's their case now. You shoulda listened to me and stayed out—"

"I—"

He held up a finger to his lips, shushing her again. "You shoulda listened." He walked off to his own car. He glanced at her with his close-together eyes but they were expressionless. He got inside, started the engine, and drove off.

Other cars were leaving. More of the nondescript sedans, some city blue-and-white police cars. And the small Emergency Service Unit trucks. The ESU men and women, like soldiers after a battle, were taking off their vests and loading the guns back into their car trunks or the compartments of the trucks.

"Who was he?"

"Samuel Haarte," Sal replied. "Professional hit man."

"I'm so confused."

She watched Sal's face. She decided there was something a little crazy about him. Indoctrinated. Like with the Moonies. She had this love/hate thing with Detective Manelli but she liked him. Sal scared her.

"She killed Victor Symington," Rune told him. "Emily did."

"So she was going by the name Emily. Any last name?"

"Richter."

"Haarte usually worked with somebody named Zane. I always thought it was a guy. But it must be her. One fucking tough woman."

Sal dug around in the back of the car, found a thermos, and sat back. He poured some coffee into the lid and offered it to her. "Black. Sweet." She took it and sipped the coffee. It was so strong it made her shiver.

Sal drank directly from the thermos. "Symington—I mean Spinello—he'd be alive if he hadn't panicked. He shouldn't've took off."

"What happened?" Rune asked.

He explained. "I'm with the Witness Protection Program. You know, giving federal witnesses new identities. Spinello and another witness—"

"That guy in St. Louis I read about?"

"Right. Arnold Gittleman. Spinello and Gittleman testified against some syndicate guys in the Midwest."

"But if they already testified, why kill them?"

Sal laughed coldly at her naiveté. "It's called revenge, sweetheart. To send the message that nobody else better talk. Anyway, Spinello took off—he didn't trust us to keep his ass safe and moved down to the Village on his own. Never told his handler about it. I was part of the team in the hotel in St. Louis guarding Gittleman." His cold eyes grew sad for a splinter of a second. Not an emotion he was used to, it seemed. "I went out to get some sandwiches and beer and those assholes got Gittleman and my partners."

"I'm sorry."

He shrugged off the sympathy. "So I went undercover to nail the pricks." Sal looked at the house. "And we sure as shit did. Looks like they were the only ones too. We waited as long as we could here in case somebody else showed up. But nobody did."

"What do you mean, you waited as long as you could?"

He shrugged. "We've been cooling our heels outside here for five fucking hours."

"Five hours!" she shouted. Then it became clear. "I *led* you here! I was bait."

Sal considered this. "Basically. Yeah."

"You son of a bitch! How long've you been following me?"

"You know that old blue van in front of your loft? With all the tickets?"

"That was yours?" she asked, dumbfounded.

"Sure."

"What'd you come up in my loft for? Earlier today?"

He frowned. "Actually, at that point, we figured you were dead. I was checking it out to see if your body was up there."

"Jesus Maria . . ." She nodded to the door. Ripped into him with a sarcastic "I hope when I escaped just now I didn't totally screw up your plans."

"Naw," Sal said, sipping more coffee. "It was good it worked out the way it did. They *might've* used you as a hostage. It was—whatta you say?—convenient you got away when you did."

"Convenient?" Rune spat. "You used me. Just like Emily did. You followed me to Brooklyn to find out where Symington was. And you followed me here to catch them!"

Now Sal grew angry too. "Listen. For a week, I thought you *might've* been one of the hit team. Think about it. We have a city police report that you were on the scene just after the Kelly killing. Then, when I'm staking out the site of the hit—that tenement on Tenth Street—you go in. Then Spinello runs outside and vanishes, like you scared the crap out of him. And then we had more reports that somebody who fits your description,—except is about nine months pregnant—has broken into Kelly's apartment and ransacked the hell out of it."

"That wasn't me," Rune protested. "It was them."

"But you *did* break in."

"The door was practically open."

"Hey, I'm not after any B and E count. I'm just telling you why I didn't walk up to you and introduce myself. Shit. And when we figured out you were an innocent and I tried talking to you, your friend the redhead just about breaks my nose and some fucking bodybuilder closes my throat up."

"How were we supposed to know?"

"Anyway, yeah, they found your prints all over Spinello's safe house in Brooklyn. But we checked you out pretty good and you didn't seem like the sort that Haarte or Zane'd hire. I talked to Manelli about you and we decided you were pretty much who you seemed to be. Just a kid in over her head."

"I'm not a kid."

"Yeah, I wouldn't take points on that one. What the hell were you doing in this mess in the first place?"

Rune told him about Mr. Kelly and the money and the movie.

"A million dollars?" Sal laughed. "Gimme a break. Stick with lotto. Or numbers. Better odds, sweetheart." He nodded. "But, yeah, that's what Manelli was thinking—that Kelly's death was a mistake. Well, whatever . . . That woman's going down. It's the prosecutor's game now. Good thing we've got a star witness."

"Who?" Rune asked. Then, when he just gave her a wry look, she said, "Hey, forget it. No way. They'll send another Haarte after me."

"Hey, not to worry," Sal said, finishing the coffee. "The Witness Relocation Program, remember? You'll get a whole new identity. You can be anybody you want. You can even make up your own name."

Sal frowned: he must have been wondering why she was laughing.

"Well, what do you think?" Rune called.

She sat sidesaddle, five feet off the ground, on a huge armature that rose phallic and rusty from a complicated tangle of industrial machinery scrap. They were surrounded by piles of pitted chrome and girders, wire, wrecks of trucks, and turbines and gears.

Richard walked around the corner. "Fantastic."

The junkyard was off Seventieth, in commercial Queens. But it was oddly quiet. They looked west, at the huge slash of orange brilliance behind Manhattan, as the sun eased through strips of dark cloud.

"You come here much?" he asked.

"Only for the sunsets."

The light hit the twisted metal and seemed to make the different shades of rust vibrate. A thousand oil drums became beautiful. Spindles of twisted iron became filaments of light and coils of BX cable were glowing snakes. Rune said, "Come on up!"

She was wearing the Spanish outfit once more. Richard climbed up next to her and they walked along the armature to a platform.

They had a magnificent view of the city.

On the platform was an old picnic basket. A bottle of champagne too.

"Warm," Rune apologized, cradling the bottle. "But it looks classy."

When they'd snuck through the fence a half hour ago, Richard had gazed at the Dobermans uneasily and stood paralyzed when one sniffed his crotch. But Rune knew them well and scratched their smooth heads. They wagged their stubby tails, sniffing at the cold macaroni-and-cheese sandwiches Rune had packed in the basket before prancing away on their springy legs.

Rune and Richard ate until dusk. Then she lit a kerosene lantern. She lay back, using the picnic basket as a pillow.

"I got another application to the New School," she told him. "I kind of threw out the one you gave me."

"You going to apply? For real?"

After a moment she asked, "I guess I'd have to take classes, wouldn't I?"

"It's an important part of going to school."

"That's what I figured. I'm not sure I'm going to do it though. I have to tell you." She snuck a furtive glimpse at his face. "See, this guy at the video store, Frankie Greek, remember him? Anyway, his sister just had a baby and she was a window designer and it turns out I can take her job while she's on leave. Only have to work half-days. Leave me free to do other stuff."

"What kind of stuff?"

"You know, stuff stuff."

"Rune."

"Oh, it'd be a radical job. Very artistic. In SoHo. Discounts for clothes. Slinky dresses. Lingerie."

"You're hopeless, you know that."

"Well, to be totally honest, I already took the job and threw out the other application too." She stared at the two or three stars whose light was bright enough to penetrate the city haze. "I had to do it, Richard. I *had* to. I was worried that if I got a degree or anything I'd get to be, like, too literal."

"We couldn't have that, could we?"

Then the stars were blocked out completely, as Richard leaned over her, bringing his mouth down slowly on hers. She lifted her head to meet him. They kissed for a long while, Rune astonished that she could be aroused by someone wearing a button-down shirt and Brooks Brothers slacks.

Very slow, it was all very slow.

Though not like slow motion in a film. More like vignettes, frame by frame, the way you'd hit a VCR pause button over and over again to watch a favorite scene.

The way she'd watched *Manhattan Is My Beat*.

Freeze-frame: The cloth of his collar. His smooth neck. His paisley eyes. The white bandage on her hand.

Freeze-frame: His mouth.

"We going to be safe?" he whispered.

"Sure," Rune whispered. She reached into the pocket of her skirt and handed him the small, crinkly square of plastic.

"Actually," he said, "I meant because we're twenty feet in the air."

"Don't worry," Rune whispered. "I'll hold you real tight. I won't let you fall."

Freeze-frame: She wrapped her arms around him.

CHAPTER TWENTY-SEVEN

███ "I don't howl."

In the loft Sandra was putting explosive red polish on her toenails. She continued sourly. "That was the deal. Remember? I don't howl when I'm in bed with a guy and you clean up after yourself."

She nodded at the mess Rune had made when she was frantically packing. "I have somebody over, I'm quiet as a mouse. *He* howls, there's nothing I can do about it. But me, I ask you, am I quiet, or what?"

"You're quiet." Rune bent over and picked up clothes, swept up the broken glass.

"Do I howl?"

"You don't howl."

"So where were you last night?" Sandra asked.

"We went to a junkyard."

"Brother, that boy's got a way to go." Sandra glanced up from her artistic nails, examined Rune critically. "You look happy. Got lucky, huh?"

"Didn't your mother teach you not to pry?"

"No, my mother's the one who taught me *how* to pry. So, you get lucky?"

Rune ignored her and repacked her clothes, put the books back on the shelf.

She paused. On the floor beside the bookcase was the shattered cassette of *Manhattan Is My Beat*. Rune picked it up. The loops of opaque tape hung out of the broken plastic reels. She looked at it for a moment. She was thinking of Robert Kelly. Of the movie. About the million dollars of bank loot that was never really there—never there for *her* to find anyway.

She tossed the cassette into the trash bin. Then glanced at Sandra's side of the loft. She picked up the good-bye note she'd written to her roommate. It was unopened. "Don't you read your mail?" she asked.

The woman glanced at it. "Whatsit? A love note?"

"From me."

"What's it say?"

"Nothing." Rune threw it out too. Then she flopped down on her pillows, staring into the blue-and-white sky. She remembered the clouds in New Jersey floating over the trimmed grounds of the nursing home as she crouched next to Raoul Elliott's wheelchair. They'd seemed like dragons and giants then, the clouds. She stared at them for a long time now. After the horror of the last few days she expected them to look merely like clouds. But, no, they still seemed like dragons and giants.

The more things change, the more they stay the same.

An expression of her father's.

She thought about the old screenwriter, Raoul Elliott. Next week she'd go out and visit him again. Bring him another flower. And maybe a book. She could read to him. Stories are the best, he'd said. Rune agreed with him there.

Five minutes later Sandra said, "Shit. I forget. Some

geek from that place you work, or used to work, the video store? Looked like a heavy-metal wanna-be."

"Frankie?"

"I don't know. Maybe. He came by with a couple of messages." She read a slip of paper. "One was from this Amanda LeClerc. He said he couldn't understand her too good. She's, like, foreign and he was saying if they come to this country why don't they learn to speak-a the language."

"The point, Sandra?"

"So this Amanda person, she called and said she'd heard from this priest or minister or somebody in Brooklyn. . . ." Sandra, juggling the nail polish, smoothed the wrinkled note.

Rune sat up.

A minister?

Sandra was struggling to read. "Like, I'm really not programmed to be a message center, you know. Yeah, okay. I got it. She said she talked to this minister and he's got this suitcase. It was somebody's named Robert Kelly's."

A *suitcase*?

"And he doesn't know what to do with it, the minister. But he said it's, like, very important."

Rune screamed, "Yes!" She rolled on her back, and her legs, straight up in the air, kicked back and forth.

"Whoa, take a pill or something." Sandra handed her the message.

She read it. St. Xavier's Church on Atlantic Avenue. Brooklyn.

"Oh, and here's the other one." She found another slip in her purse.

It was from Stephanie. She was out of the hospital and feeling a lot better. She'd stop by later.

"All right!" Rune cried.

"I'm glad *somebody's* happy." Sandra added, "I'm depressed. Not that anybody cares." She continued to paint her nails carefully.

"I've got to call Richard. We're taking a trip."

"Where?"

"Brooklyn!"

"Old folks homes, junkyards . . . Why am I not surprised? Hey, don't hug me! Watch the polish!"

■

Rune got Richard at home.

This was weird. It was the afternoon. What was he doing home?

She realized that he hadn't told her exactly *where* he wrote his boring meet-your-CEO scripts.

Rune was on the street, calling from the pay phone. "Hey, how come you're home? I thought you worked for a company. With what's her name? Too-tall Karen?"

He laughed again. "I do mostly freelance. I'm sort of an independent contractor."

"We need to go to Brooklyn. A church on Atlantic Avenue. Can you drive?"

He said, "You're home now?"

"I'm in my office."

"Office?" he asked.

"My exterior office."

"Oh." He laughed. "A pay phone."

"So, can we go?"

"What's going on in Brooklyn?"

She told him about the minister's message, then added, "I just called him—the priest Amanda found. I sort of told him a white lie."

"Which was?"

"That I'm Robert Kelly's granddaughter."

"That's not a white lie. It's a full-fledged lie. Especially to a man of the cloth. You oughta be ashamed.

Anyway, I thought you were going to forget about the money."

"I did. Forgot completely. It was *him* called me." She persisted. Said that Mr. Kelly'd been living in a home attached to the church until he found an apartment. And that he'd left a suitcase with the minister for safekeeping. He didn't want to carry it around until he was settled. It was—are you listening? He said it was too valuable to him to just carry around the streets of the city."

Another pause.

"It's too crazy," Richard said.

She added, "And get this. I asked him if there was a cemetery nearby—like in the movie *Manhattan Is My Beat*. See, Dana Mitchell, the cop, buries the money in a new grave. And there is!"

"Is what?"

"A cemetery. Next to the church. Don't you see? Mr. Elliott told Mr. Kelly about the church and Mr. Kelly went there and dug up the money."

"Okay," he said dubiously. Then he asked, "You're at your loft?"

"Will be in five minutes."

He said seductively, "You going to be by yourself?"

"Sandra's there."

"Bummer. Can't you send her out to buy something?"

"How 'bout we go to Brooklyn now. Then we'll think about some privacy."

"I'm on my way."

■

Rune reached the stop of the stairs in her loft and stopped.

"Stephanie!"

The redhead smiled wanly. She sat in Rune's half of the loft, on a pile of pillows. She was pale—paler than usual—and she wore a scarf that partially covered a bruise on her neck. There was also large bandage on her temple and an eggplant-colored mark on her cheek.

"Ohmygod," Rune blurted out, examining her. "You *do* bruise, don't you?" She hugged the woman carefully. "You look, well. . . ."

"I look awful. You can say it."

"Not for somebody who got run over by a cab."

"Hey, there's a compliment for you."

There was dense silence for a moment. "I don't know what to say, Steph." Rune was nervous and she did busywork, straightening up clothes. "I got you involved in this whole thing. I almost got you killed. And it was so stupid—we were running from a federal marshal."

"A what?" Stephanie gave a laugh.

"That guy in the subway, the one you hit—I thought he was working for *them*. But it turned out he was a U.S. marshal. Isn't that radical? Just like the Texas Rangers."

She told Stephanie about Haarte and Emily.

"I heard something about it on the news, in the hospital," Stephanie said. "A shooting at this town house. I never guessed you were involved."

Rune's eyes were excited again. "Oh, oh, and talk about adventures . . . They want me to be the star witness."

"Isn't that scary?"

"Sure. But I don't care. I want that bitch to go away for a long time. They killed Mr. Kelly. And they tried to kill me—and you too."

"Well, I'm pretty sure there'll be plenty of cops to look out for you."

Rune wandered to the bookcase, replaced some of the books she'd packed to take home. "I called the video store. They told me you quit."

"That Tony," Stephanie said, "what an asshole. I couldn't deal with him—not the way he treated you."

Rune grinned coyly. "So, you want a hundred thousand dollars?"

"What?"

Rune told her about the minister. "Little Red Hen, remember? You believed in me. If there really is any money, you'll get some of it."

Stephanie laughed. "You think there is?"

"I'm not sure. But you know me."

"Optimist," Stephanie supplied.

"You got it. I—"

Plop.

Rune cocked her head. She heard the sound again. A drip. Soft. *Plop.*

She glanced at where it was coming from—Sandra's side of the apartment.

"You don't really have to give me anything, Rune."

"I know I don't *have* to. But I want to."

Plop, plop.

Damn! Sandra'd spilled her nail polish. There was a big red stain on the floor.

"Jesus, Sandra!"

Rune turned the corner and stopped. There was her roommate in her thick white bra and black panty hose, eyes staring at the apex of the glass ceiling. She lay on her futon. The bullet hole in her chest was a tiny dark dot. The stain wasn't nail polish. It was the blood that was trickling down her arm and onto the floor.

Stephanie stood up and pointed the gun at Rune. She said, "Come on back over here, love. Let's have a little talk."

CHAPTER TWENTY-EIGHT

"You're Haarte's partner," Rune whispered.

She nodded. "My name's Lucy Zane," the woman said coldly. "Haarte and I worked together for three years. He was the best partner I ever had. And he's dead. Thanks to you."

"Then who's Emily?"

"Just backup. We use her sometimes for jobs on the East Coast."

Rune, sitting down on the cushions, shaking her head. Everything floating in front of her—a big soup. Richard, the money, Pretty Boy, Emily, and Haarte. Robert Kelly. She felt the slamming of her heart in her chest as the hopelessness arose again. And she lowered her face into her hands. Whispering: "Oh, no, oh, no."

She was too numb for tears. Not even looking up, she said, "But your job at the video store? How'd you get the job?"

"How do you think? I fucked Tony."

"I hope it was disgusting," Rune spat out.

"Was. But it didn't last long. A minute or two."

"But you were my friend. . . . You helped me get the clothes. . . . Why? Why'd you do that?"

"I got close to you so we could set you up. Haarte and I killed two U.S. marshals in St. Louis. That put a lot of heat on us. And we fucked up the Spinello hit in the Village. So we needed a fall guy. Well, fall *girl*. You got elected. Almost worked too."

"Too bad the cab had good brakes," Rune said coldly.

"We're lucky sometimes. Even people like me."

Rune shook with anger and fear.

Stephanie continued. "I heard from Emily. The judge denied her bail request. But she said to say hello. She hopes you and I'd have a nice visit. And I think we will. Now, there's one thing I've got to know. Did you tell the cops or marshals anything about me?"

A click and a grind sounded behind them. Rune's eyes flashed for a second.

Richard.

Stephanie glanced at the sound, then turned back to Rune.

"Tell me," she said. "And I'll let you go."

"Bullshit." Rune scrabbled away into the cushions as if they'd protect her from the black gun.

"I'll let you go," the woman said. "I promise."

"I'm the only witness. How can you let me go? You *have* to kill me." She looked at the clouds outside the loft, the dragons, the giants, the trolls, marching past, miles high, not caring a bit for what was going on down on earth.

The grinding started again. The elevator was coming up.

"You must've told them about me after the accident. Did the marshal I hit in the subway think I was part of them? Did you tell them my name?"

"It's not real."

"No, but I've used it before. I can be traced through it."

Chains, clinking chains. And the grind of metal on metal. Another loud click, a scrape.

"Who's coming to visit, Rune?"

"I don't know."

Stephanie glanced at the stairway. Then back at Rune. She said, "So, what do you have in your hand."

Rune couldn't believe that the woman had seen her. Oh, she was good. She was very good.

"Show me," Stephanie persisted.

Rune hesitated, then held up her hand and slowly opened the bandaged fingers. "The piece of stone. From the Union Bank Building. My souvenir. The one I picked up when you were with me that day down in Wall Street."

"Now, what were you going to do with it?"

"Throw it at you," Rune responded. "Smash your goddamn face."

"Why don't you just toss it over there." Lucy Zane held the silenced gun very steadily on Rune's chest.

Rune pitched the stone away.

Just as Richard climbed the stairs and said, "Hi."

He froze, seeing the gun in Stephanie's hand. "What is this?"

Stephanie waved him in. "Okay. Just stand there." She backed up so that she could keep them both covered. She held the gun out straight. It was small and its black metal gleamed in the sunlight. The short cylinder of the silencer was dark too.

Her voice now had an edge to it. "I don't have much time. Who'd you tell about me, Rune? And what did you tell them? I want to know. And I mean now."

"Let him go."

Richard said, "What the hell is this? Are you two joking?"

Stephanie's left hand went out toward him. Palm up. The nails were done in careful purple-pink. "Shut up, asshole. Just shut up." To Rune: "*What* did you tell them?"

"God," Richard whispered, looking at Rune.

Rune sank back into the cushions, put her hands over her eyes, sobbing. "No, no . . . I don't give a shit about you or Emily or anybody. I won't testify. I'll tell them it wasn't Emily or you. Mr. Kelly's dead! Spinello's dead! Just leave us alone."

Stephanie said patiently, "Maybe I'll consider that. You have to understand, Rune. I like you. I really do. You're . . . charming. And I was really touched you were going to give me some of that ridiculous money. That almost choked me up. But you have to tell me. This's just business."

"All right . . . I didn't tell anybody anything about you."

"I don't believe you."

"It's true! All I did was write about you in my diary. I mentioned you and Emily." She sat back, hand in her lap, small, defeated. "I thought you were my friend. I described you and wrote how nice you were to help me buy some clothes."

If this choked her up too, Stephanie's expression didn't show it.

"Where is it?" the woman asked. "The diary. Let me have it and I'll let you go. Both of you."

"Promise?"

"I promise."

Rune debated then walked to her suitcase, rummaged through it. "I can't find it." She looked up, frowning. "I thought I packed it." She opened her leopard-skin bag, looked through that too. "I don't know. I . . . oh, there it is. On the bookcase. The second shelf."

Stephanie eased over to the bookcase. Touched a notebook. "This one?"

"No, the one next to it. On its side."

Stephanie pulled the book off the shelf and flipped it open. "Where do you mention—"

An explosion. The first bullet broke a huge chunk out of the blue-sky wall and sent fragments of cinder block raining through the room.

The second shattered a panel of glass in the ceiling.

The third tore apart a dozen books, which pitched through the air like shot birds.

The fourth caught Stephanie squarely in the chest as she was turning, shocked, mouth open, toward Rune.

There may even have been a fifth shot. And a sixth. Rune wasn't sure. She had no idea how many times she pulled the trigger of the gun—the one that Rune had pulled from the accordion folder she'd thrown away earlier—tossed into the trash can beside her bed.

All Rune saw was the smoke and dust and paper flecks and clouds and blue sky of concrete and broken glass flying through the loft around Stephanie—beautiful, pale Stephanie, who spiraled to the floor.

And all Rune heard was a huge ringing roar from the gun. Which, after a few seconds, as Richard scrambled from the floor and started toward her, was replaced by an animal's mad screaming she didn't even know was coming from her.

CHAPTER TWENTY-NINE

Head bowed at the altar, Rune was motionless.

Kneeling. She'd thought she could remember all the words. But they wouldn't come to her and all she could do was repeat over and over again, in a mumbling whisper, "We yield thee praise and thanksgiving for our deliverance from those great and apparent dangers wherewith we were compassed."

After a moment she stood and walked slowly up the aisle toward the back of the sanctuary.

Still whispering, she said to the man wearing black minister's robes, "This is a totally radical church, Reverend."

"Thank you, Miss Kelly."

At the door, she turned and curtsied awkwardly toward the altar. The minister of St. Xavier's glanced at her curiously. Maybe curtsying—which Rune had just seen a character do in some old Mafia movie—was only for Catholics. But so what? she decided. Stephanie was right about one thing: short of devil worship and animal sacrifices, ministers and priests probably aren't all that sensitive about technicalities.

They left the sanctuary.

"Your grandfather didn't mention any children when he stayed with us in our residence. He said his only relative was his sister but she'd died a few years ago."

"Really?" she asked.

"But then," the minister continued, "he didn't talk much about himself. He was a bit mysterious in some ways."

Mysterious . . .

"Yep," she said after a moment. "That was Grandfather. We used to say that about him. 'Wasn't Grandfather quiet.' All of us would say it."

"All of you? I thought you said there were just two of you. You and your sister."

"Oh, well, I mean all the kids in the neighborhood. He was like a grandfather to them too."

Watch it, Rune told herself. It's a minister you're lying to. And a minister with a good memory.

She followed the man through the rectory building. Filled with dark wood, wrought iron. The small yellow lights added a lot of churchy atmosphere to the place, though maybe they used small-wattage bulbs just to save money. It was very . . . well, *religious* here. Rune tried to remember a good movie she'd seen about religion and couldn't think of one. They tended not to have happy endings.

They walked into a large dormitory, newer than the church, though the architecture was the same—stained glass, arches, flowery carvings. She looked around. It was some kind of residence hall for senior citizens. Rune glanced into a room as they passed. Two beds, yellow walls, mismatched dressers. Lots of pictures on the walls. Homier than you'd think. There were two elderly men inside the room. As she paused, looking in, one of the men stood up and said, " 'I am a very foolish fond old man, fourscore and upward, not an hour more or less, and, to deal plainly, I fear I am not in my perfect mind.' "

"I'll say you're not in perfect mind," his friend chided. "You've got it all wrong."

"Oh, you think you can do better?"

"Listen to this."

His voice faded as Rune and the minister continued down the corridor.

"How long was Grandfather here?" Rune asked.

"Only four, five weeks. He needed a place to stay until he found an apartment. A friend sent him here."

"Raoul Elliott?" Rune's heart thudded harder.

"Yes. You know Mr. Elliott?"

"We've met once."

So, Elliott had been confused. He hadn't sent Mr. Kelly to the Florence Hotel but here—to the church. Maybe Mr. Kelly was staying in the Florence when he visited the screenwriter and the poor man's mind just confused them.

"Wonderful man," the priest continued. "Oh, he's been very generous to us here at the church. And not only materially . . . He served on our board too. Until he got sick. A shame what's happened to him, isn't it? That Alzheimer's." The minister shook his head then continued. "But we have so few rooms, Robert didn't want to monopolize one—he wanted to make it available for somebody less fortunate. So he moved into the Hotel Florence for a while. He left the suitcase here, said he'd pick it up when he moved into a safer place. He was worried about break-ins. He said the bag was too important to risk getting stolen."

Rune nodded nonchalantly. Thinking: *One million dollars.*

She followed him to a storage room. The minister

unlocked the door with keys on a janitor's self-winding coil. Rune asked, "Did Grandfather spend much time in the church itself?"

The minister disappeared into the storage room. Rune heard the sound of boxes sliding along the floor. He called, "No. Not much."

"How about the grounds? The cemetery? Did he spend much time there?"

"The cemetery? I don't know. He might have."

Rune was thinking of the scene in *Manhattan Is My Beat* where the cop, his life ruined, was lying in his prison cell, dreaming about reclaiming his stolen million dollars, buried in a cemetery. She remembered the close-up of the actor's eyes as he wakened and realized that it had just been a dream—the blackness of the dirt he'd been digging up with his fingers becoming the shadows of the bars across his hands as he woke.

The minister emerged with a suitcase. He set it on the floor. "Here you go."

Rune asked. "You want me to sign a receipt or anything?"

"I don't think that'll be necessary, no."

Rune picked it up. It was as heavy as an old leather suitcase containing a million dollars ought to be. She listed against the weight. The minister smiled and took the case from her. He lifted it easily and motioned her toward the side door. She walked ahead of him.

He said, "Your grandfather told me to be careful with this. He said it had his whole life in it."

Rune glanced at the suitcase. Her palms were moist. "Funny what people consider their whole life, isn't it?"

"I feel sorry for people who can carry their homes around with them. That's one of the reasons the church has this residence home. You really feel God at work here."

They walked to his small office. He bent over the

cluttered desk and sorted through a thick stack of envelopes. He said. "I wished Robert had stayed longer. I
liked him a lot. But then, he was independent. He
wanted to live on his own."

Rune decided that she was going to give the church
some money. Fifty thousand, she decided. Then, on a
whim, upped the ante to a hundred Gs.

He handed her a thick envelope addressed to "Mr.
Bobby Kelly."

"Oh, I forgot to mention . . . this came for him care
of the church a day or so ago. Before I got around to
forwarding it, I heard that he'd been killed."

Rune stuffed it under her arm.

Outside, he set the suitcase on the sidewalk for her.
"Again, my sympathies to your family. If there's anything
I can do for you, please call me."

"Thank you, Reverend," she said. Thinking: You just
earned yourself two hundred thousand.

Little Red Hen . . .

Rune picked up the suitcase, walked to the car.

Richard eyed the bag curiously. She handed it to him,
then patted the hood of his Dodge. He lifted the bag and
rested it on the car. They were on a quiet side street but
heavy traffic swept past at the corner. Superstitiously
they both refused to look at the scuffed leather bag. They
gazed at the single-story shops—a rug dealer, a hardware
store, a pizza place, a deli. The trees. The traffic. The sky.

Neither touched the suitcase, neither said anything.

Like knights who think they've found the Grail and
aren't sure they want to.

Because it would mean the end of their quest.

The end of the story. Time to close the book, to go to
bed and wake up for work the next morning.

Richard broke the silence. "I didn't even think there'd
be a suitcase."

Rune stared at the patterns of the stains on the

leather. The elastic bands from a dozen old airline claim checks looped through the handles. "I had some moments myself," she admitted. She touched the latches. Then stepped back. "I can't do it."

Richard took over. "It's probably locked." He pressed the buttons. They clicked open.

"Wheel . . . of . . . Fortune," Rune said.

Richard lifted the lid.

Magazines.

The Holy Grail was magazines and newspapers.

All from the 1940s. *Time, Newsweek, Collier's.* Rune grabbed several, shuffled through them. No bills fluttered out.

"A million ain't going to be hidden inside of *Time*," Richard pointed out.

"His whole life?" Rune whispered. "Mr. Kelly told the minister his whole life was in here." She dug to the bottom. "Maybe he put the money into shares of Standard Oil or something. Maybe there's a stock certificate."

But, no, all the suitcase contained was newspapers and magazines.

When she'd gone over every inch of it, pulled up the cloth lining, felt along the moldy seams, her shoulders slumped and she shook her head. "Why?" she mused. "What'd he keep these for?"

Richard was flipping through several of them. He was frowning. "Weird. They're all from about the same time. June 1947."

The laughter startled her, it was so abrupt. She looked at Richard, who was shaking his head.

"What?"

He couldn't stop laughing.

"What is it?"

Finally he caught his breath. His eyes were squinting as he read a thumbed-down page. "Oh, Rune . . . Oh, no . . ."

She grabbed the magazine. An article was circled in blue ink. She read the paragraph Richard pointed at.

Excellent in his role is young Robert Kelly, hailing from the Midwest, who had no intention of acting in films until director Hal Reinhart spotted him in a crowd and offered him a part. Playing Dana Mitchell's younger brother, who tries unsuccessfully to talk the tormented cop into turning in the ill-gotten loot, Kelly displays striking talent for a man whose only experience onstage has been a handful of USO shows during the War. Moviegoers will be watching this young man carefully to see if he will be the next member of the great Hollywood dream: the unknown catapulted to stardom.

They looked through the rest of the magazines. In each one, *Manhattan Is My Beat* was reviewed and, in each, Robert Kelly was mentioned at least several times. Most gave him kind reviews and forecast a long career for him.

Rune, too, laughed. She closed the suitcase and leaned against the car. "So *that's* what he meant by his whole life. He told me the movie was the high point of his life. He must never have gotten any other parts."

Stuffed in one of the magazines was a copy of a letter written to Mr. Kelly from the Screen Actors Guild. It was dated five years before.

She read it out loud. " 'Dear Mr. Kelly: Thank you for your letter of last month. As a contract player, you would indeed be entitled to residual payments for your performance in the film *Manhattan Is My Beat*. However, we understand from the studio, which is the current owner of the copyright to the film, that there are no plans for its release on videotape at this time. If and when the film is released, you will be entitled to your residuals as per the contract.' "

Rune put the letter back. "When he told me he was going to be rich—when his ship came in—*that's* what he meant. It had nothing to do with the bank robbery money."

"Poor guy," Richard said. "He'd probably be getting a check for a couple hundred bucks." He looked up and pointed behind her. "Look."

The sign on the dormitory read ST. XAVIER'S HOME FOR ACTORS AND ACTRESSES. "That's what he was doing here. It had nothing to do with the money. Kelly just needed a place to stay."

Richard pitched the suitcase into the backseat. "What do you want to do with them?"

She shrugged. "I'll give them to Amanda. I think they'd mean something to her. I'll make a copy of the best review for me. Put it up on my wall."

They climbed into the car. Richard said, "It would have corrupted you, you know."

"What?"

"The money. Just like the cop in *Manhattan Is My Beat*. You know the expression, 'Power tends to corrupt, absolute power corrupts absolutely'?"

Of *course* I've never heard of it, she thought. But told him, "Oh, sure. Wasn't that another one of Stallone's?"

He looked at her blankly for a moment then said, "Well, translated to capitalistic terms, the same truth holds. The absoluteness of that much money would have affected your core values."

Mr. Weird was back—though this time in Gap camouflage.

Rune thought about it for a minute. "No way. Aladdin didn't get corrupted."

"The guy with the lamp? You trying to make a rational argument by citing a fairy tale?"

She said, "Yeah, I am."

"Well, what about Aladdin?"

"He wished for wealth and a beautiful princess to be his bride, and the genie gave him all that. But people don't know the end of the story. Eventually he became the sultan's heir and finally got to be sultan himself."

"And it was Watergate. He got turned into a camel."

"Nope. He was a popular and fair leader. Oh, and radically rich."

"So fairy tales may not *always* have happy endings," he said like a professor, "but sometimes they do."

"Just like life."

Richard seemed to be trying to think about arguing but couldn't come up with anything. He shrugged. "Just like life," he conceded.

As they drove through the streets of Brooklyn, Rune slouched in the seat, put her feet on the dash. "So that's why he rented the film so often. It was his big moment of glory."

"That's pretty bizarre," Richard said.

"I don't think so," she told him. "A lot of people don't even have a big moment. And if they do, it probably doesn't get put out on video. I'll tell you—if *I* got a part in a movie, I'd dupe a freeze-frame of me and put it up on my wall."

He punched her playfully on the arm.

"What?"

"Well, you saw the film, what, ten times? Didn't you see his name on the credits?"

"He had just a bit part. He wasn't in the above-the-title credits."

"The what?"

"That's what they call the opening credits. And the copy we watched was the bootleg. I didn't bother to copy the cast credits at the end when I made it."

"Speaking of names, are you ever going to tell me your real name?"

"Ludmilla."

"You're kidding."

Rune didn't say anything.

"You *are* kidding," he said warily.

"I'm just trying to think up a good name for somebody who'd do window displays in SoHo. I think Yvonne would be good. What do you think?"

"It's as good as anything."

She looked at the bulky envelope the minister had given her. The return address was the Bon Aire Nursing Home in Berkeley Heights, New Jersey.

"What's that?"

"Something Mr. Elliott sent to Mr. Kelly at the church."

She opened the envelope. Inside was a letter taped to another thick envelope, on which was printed in old, uneven type: *Manhattan Is My Beat,* Draft Script, 5/6/46.

"Oh, look. A souvenir!"

Rune read the letter out loud. " 'Dear Mr. Kelly. You don't remember me, I'm sure. I'm the nurse on the floor where Mr. Raoul Elliott's room is. He asked me to write to you and asked if you could forward the package I'm enclosing here to the young girl who came to visit him the other day. He was a little confused as to who she was—maybe she is your daughter or probably your granddaughter—but if you could forward it, we'd be most appreciative.

" 'Mr. Elliot has mentioned several times how nice it was for her to come visit and talk about movies, and I can tell you her visit had a very good effect on him. He put the flower she brought him by his bedside and a couple times he even remembered who gave it to him, which is pretty good for him. Yesterday he got this from his storage locker and asked me to send it to her. Thank her for making him happy. All best wishes, Joan Gilford, R.N.' "

Richard, driving through commercial Brooklyn, said, "What a great old guy. That was sweet."

Rune said, "I think I'm going to cry."

She tore open the envelope.

Richard stopped for a red light. "You know, maybe you can sell it. I heard that an original draft of somebody's play—Noël Coward, I think—went for four or five thousand at Sotheby's. What do you think this one'd be worth?"

The light changed and the car pulled forward. Rune didn't answer right away but after a moment said, "So far it's up to two hundred and thirty thousand."

"What?" he asked, smiling uncertainly.

"And counting."

Richard glanced over at Rune then skidded the car to a stop.

In Rune's lap were bundles of money. Stacks of wrapped bills. They were larger than modern Federal Reserve notes. The ink was darker, the seals on the front were in midnight-blue ink. The paper wrappers around the stacks were stenciled with *$10,000* in a scripty old-time typeface. Also printed on them was *Union Bank of New York.*

"Thirty-three, thirty-four . . . Let's see. Thirty-eight. Times ten thousand is three hundred and eighty thousand dollars. Is that right? I'm *so* bad with math."

"Christ," Richard whispered.

Cars honked behind them. He glanced in the rearview mirror, then pulled to the curb, parked in front of a Carvel ice cream store.

"I don't understand . . . what . . . ?"

Rune didn't answer. She ran her hand over the money, replaying the great scene in *Manhattan Is My Beat* where Dana Mitchell is inside the bank and opens the suitcase of money—the camera cutting between his face and the stacks of bills, which had been lit to glow like a hoard of jewels.

"Raoul Elliott," she answered. "When he was researching the film he must have found where the loot was hidden. Maybe it *was* buried there. . . ." She nodded back toward the church. "So he donated a bunch back to the church and they built the home for actors. The minister said he'd been very generous to them. Raoul kept the rest and retired."

Two tough-looking kids in T-shirts and jeans walked by and glanced in the car. Richard looked at them then reached over Rune, locked the door, rolled up the windows.

"Hey," she protested, "what're you doing? It's hot out."

"You're in the middle of Brooklyn with four hundred thousand dollars in your lap and you're just going to sit there?"

"No, as a matter of fact"—she nodded toward the Carvel store—"I was going to get an ice cream cone. You want one?"

Richard sighed. "How 'bout if we get a safe deposit box?"

"But we're right here."

"A bank first?" he asked. "Please?"

She ran her hand over the money again. Picked up one bundle. It was heavy. "After, can we get an ice cream?"

"Tons of ice cream. Sprinkles too, you want."

"Yeah, I want."

He started the car. Rune leaned back in the seat. She was laughing. Looking at him, coy and sly.

He said, "You're looking full of the devil. What's so funny?"

"You know the story of the Little Red Hen?"

"No, I don't. How 'bout if you tell it to me?"

Richard turned the old car onto the Brooklyn Bridge and pointed the hood toward the turrets and battlements of Manhattan, fiery in the afternoon sun. Rune said, "It goes like this . . ."